TALE OF A SHADOW

Unseen, unheard, unloved
and unfinished...

Adacus May

For my siblings x

CONTENTS

INTRODUCTION

If we believe that we reap what we sow then kindness and compassion should lead to rich rewards in our lives while manipulation and greed should perhaps result in the comeuppance we deserve. Good will always triumph over evil but what if you don't recognise the good when it comes and can't find anything in yourself to repay it?

In a small sliver of space between earth and sky, Nancy Sullivan travels the difficult road of hardship and poverty in a world dominated by men, her only escape from it, the joy she finds in learning and books. Just like her beloved *David Copperfield*, Nancy longs to be the hero of her own life, but things are not always as they seem, and her own resilience and determination in the face of misery and social injustice may count for nothing as she grows up should she be blind to the transformative power of the human connections that can foster love, friendship and loyalty.

As a prequel to my first novel *Cold Canvas* (featuring Nancy as a young woman living in Boston as she searches for love and a sense of self) ***Tale of a Shadow*** tells the story of her life leading up to that time, beginning in the dark period after Ireland's great famine, then the years that follow the Sullivan family's unexpected emigration to a new life in America and all that entails.

Tale of a Shadow does not delve deeply into the political or religious dynamics of Ireland at the time - I leave others to do justice to that - but focuses on the Sullivans as they navigate the brutal grasp of poverty and then experience life as foreigners in a new country where ultimately their destiny is shaped by the people they meet.

Whilst this is a complete work of fiction, it includes some places and people that actually existed and events that took place in the mid-nineteenth century. All names, characters, places, events and incidents in this book are either the product of my imagination or have been used in a fictitious manner for dramatic effect.

THANKS

Special thanks to Seán Ó Súilleabháin (author of a number of books about Ireland) for his invaluable help with some of the County Leitrim words and dialect. I am very grateful for his guidance in helping to bring authenticity and integrity to the dialogue and all that is correct is down to Seán. Any licence that has been applied in the interests of making the dialogue practical for the reader to navigate is solely down to me.

As always, huge thanks to friends and family who encouraged and supported me throughout the writing of this book and for being willing to give me their feedback and insights along the way.

GLOSSARY of CO. LEITRIM WORDS

Basting *A beating*

Bladdering (stop your bladdering) *Stop talking nonsense*

Brawl (he's a right brawl) *He's a right fool*

Clab (shut your clab) *Shut your mouth*

Cnat *A sly little youngster*

Duderal (he's an awful duderal) *An awful idiot or numbskull*

Gombeen (he's a right gaimbín) *He's a right chancer*

Kippings (cipíns) *Small sticks that can be used a kindling*

Lob (he's a lob of money) *He's a big lump of money*

Poreens (póiríns) *Small potatoes*

Sim-saming (stop your sim-saming) *Stop your whinging/complaining*

Slanus grass *Long stringy grass*

Whisht (will you whisht) *Will you listen/hush*

PART I: IRELAND
1858

CHAPTER 1

The Skib

An almost indiscernible twitch of the sacking gave him away as she crept slowly and quietly towards her friend, stooping low and holding her breath, hands clasped behind her back for fear that even the sound of them brushing against her dress would alert him. Wet grass made a gentle whooshing noise as it brushed against her heavy boots so she slowed her pace even more, moving silently like a cat closing in on its prey, then taking hold of one corner of the empty sack, she slowly lifted it, careful to make no sudden movements. The face staring up at her showed no regret, only pleasure at being found, and he didn't run but stayed perfectly still in happy surrender in their game of hide and seek, his dark, round eyes shining out mischievously at her, his ears blushing pink like sea thrift giving away his obvious pleasure at their play. 'Found you Faerie!' she whispered triumphantly.

In a bright sliver of space between cold, damp

earth and the heavy skies that hung above them, their tribe of two made its own special place in the world where there were no fights or shouting, no space given over to the cold slap of misery. Faerie never said cruel things to her, in fact he never said anything at all, instead always staying silent, listening intently to her like his life depended on it, hanging himself on the edge of every single word until the last before moving closer to her, eager for more sustenance. When she needed him to answer, give her what she needed, she would speak it for him. *Poor Nancy, thems s'cruel t'you. Yer the prettiest girl in the whole o' Kinlough. Yer da's a duderal an' yer ma's a witch.* Delighting in the other's happiness and the small pleasures that came to them in this meagre life, they spent their days escaping to places where they were taller beings, adventurers, imagined themselves as a faerie king and queen in their fine clothes driving a chariot through the forest or on a ship tossed by the waves in Donegal Bay. They shared their dreams, understood each other's place in things, accepted it.

'Girl! Girl! Whar you at?' The irritation in Michael Sullivan's miserably thin voice was carried to her on the wind. She had been sent out to fetch water half an hour ago so where was she? Nancy raised her finger to her lips as a sign to her friend to stay quiet. 'Next time A'll hide an' you come find me.' Faerie stayed quiet but blinked his dark eyes slowly in his understanding of her instruction. Their game over, she turned back to the cottage picking up the half-filled bucket on the way, in her rushing unable to keep it steady, slopping and splashing its contents.

Her father was waiting at the door. 'Get yerself inside, you anger yer mother an' A get the brunt o' it. You raise ructions in this house.' He went to cuff her as she passed him but with such little conviction that she was able to dodge him easily like she usually did.

The air inside the cottage was thick and heavy, filled with the pungent fruity smell of the peat turves burning in the hearth and the suffocating string of claggy smoke that hovered just above her head. Crossing the floor towards her mother, she could feel the damp rising up through her boots from the flattened earth beneath her feet as the cold of it met the heat in the air. Kitty Sullivan was slumped over their large wooden table picking through a glutenous heap of dulse, almost a daily routine now with few variations and eaten so often that the fishy, salty taste would rise up in Nancy's throat even at the thought of it. It was practically dulse or nothing now, with no meat or fish for over a month, even the cornmeal sack was almost empty. With little chance of replenishing any of their supplies unless her father found work, if their small potato plot did badly again, it would be a long difficult winter with no chance of any delicious lumpers to fill her belly.

Kitty turned towards her daughter with no kindness or warmth in her face. 'How can it tek s'long t'bring one bucket o' water? It'll serve you right if you chew on grit, bring it here, A'm after washin' this.' Nancy passed her mother the bucket and watched transfixed as she doused the slippery dulse, lifting the shiny red tentacles up and down before finally dropping it into the cooking pot. 'Bring me more water an' be quicker 'bout it this time. Then be after fetchin' me some nettles. Gwan now.' Nancy hated picking nettles, grasping them did nothing to lessen the sting to her fingers, so she would have to gather the skirt of her dress and use it as a guard against their vicious toothed hearts.

'The chile hasn't been s'well these last weeks Kitty. See how thin she be, thar's little strength in her an' the cold's teken the rest.'

Kitty whipped around to look at her mother-in-law who sat in a chair by the hearth holding the sleeping Isaac in her arms, small and diminished herself from lack of food.

'Thin? Right you be 'bout that. Wur all thin auld woman.'

Frances Sullivan held her tongue but gave her granddaughter a guarded look that said *stay quiet* and she did.

Keeping her eyes lowered and her mouth

firmly shut, Nancy took the bucket from her mother's hand, on her way out of the cottage, looking up into the face of her father who still stood awkwardly on the threshold. Not much of a man really, he may have regarded his mother but he feared his wife's wrath more, so chose to say nothing when the two women were at odds. He should take granny's side in an argument, after all they lived in her cottage, but the young and innocent have no understanding of the dire consequences such misplaced, foolish loyalties can bring about.

He had no work again today, there had been little day-labour for the last two weeks so he cut peat or hunted corncrakes or even rats – no one laid claim to vermin - and once skinned, gutted and cut up with all their distinguishing characteristics removed, he could pass one off to his family as a riskily poached hare. Some days he would take Nancy with him believing that a hungry-looking child might earn him favour if he were ever to be caught when he was up to no good. Other times he would go off alone at night to try and spear salmon or eel in the lough or cast a line in the bay but his eyesight was poor and his reactions slowed from years of drinking so he often returned empty-handed. Still, dulse was always in plentiful supply.

The baby was sick, hungry and sick, and she had watched an inevitable quiet settle on him these past two days. He seemed to her asleep even when he was awake and when she pulled faces at him, his smile was distant and his eyes had no light in them. She would bring him a nettle bug if she could find one, put it in a jar and use a long blade of slanus grass to make it jump, that would make him laugh. Water first, bug later, and setting off towards the stream her spirits began to lift the further she got from the cottage. Just one room really, insulated by thick clay and stone walls with a solid timber and thatched roof, it mostly offered them an effective defence against the wind and rain. Its cold, earth floor gave way to a row of flat stones that formed the hearth, above it, a hole through the roof allowed a fire to be lit day and night. Just one small window, with all its panes intact, allowed in a welcome source of light when the door was closed which was most of the time, and a pretty yellow linen curtain, artfully hand embroidered by mamo, and the room's only adornment, helped to keep out the draught that seeped in around its frame. The furniture was all made by her grandfather and built for practicality with little thought for comfort. Chairs were rigid and unyielding to the body; surfaces were rough and the curse of splinters was to be expected. It all kept bodies and food off the floor, nothing more. She could just remember a time when pretty cups and plates painted with dainty blue flowers and winding leaves lined the shelf by the window, all gone now, she didn't know why mamo had put them away.

They had moved to Kinlough from Augharrow a year ago when, like so many small holders, her father could no longer produce sufficient food for them to live on let alone to settle their dues with the landlord. They had somehow managed to hang on during the long hunger years but with rents rising and any money they had wasted on her father's drinking and gambling, like countless other families, eviction had come and they had been abandoned to their fate. Mamo had taken them in and saved her son from the humiliation of his family being sent to the workhouse in Ballyshannon, or having to live on a tenant farmer's land to labour for nothing more than the scrapings of food and a bed, but Nancy could see there was no gratitude from her parents for it and the cottage very quickly seemed to become her mother's domain with her granny pushed to the edges like an unwelcome guest in her own home.

The Sullivans kept to themselves, habits learned from the years of the great hunger when no one was to be trusted, when a desperate man would claim for himself things over which he had no right or business, besides Michael assumed a man would do unto him exactly what he would do unto them, so he stayed vigilant. As for Kitty, she didn't see anything to be gained from friendships or getting to know other folk, they were an open door to meddling and gossip as far as she was concerned. The only regular visitor to the cottage was mamo's beloved Annie. Their mothers had been friends and the two women had grown up close. Courting the two youngest Sullivan boys, marrying in the same church within a year of each other, inextricably bound together by the happiest and saddest of times. Annie worried for her friend, Michael showed no care for her and Kitty was selfish and looked out for her own needs first, so anything her growling stomach could manage without, she would bring to Frances and the child. But as age took a tighter hold on her, Annie made the walk to the cottage less often, so most weeks would come and go, Nancy seeing no one except her family and Faerie. If she were to meet a stranger, she was to run as fast as she could and, if followed, she should scream and her parents would come to find her. She didn't know why, she would be glad to see another face, but every stranger was to be treated like the dreaded Pooka coming up in ever-changing shapes from the bog; if it was angry she might be taken away, lost never to be found.

Approaching the stream she spotted a fat nettle bug for Issy, she must have it and in an instant, the water was forgotten. She could wrap it in leaves and put it in her pocket but in her haste to catch it, she slipped on the muddy bank and slid into the cold water dropping the bucket which began to skip down the stream. Scrambling to her feet, the image of her mother's angry face before her, she knew she must not lose it. 'Faerie, Faerie, help me!' She called out but a gust of wind whipped away her voice and he didn't come. She ran as fast as she could along the bank to get ahead of the bucket which was gaining speed now until, with a loud clunk, it caught on a rock that blocked its journey downstream. Wading in up to her knees, the water was soaking her dress and pulling her down, the movement of the water rocking her on her feet. The wild kelpies must not get hold of her and carry her away under the water to be lost forever in a watery grave, so concentrating hard to steady herself, she reached down and caught hold of the bucket's handle - closing her eyes so she would not see the black eyes and flowing manes of the kelpies and they would not see her - then heaved it backwards through the water until she and it were safely on the bank. Lying back on the grass, she lifted both her feet into the air to empty her water-logged boots then sitting up, picked up a twig from the ground beside her and threw it into the water, watching as it danced its way down the stream. Then two more twigs, setting them off together to see which would travel fastest, the longest twig won.

The nettles! She had already been gone too long; her mother's anger would spill over and they would all pay the price. She would have to go a little further downstream to get them and the bug would have to wait but her hands were getting cold as the pressure of the hard handle turned her fingertips white, so stopping every few steps, she put down the bucket and rubbed them together to ease the dull ache that had taken hold. Eventually reaching a good, thick patch of nettles, she picked them quickly, her cold fingers in their numbness not even feeling their sting. Wrapping them in her skirt - hitched up to keep them from falling out - she picked up the bucket and began her slow progress home.

When she arrived back the cottage door was shut, so putting down the bucket and holding on to her skirt tightly, she reached up, lifted the latch and pushed it open. In years to come vivid nightmares would bring back the moment when three figures stood as silent shadows around the kitchen table. No one noticed her come in as they stared down at the contents of the skib on the table. Were there potatoes today? Not tall enough to see down into it, Nancy climbed up on the bench to get a better look but it was not the waxy skin of potatoes that filled the skib but the waxen face and limbs of her brother. No one spoke; there was no breath in the room. She leaned in and gently pinched her brother's cheek but it was cold and no colour came to it. Then she tickled him behind his ear where the hair curled into its shadows but his blued lips didn't move. 'Will we fetch Issy some porridge?' She looked up into mamo's face. 'He can't ate chile, he's left us.' Kitty picked up some of the nettles that had spilled from Nancy's skirt onto the table, and turning away, placed them in a pot ready to wet them for the tea. As her father stared at Kitty's turned back, he seemed to sway on his feet, then slowly pulling the blanket up and over his son's face he cleared away what was bubbling up in his throat before falling heavily into mamo's chair by the fire and staring into the flames.

Nancy reached in under the blanket and took hold of one of Issy's wrists lifting it and gently moving it backwards and forwards, his hand flapping like he was waving goodbye, like he used to when she would leave him. She thought he would join in, that his arm would come back to life, but it didn't. 'Come away chile.' Mamo reached across the table and took Nancy's other hand helping her to climb down off the bench as she let go of Issy for the last time. Still her parents didn't speak.

Mamo pulled back the heavy curtain that separated the kitchen from where they slept and led Nancy to their bed, lightly tracing her fingers along the cover of her bible on the bedside table as she passed it. 'Come an' lie down wi' me.' Nancy didn't understand what was happening - the strangeness of everything - but followed her grandmother as she almost fell onto the bed, a loud sob escaping her like the sound of a dog whipped. She pulled Nancy down onto the bed next to her and held her so close that she could smell the smoke in her grandmother's hair and the sweet milky-ness of her brother who had been nestling at her breast. Pushing off her wet boots easily, she moved her feet to warm her icy toes against mamo's skirt.

'The gud Lord has teken yer brother.'

'Teken him whar?'

'T'heaven darlin'.'

'When's he comin' back?'

' Issy can't come back darlin'.'

'Why not?'

'Please chile, ask n'more questions.'

Nancy considered her grandmother's words. She knew of no journeys where you didn't have to come back. If she went to the stream, she had to walk back. If she chased Faerie too far, she had to run back. If she went with her father to the bay, they would be sure to travel home before dark. She didn't understand, you always had to come back from where you had gone. As she lay quietly in the dim light trying to make sense of where Issy was, mamo said nothing more but held on to her tightly, as the chill of her parents' continuing silence crept in around the edges of the curtain.

Finally, her father spoke. 'N'one need know 'bout it.' His voice was low and steady; it didn't sound like him at all. 'A'll find a sef place t'lay him t'rest.'

Nancy heard her mother set the tea down on the table then she counted seven of mamo's breaths before, at last, she spoke too. 'Don't be markin' its place an' be sure t'bury him deep, thar still be devilish flesh-aters in these parts an' we don't want them comin' fer the boy.'

'No flesh-aters have roamed this place fer years Kitty, if ever, yer wild imaginins will do n'gud.'

'Yer t'bury him deep A telly, A'm not havin' him touched by man or beast.'

Her father did not reply but she heard his dragging footsteps, then the cottage door opening and closing quietly behind him as he went out. Loud, steady breathing told her that mamo had fallen asleep so she slid gently from under the weight of her arm careful not to wake her then, standing with her nose touching the dusty curtain, pulled back the edge and peered out to see what was on the other side. The skib that had cradled her precious brother was gone, in its place, a steaming plate of dulse.

CHAPTER 2

Fair Brigid

Waking to the sickly smell of porridge, alone in the bed, Nancy could still feel the edges of the warmth from where mamo had been lying next to her and moved her legs under the covers further into it for comfort. The bed next to her where her parents and Issy slept was empty. Issy. She remembered mamo's words but she could not be right, he would come back or she would find him. Then mamo's face appeared around the curtain. 'Come an' ate chile, tis past seven an' thar's work t'be done, be quick.'

It felt like she was lifting the weight of the whole sky above her as she pushed back the covers and pulled herself up, toes searching for the small rag rug by the bed to give her some brief respite from the cold floor. Tiptoeing forward she pulled back the curtain to where the three shadows sat silently at the table.

'C'mon, it gets cold.' Her mother spoke without looking at her as she dropped a spoonful of the thick yellow paste into a bowl and pushed it across the table towards her husband. Nancy climbed up onto the bench and sat across from mamo, her chin almost resting on the table, as a bowl was shoved towards her and the spoon fell out spilling with it some of the porridge. Tutting, Kitty ran her fingers along the table surface and scooped up what was spilt, plopping it back into Nancy's bowl before loudly licking her fingers one by one.

Nancy observed her mother. She thought her face pretty like a faerie princess but in its cold arrangement, mean like an evil witch. Her hair was crow-black and her eyes nearly as dark, dark enough to cast spells on you if you were bad or did not bring the water quickly enough or picked the wrong nettles. Her skin was pale with a scattering of freckles that crossed her nose and cheeks, and dark shadows cupped her eyes making them look even more cruel. She was taller than her father by some measure, at least a tallow's length, so she had no chance of looking dainty unless she was sitting down. Her hands were too big with long fingers and nails that were bitten down to no more than ugly nubs, blackened from making devilish potions whenever there was a full moon, but although her limbs were unladylike in their composition, the flow of her body curves were soft and feminine as a woman's should be.

By the hearth, damp boots steamed and

creaked with the heat from the fire, next to them the skib, sitting empty on its stump, forlornly resigned now from its service as a cradle. She looked around the table but no one looked up and no one spoke Issy's name. Why had her mother sent her out for the water and the nettles yesterday, if she had stayed at home, she would have told Issy not to leave. It was all her mother's fault, Nancy had thought her mother loved him, but she didn't. She wanted to hurt Kitty for not saving him and for not caring that she couldn't save him, but instead of striking out, she reached in under the hem of her dress and dug her fingernails into her leg taking on the pain that her mother should have been feeling. The pain in her leg, stopped the pain in her head, stopped her thinking. With the breaking open and pulling away of her skin she felt raw now like a skinned hare, no longer resembling what she once was, all her softness stripped away from her.

Then her mother's sharp voice scraped her stripped flesh again. 'We need more dulse unless yer able t'provide somethin' better fer yer family.' Kitty spoke to her husband without raising her head from her porridge.

'Thar wur n'more than a skiff o' rain in the night an' the weather is set fair fer the day, s'the girl an' me'll walk t'the bay, the tide fevours us an' thar'll be mussels an' cockles t'be had.'

Kitty just made a low moaning noise by way of

a response.

Mamo protested. 'Must you tek Nancy the day? Me boots aren't dry yet an' she shudn't mek such a long walk wi'out them.'

Michael cast his eyes towards mamo's boots drying by the fire. 'Stuff them wi' grass; it'll stop them slippin' s'much an' might speed her up a bit. Up t'you, boots or no boots, meks no difference t'me.' Now resting his eyes on Nancy he spoke in a dull, lifeless voice. 'Mek haste an' ate, A'm after leavin' the half hour.'

After hurrying breakfast and with the porridge still stuck in her throat, Nancy was sent out to pick handfuls of grass from under trees that had sheltered it from the rain. Sitting her up on the table, mamo helped her to push the grass down into the toe of each boot, before adding a thick layer across the bottom too. As they were fastened, Nancy thought the grass felt nice as the heat from the boots warmed it.

'Hurry girl, time wur goin'.' Michael thrust a sack into her hands as he flung a bag over his shoulder that he had fashioned from salvaged fishing net found in the bay; it served them well enough to transport the dulse and it had cost him nothing.

The walk to the bay usually took about an hour, that's what mamo said, but Nancy had no way of measuring the time except she knew her father walked very fast so perhaps they made the journey more quickly than that. She always found it hard to keep pace with him and normally counted two steps to his one, but today as they set off, it was more like three as she struggled with the weight of the grass-filled boots. She was careful to trail behind him a little as usual, better that way, so as not to annoy him with her stuttering progress. Faerie had come to her this morning when she was picking the grass but he had stayed at a distance like they agreed he would when her father was about. Her father didn't like Faerie and Faerie didn't like him. She needed to tell her friend about Issy, to hold his precious name in her mouth and then gently pass it over to someone who cared about him too, but that would have to wait until they were home again.

As they trudged on over the uneven ground, the grass that had at first cushioned her feet began to lose its dry softness as it mashed inside her boots, she didn't like the feel of it but said nothing to her father for fear it would make him angry. Moving almost silently, they followed the snaking line of the black river, staying close to anything that would give them cover along the way as they moved over grass, then stones, then boggy ground in an ever-repeating sequence. All the while her father's eyes hardly left the ground and he didn't walk upright but stooped, like he carried a heavy weight on his back. Then as they approached the oak tree that marked the halfway point, he slowed his pace, looking up into its branches. They had passed the tree only three days ago on their last trip to the bay and there had been no nuts in sight, but still now he moved closer to it, his face almost touching the trunk. Squinting, he kept looking up, a bag of acorns would win him favour with Kitty and perhaps lift her spirits a little after the boy. 'The lower branches have been stripped but thar be nuts on the higher ones.' He looked expectantly in Nancy's direction. 'You'll need t'climb up girl an' throw the nuts down t'me.' Nancy dropped her sack on the ground and approached the tree. 'C'mon A'll lift you up.' Her father laced his fingers together and cupped his hands. 'Put yer foot here an' A'll push you, then catch hold o' the nearest branch.' No sooner had she put her right foot in his hands, he flung her up as she grabbed for a branch and hung in mid-air, legs flailing about looking for a foothold. The boots were too big and stiff and she couldn't steady herself to stand on a branch so carefully, using twigs like handles, she lowered herself onto her knees hugging the branch below her.

'Climb out further, that-a-way.' He jabbed a finger in the air pointing to where the trees foliage was thickest.

As she began to crawl, leaves got in the way and twigs skewered the knots in her hair as she pushed through them, the rough bark scratching her legs and the skirt of her dress catching under her knees bringing her to a sudden halt and almost toppling her out of the tree.

'That's it girl, yer nearly thar.'

As the branches thinned out into thick twigs they began to bend under her weight so she didn't look down. Twisting and picking each acorn, she dropped them to the ground while her father circled the tree looking for more bounty. 'Come this-a-way, over onto this branch.' He pointed to another cluster of nuts as she slowly reversed along the branch she was on and then carefully out onto the next.

'That'll do. You can come down.'

She backed up again towards the trunk and manoeuvred herself until she was sitting on the branch above her father's head. He stretched out his arms 'Jump!' Shuffling to the edge of the branch she hesitated; would he catch her? 'Jump A says, yer wastin' time.' She closed her eyes and let go and the hare was caught.

Her father had filled his pockets to bulging with the nuts and she could tell that he was satisfied with their haul, mamo would soak and roast the acorns and her mother would be pleased to have this dark, muddy treat to drink. As they continued their progress towards the bay, her father still walked ahead like a man alone, except that he looked over his shoulder from time to time to make sure she wasn't falling behind.

Finally, the lush green gave way to lines of grey, of yellow, of blue as the rushing sound of the sea filled her head. Standing at the cliff edge, they looked down at the sand that stretched out below them and the distant figures that already dotted the beach, then her father gripped her arm and she thought he was going to push her over the edge but instead he pulled her towards him and propelled her down the cliff path almost lifting her off her feet in his urgency to catch up with the thieves that had got ahead of him. They would have to walk much further for the dulse today. Michael considered how they could achieve the best haul. 'A'll walk t'wards Tullaghan.' He pointed down the beach. 'Thar'll be mussels t'be had fer thems that's clever. You go up the beach t'wards Bundoran, spake t'no one an' if anyone tries t'steal what you gather, tell them you've the fever an' run. As soon as the tide begins t'turn back on itself, mek yer way back t'this point here.' He stamped his foot on the sand and then with the toe of his boot drew a large circle in it. 'Don't keep me waitin' or A'll be leavin' wi'out you.' With that, he was gone and she was left alone with the strangers on the beach who she thought had been observing them both with too much interest.

A little way off, two young fellas were wading in amongst the rockpools, searching for the red gold. Working quickly and efficiently, she watched as one stripped the dulse while the other managed their net, dousing it in the seawater and pushing the dulse down inside it so as to get as much in as possible. To their right, she could see an old man dragging a net of dulse almost as big as his shrunken body across the sand, and she didn't know how he would ever get off the beach and up the cliffs. He didn't look strong enough to have torn the dulse from the rocks, if he had collected what had been washed up on the beach, he might be sick, perhaps he didn't have a mamo like hers to tell him to never pick up dulse from the sand.

Further along the shoreline a woman and a small boy were digging for cockles, the woman slowly walking backwards dragging a stick through the wet sand while the boy crouched down on his haunches, face almost touching the sand, as his small fingers searched for tiny treasures in the fleeting furrows before they disappeared. All the while she could see they kept their nervous eyes on a man who was watching them from a little way off. He wasn't collecting dulse or digging for cockles, he didn't seem to be doing anything at all except standing with his hands in his pockets, watching.

She looked up the beach to where she hoped there would be fresh rockpools to plunder and dropping the sack onto the sand she sat down on it to take off the boots. Her progress would be quicker without them and anyway, she liked the feel of the soft sand, but now as she pulled at them they wouldn't budge as mashed, sticky, grass held on to her feet and worked against the rough leather of the boots. She didn't want to unfasten them, the laces were too difficult for her, so in turn, using the toe of one boot she pushed against the heal of the other loosening her feet from their hold sufficiently to be able to pull them off. Her feet were delivered onto the beach like two mossy, knotted logs so burying them in the sand, she scrubbed them backwards and forwards to wipe away the grass that had stuck to them gluing her toes together, but they were still stained green; she was part leprechaun.

She looked down the beach in the direction of her father who was now almost out of sight. The man who had been watching the woman and boy now seemed to be looking in her direction and appeared to be closer to her than before. The sun was in her eyes and she couldn't read the blank silhouette of his face, but she could feel his eyes were on her. *If you meet a stranger run as fast as you can...* She jumped up, put the boots in the sack and headed off up the beach as fast as she could, looking back over her shoulder to make sure no one was behind her. Happy that she wasn't being followed she slowed down and headed for an outcrop of shiny grey rocks. Approaching them, she checked the waves were still drawing back, she had time, then clambering over a small cluster of rocks, she stepped carefully into a pool of clear water where a few glistening tendrils floated just above the low waterline. Putting her sack on the rocks she opened its mouth to receive the dulse.

As she tugged at the first patch a tiny, speckled crab scurried out from its fronds, dropping into the water and taking refuge in a crack in the rocks below the waterline. It would nip her if she reached her fingers in after it so reluctantly she let it be. A few small handfuls later she had cleared what she could, the rest too difficult to reach or too firmly anchored for her to pull away. She would need to go on further if she was going to fill the sack so climbed over the next mound of rocks knowing she must watch the tide or she would be cut off, the cliffs were sheer here and there was no way off the beach. Hauling the sack behind her she carefully navigated the uneven surface of the rocks until she was able to drop into a shallow pool on the other side. To her delight, hundreds of tentacles danced in the water here hidden from sight, plenty to fill her sack which she would set about feeding as quickly as possible. The rocks on this part of the beach seemed to reach out from the cliffs to the shoreline like a long, gnarled finger, and as her eyes followed its line up to the cliff, there was a wide-open mouth in its face, a dark cave that looked like it would swallow you up. A gaping hole big enough for a giant; a hideous fomorian might lurk there angry that she was stealing from its beach. Then something moved in the shadows.

'Who's thar? A've the fever! Don't come near me.'

No reply came, the shadow shifted but did not show itself or speak, the darkness becoming more solid where it stood.

'Stay away!'

The shadow shifted again. Then a soft low voice said, 'Sweet Brigid.'

Nancy stood perfectly still, perhaps it would not see her if she stood as lifeless as stone, anyway it was looking for someone else.

'Sweet, sweet Brigid. I have been waiting for you.'

A tall figure stepped out into the light, she recognised the silhouette, it was the man from the beach. How had he got ahead of her? Pooka; the shapeshifter, suddenly appearing from nowhere. His soft black hat was tipped forward obscuring his face, the dark blue vest and trousers and white linen shirt he was wearing, the cleanest she had ever seen. His hands were pushed down into his pockets, his elbows spreading his long black coat out wide like dark angel wings; he was more Tuath Dé than fomorian!

'A'm not Brigid, stay away.'

The man laughed. 'I only want to talk a while

with you. See, I shall sit here at a distance, you have nothing to fear.' He didn't move closer to her, sure that she would bolt if he did, but lowered himself slowly and sat on a rock never taking his invisible eyes from her.

'Me da is down thar an' he'll batter you, don't come near me.' She pointed into the blank distance.

He laughed again and slowly turned his head to look down the beach. 'Your father is nowhere in sight Brigid and cannot come to your rescue.'

Nancy wanted to run but he could easily cut her off. She looked over her shoulder towards the shore; the tide was still pulling out; it wasn't time yet.

'Do not worry, the tide does not turn yet, your father will not expect you.' He couldn't have heard her father's instructions to her, how did he know what he had said?

'A want t'go.'

'Nothing holds you here. Go if you wish.'

It must be a trick; she would make move to escape and he would grab her and take her into the depths of the dark cave where other-worldly creatures lurked and she would be lost forever. So she didn't move, as in her freedom to run, he somehow held on to her.

'Very well then.' He removed his hat and smiled at her. To her surprise, his hair was light and his eyes were coloured like the rocks on the beach, shining grey and flinty, but not unkind in their looking. His skin was smooth and evenly coloured, not weathered and smudged by the wind and sun.

'So fair Brigid, she of pretty words and poetry, what do you have to say?'

'Me name's not Brigid.'

'Your parents have named you other then?'

'A'm called after me great granny.'

'Who was called Brigid?'

'She wur called Nancy.' As her name fell from her lips she realised he had tricked her into giving her true self away.

'Nancy is it? You will be Brigid to me. Would you like to sit a while and hear a story?'

She liked mamo's stories but she didn't want his. 'A don't want a story.'

'You don't even know what my story is about, there is magic and wonder to be found in words, are you sure you would not like to hear?'

Nancy hesitated. 'Me da'll give me a bastin' if A don't bring the dulse.'

Suddenly the man stood up and began to walk towards her, frightened, she closed her eyes and screamed as loud as she could but he ran towards her and clasped his hand over her mouth silencing her. He was going to finish her. Opening one eye, she looked up into her killer's face but saw he was smiling at her, and with that, her rigid body softened and her muffled screams left her. Letting go and without speaking, he turned and began tearing at the clumps of dulse, stealing what was rightfully hers. She watched him without moving as her feet sank into the wet sand further anchoring her to the spot, then having piled his harvest of dulse up on the rocks, he opened her sack and pushed the slippery tendrils inside.

'There, your father will be very pleased with you, I have saved you from a beating.'

Nancy was confused, why was he helping her?

'See, now the tide begins to turn, I will carry it down the beach and leave you before your father comes into sight.'

He threw the sack over his shoulder like it weighed no more than a feather, climbed over the rocks and jumped down onto the sand on the other side. 'Are you coming sweet Brigid?'

She must get back to her father or there would be trouble for her, so pulling her feet from the sucking sand, she followed him, walking separately but keeping a close eye on her sack. He said nothing more to her but looked at her and smiled from time to time as they made steady progress down the beach until they had almost reached the circle in the sand. Her father was not yet in sight; he would be the one to keep her waiting not the other way around and it made her smile to herself. The man dropped the sack, tipped his hat, and left her without saying a word.

Watching after him, she saw him deftly climb the path up the cliffs until he reached the top, then turn and wave at her. Taking hold of the sack and using all her weight against it, she dragged it backwards the last little distance to where she was to meet her father, falling down on the springy heap just as he came into view. Even from a distance she could see the spoils in his net, he would be happy, they would all be happy tonight and the next day and the next.

As Michael Sullivan approached he stared at the bulging sack and Nancy thought she even saw him smile. 'Sure, that's a horrible grand job you've done, 'though how you wur able t'carry it all, A don't know.' He considered the abundance of their combined haul and the challenge of the long walk home. 'We'll switch. You tek the net an' A'll tek the sack.' He looked down at her green feet. 'Whar be yer boots?'

Nancy had forgotten about the boots which were buried deep under all the dulse. He would be angry. 'A put them in the bottom o' the sack.'

Her father looked at the sack and then at her and she expected he would make her walk home in her bare feet but instead, he took a small knife from his coat and cut the stitching of one corner, then pushing his hand in, felt around for the boots and tugged them out one at a time through the hole before knotting it to stop the contents falling out. 'Mind, yer t'mend the sack this evenin' girl.'

CHAPTER 3

The Big House

Stepping out from the shadowing of the birch trees that lined its long winding approach, Nathaniel looked up at the house. In all its excesses his grandfather had built it to impress and be a lasting monument to his success. All who visited would declare it handsome, fitting, most elegant. Eleven limestone steps ensured a dramatic approach to the grand portico which was made up of four ashlar columns that supported a cornice embellished with simple carved roundels, while crowning the round-headed door, incongruous in its mimicry, was an ornate venetian-style window with limestone sills. Symmetrical windows, appearing like blank staring eyes in the sunlight, punctuated the impressive breakfront of the house, diminishing in size as they stacked themselves up to the roofline, in one of them, his mother appearing as the inky black pupil, spying on him as he approached. Spotting her, Nathaniel took a cursory look down at himself, the long grass had swept away any evidence of sand on his shoes but he was careful to brush away any other residue on his clothes that could incriminate him. No sooner was he through the door, the walls and ceiling of the large entrance hall closed in as his mother appeared in front of him. 'Your father has been waiting for you. Where have you been? You were promised to be here to meet with Mr. Hamilton more than two hours ago and he has had to conclude the estate business without you.'

'As my father knows, I have little to offer when it comes to estate affairs either in useful insights or indeed the vaguest of interest.'

'It is your duty to take an interest, not a choice.'

'Ah well mother we may not agree on that point. In any event, we share little in common when it comes to ideas on how to run the estate, I do not think my father cares to hear my opinion in these matters.' He tried to move past her but she blocked his path, she was not finished with him.

'I do not understand why you insist on vexing your father so? You create an unnecessary disquiet in this house which we all have to endure.'

'I am so sorry for your suffering.' It was said with sarcasm. 'My father knows that I am more than happy to step aside in favour of Henry, my brother would want it, he would as quickly trample over me as blink his eye if it would gain him the prize of being my father's heir.'

'That is not the point. You are the eldest, it is your birthright.'

'A birthright that I will never value nor want.'

'That is ridiculous. What do you expect to do with your life? How do you intend to honour this family's good name? By reading your poetry books or gazing at the stars? None of it of real life or any use to man or beast.'

'In those words mother you prove my point. I am made different is all I can say, when the potions of life mingled together, something different was concocted in my case. I find more sense in nature and its spiritual gifts than any deed papers or ledgers, perishable promises, or self-serving numbers on worthless paper. My father will never seek to balance his books on the poor souls whose plight it has been to be cut off from the basic rights of human beings to have a roof over their heads and food on their tables. They seek only the security of a home but live pitifully under the threat of eviction or forced emigration.'

'You know your father to be a fair and decent man but these people should not expect handouts.'

'These people? Handouts? Like the handout my father received from grandfather?'

'I will not have you speak of your father so

disrespectfully.'

'I yearn to respect the man but I will never respect the money that he did not earn or make any sacrifice for and uses ill. When any man is more money than soul I lose interest. Ask me instead to admire the man who works hard for his family and the mother who gives up her own food to feed her child. This is where I place my respect.'

'Hah! I suppose you would rather keep company with low-living wretches; violent agitators or rioters!'

'They protest with the integrity of a just cause in the face of government rule that is cruel beyond measure and perpetuated by mis-guided patriots like my father. Did you know that just this last week a boy of no more than twelve years was transported for the most heinous crime of stealing a loaf of bread?'

'There is no place in a civilised society for people of low morals and criminal intent. The law must prevail or there will be rampant disorder.'

'A twelve-year-old boy mother.'

Ellen Collins shrugged her shoulders dismissively 'What do you expect me to say? That I applaud the parents who raised a thief?'

'No. That you grieve for the mother who has lost her son. That you fear for the child who sails to a foreign land without anyone to care whether he ever sets foot on land again; lives or dies.'

'I will not argue with you. You are irrational

and too emotional by far to have a sensible conversation. Go to your father. He awaits you in his study and you should pray that his mood has softened this last hour.' She stepped aside to let him pass.

Nathaniel took the long, bleak walk to his father's study already knowing the inevitability of what was to come. He knocked and waited, just as he had as a child, never having had the freedom of spirit or the encouragement to ever enter unannounced. His father's heavy voice came from the other side of the door. 'Enter.'

Sitting at his desk studying a property deed that was spread open on it covering its whole width, his father didn't look up, continuing with his reading.

'Sit.'

Nathaniel sat down, ready to take his punishment.

'What was so important that you could not keep your commitment to meet with Mr. Hamilton and I this morning?'

'I am sure Mr. Hamilton would not have felt my absence very acutely.'

'Do not be impertinent. You have responsibilities and you cannot be so casual in your affairs sir. I ask again. Where were you?'

'Surveying some of our tenants father.'

'For what purpose?'

'For understanding.'

'Understanding of what?'

'Their plight.'

'Their plight?...'

He finally raised his myopic eyes and looked out at his son through the thick lenses perched on his nose, the black rim of his glasses drawing hard lines around his beady eyes, shrinking his irises and their pupils to small black dots, reminding Nathaniel of the frog spawn he and Henry had gathered as boys from the big pond. 'And what do you surmise about their plight I wonder?'

'That no man should be separated from the opportunity to live a decent and prosperous life simply by trick of their birth.'

Now Matthew Collins removed his glasses and sat back in his chair. 'Those are fine words for a man, who by trick of his birth as you put it, need not ever worry about such things. You survey the wretched from a lofty and privileged position sir. I am sure these poor mites are most grateful to be pitied by you, that will surely satisfy any hunger felt in their bellies.' The meter of his father's voice didn't alter and its pitch remained low and measured, his composure never visibly faltering other than the fat vein pulsing below his left eye which gave him away. Nathaniel knew he must not let his tongue run away with him the way he allowed it to with his mother and although he steadfastly held his father's gaze, he was the first to surrender, dropping his eyes to the floor, bringing their futile parrying to an end.

'I do not begin to understand your lack of ambition nor your reluctance to apply yourself in any useful way to business. Such ridiculous ideologies are cheap to a man who has never had to earn his place in the world.' He leant forward in his chair. 'Hear this, you have six months to prove to me that you are willing to contribute to the fortunes and good reputation of this family. Beyond that sir, you will find yourself cut-off without a penny and then you will see what it is for a man to prosper by living on his own wits. I leave this house and the care of your mother in your hands while I am away in Spain these next two weeks, do not give me cause to regret it. Hamilton has the full schedule of works and you would do well to work with him to ensure all is managed satisfactorily. Now get from my sight and consider your options carefully, all that is ahead in your future is up to you.'

As his father went back to his deeds, Nathaniel stood to leave. 'Do you care for me at all father?' He hadn't intended to say it but it was out of his mouth now and there was no going back.

'What nonsense is this? I wonder if you are not a little unwell.' His eyes only momentarily flickered in his son's direction before fixing themselves again on the papers that demanded his attention.

'I am quite well father.'

'You are my son and heir, there is nothing greater than that and no more to be said, now go.' His voice was flat and careless in its tone, the slap of his cold words, like a physical blow. As Nathaniel opened the door to leave, Henry was lurking in the corridor with no credible excuse for being there except his blatant eavesdropping. His brother's smile was fake at the best of times but now, coupled with his obvious embarrassment at being caught in the act, he grinned at Nathaniel like an imbecile. Neither brother spoke in their understanding of what was at play and as Nathaniel pushed past his brother, he stiffened his shoulder giving him a hard shove, while inside the study, Matthew Collins stared at the closed door, disturbed by something unfamiliar but sharply felt.

The day had started so promisingly for Nathaniel, now it lay in tatters. Back in the sanctuary of his room, he leant against the door, muscles snapped shut and rigid as his anger held on to him, then crossing the room to the fireplace, he picked up a poker and smashed it against the wall again and again, denting the wood panelling until finally his anger burst and leaked away, the sound of splintering wood bringing him to his senses as he collapsed into an armchair breathless and spent. What life was this, how could he live it? He thought of Brigid and all those poor souls who would be grateful to have such a wretched life as his. Exhausted, his tired eyes drifted around the room looking for compass or some small stepping stone to a happier state of being, before settling on the stack of books on the table by his chair. Picking up *Songs of Innocence* from the top of the pile he opened it, smiling to himself as favoured pages fell open from hours of reading making their own selection for him now, the book choosing exactly what he needed.

Can I see another's woe,
And not be in sorrow too?
Can I see another's grief,
And not seek for kind relief?
Can I see a falling tear,
And not feel my sorrow's share?...

CHAPTER 4

Under Mamo's Skirt

She had found the place where her father had taken Issy, a little way from the cottage, hidden between an elm tree and a green mossy mound where sunny ragwort claimed the ground. A circle of grey stones marked out the tiny, Issy-sized grave and as the two friends sat on the ground next to where he lay, each quietly contemplated his departure without the words to express the pain and confusion of his leaving. Faerie had watched on quietly as Nancy slowly circled her brother picking daisies for a chain to lay across the cold stones, all the while the side of her bare foot tracing their edges so she could feel something of him. Then, hands full of flowers, she had sat down on the ground as her small fingers began linking head to stem, head to stem.

'Mamo says he's not here Faerie; he be gone t'heaven whar the angels are. Tis above the earth we stand on, higher than the trees but we can't see it. A didn't think he'd g'away an' not come back. A don't understand.' She looked upwards and so did Faerie but there was nothing but sky and clouds.

'Don't understand what Brigid?'

She froze. From behind the tree the silent shadow of a dark angel wing emerged, the man following it, until he stood towering just a nettle's height away from her. She didn't answer, afraid to look at him, all the time keeping her eyes fixed on Faerie for reassurance.

'Come now fair Brigid, have you forgotten me so quickly?' He moved a step towards her and then sat down on the grass, dropping his wings and crossing his legs under him. He was too close. His knee was almost touching the edge of her dress that was spread out on the ground and she shuffled a little further away because of the nearness of him. He folded his clean, white hands in his lap and then just looked at her.

'What d'you want? A'll shout me da.'

'I hope you would favour my company over his. From my understanding he is not a man of any merit or obvious virtues and looks out for his own interests before those of his family. He gives little regard to your happiness Brigid.'

'You don't know 'bout him.'

'I know about lots of things.' He looked into her eyes. 'Is this where your brother lies?'

She hesitated, how did he know? She nodded.

He looked at the pathetic circle of stones, not

much to show for the sum of a life, then leaning forward whispered. 'Bright One, every day the fire of your hope rises with the sun and your brother will live in that light for eternity. Take your strength from the promise that every new dawn brings, trust me fair Brigid, new life will always spring up around you.' She didn't know what he was talking about, he spoke strangely and confusingly, but she liked the sound of his words and savoured his voice that was as pleasing as salt to potatoes.

He sat back from her as his tone changed and all the lightness in his voice fell. 'You live a poor and wretched life little one, that is the truth of it, and I would like to help you.'

'A'm not t'spake wi' strangers.' It was all she could think of to say.

'It is my hope that you will consider me a friend when I tell you of my plans. Do you know what difference gold can make in this world Brigid? It brings power and choices but to my mind is often to be found in the wrong hands. I have gold Brigid, lots of money and I would like to help you if you will let me.' He reached across and laid his hand on top of one of hers, she wanted to move it but his hand was heavy and not for letting go. 'Do you think we can be friends?'

She was struck dumb by the question.

'Think about it.' He leant across, his face so close to hers now, that she could smell the sweetness of his breath. He studied the dirty face of the beauty in waiting before pulling his hand away and releasing her. Taking her opportunity to break free, she ran as fast as she could back to the cottage and almost falling through the door, found mamo sitting alone in the kitchen by the fire.

'Whar you been chile? Yer mother sent you out fer kippins an hour ago, you'd be wise not t'vex her, she's not fer reasonable behaviour the day an' carries the strap.'

She didn't care about what her mother wanted. 'A went t'see whar me da put Issy.'

'Oh chile, no gud'll come o'that, don't be causin' yerself such sufferin'.'

'A don't want him t'be alone. A want him t'come back now.'

'He's gone from this earth but he's not alone.'

She wanted to tell mamo about the man with the angel wings but just then Kitty's angry, shrieking voice came from outside and they both froze. 'Whar you girl? A know what yer 'bout. You'll be sorry fer crossin' me s'you will.'

'Get under!' Mamo lifted her dress. 'Get under, quick!' Nancy dropped to the floor and crawled under her grandmother's skirt, the heavy grey curtain coming down over her just as her mother burst through the cottage door.

'Whar's she hidin'?' Nancy could hear the breathless fury in her mother's voice.

'She's not come back here. A thought you sent her out fer kippins?'

'A did, an hour since but she's off wi' idlin' just like her father.' Kitty looked defiantly into the face of the woman who raised him. 'A'll not suffer her devilment; wait 'til A get me hands on that little cnat!'

'Sit Kitty, thar be tay in the pot.' Frances spoke softly and calmly. Kitty eyed the pot as her weariness overcame her and she dropped down heavily on the bench, the leather strap still dangling ominously in her hand. 'Yer tired, why not have some tay an' then rest fer a while, you've had much t'trouble you these last days. The girl'll catch it from me when she comes back an' A'll mek sure she does all you've instructed. Rest Kitty.'

Kitty surveyed her mother-in-law with suspicion. 'Yer too soft wi' her; A don't trust you t'punish her.'

Frances had to think quickly. 'She'll sleep here on the cold floor t'night an' won't know the comfort o' our bed, that'll teach her t'mind her mother.'

In the darkness under mamo's skirt, Nancy didn't move, as her mother considered the attraction of the opportunity to lie down and shut out the world and its miseries for a few hours. Then she heard Kitty push back the bench and the scraping sound of her footsteps very close as she lifted the pot and poured the tea. As she waited, a smell like damp earth and bog water was coming from mamo, but she couldn't lift her grandmother's skirt for air, so held her nose and breathed through her mouth to shut it out. She stayed perfectly still with nothing to break the blackness of the dark tent of her grandmother's skirt except the illumination of her faded blue drawers and bone-white stockingless legs, skin hanging loose, dripping like a candle. Nancy's toes had searched for the warmth of those legs at night when they lay in their bed but she had never thought about what they would look like and now she couldn't take her eyes off their strangeness.

'Alright auld woman.' The anger had ebbed away from Kitty's voice.

'Why not tek the tay t'yer bed, you must be dyin' wi' sleep.'

Through the dulling of the thick wool cloth of mamo's skirt, she heard her mother's footsteps come close again and then the muffled sound of her pulling the curtain across and the creak of the wood as she lay down on her bed. In the silence she waited and held her breath until eventually the darkness lifted as mamo raised the hem of her skirt and bent down to look in on her, a rush of fresher air coming to Nancy's nostrils. Her face upside down, finger to her lips, mamo spoke in a hushed voice. 'You can come out now but stay quiet.'

Nancy couldn't move.

'C'mon chile.' And reaching in mamo took hold of her arm and gently pulled her out. Nancy stood mutely in front of her grandmother looking anxiously towards the curtain where her mother lay just feet away. Mamo followed her eyes towards the curtain and back to Nancy then slowly and stiffly got to her feet before leading her by the hand, out of the cottage and far enough away so that their voices wouldn't be heard.

'You understand yer t'sleep on the floor t'night chile? Tis the only way t'satisfy yer mother's anger.'

'But A can't sleep wi'out you mamo.' Nancy began to cry.

'Don't be cryin.' D'you trust me t'tek care o' things?

Nancy nodded.

'Then dry yer tears. All will be well.' She smiled and touched her granddaughter's face gently, smoothing her wet cheek.

'Now listen t'me, you must be gud. Don't be answerin' yer mother back, best you don't speak at all unless she demands it o' you. Be after doin' whatever you can t'please her. D'you understand?'

Nancy nodded again.

'Grand. Now help me back t'the cottage an' then go an' fetch the kippins, an' mek sure thar dry, yer mother'll be after dampin' the fire if thar wet.'

That night Nancy lay on the cold ground in the dark as the moon cast a thin, glowing line of silver across the floor and the dim light from the fire threw shadowy dancing shapes onto the walls that frightened her. She put her hands over her face and closed her eyes to shut them out but she couldn't keep them closed and they would spring open again - closed, open, closed, open - then looking out between her fingers she saw mamo sitting in the chair by the fire. Her grandmother raised her hand as a signal not to move from where she was and Nancy stayed still, then closed her eyes and fell asleep.

CHAPTER 5

The Sovereign

Waking at dawn, she lay still on the floor tracing her eyes along the beam of yellow-infused light from the window that had replaced the silver line of the moon, settling itself on mamo's empty chair. Only they would know that she had been there, that they had been together through the night. Remembering what mamo had told her she intended to be especially helpful to her mother today, starting with setting out the dishes for breakfast but just as she was taking the bowls from the shelf, mamo appeared from behind the curtain, giving her a knowing smile. A little unsteady on her feet, in her stumbling, the contents of the gizunder she was carrying splashed on the floor, so abandoning the dishes, Nancy went to her grandmother and took her arm, helping her to the chair.

'Thanky chile. Tek this an' empty it. Then bring the bucket s'A can boil water fer the tay.'

Nancy took the po from mamo concentrating

on holding both its handles tightly so as not to spill any of the putrid yellowness on herself, then setting it down carefully on the floor by the door, she lifted the latch to the brutal chill of a new day. Once outside, walking slowly and steadily, she went around to the back of the cottage and emptied the foul liquid down the stinking hole that swallowed everything disgusting, taking the opportunity to do her own business while she was about it. When she went back into the kitchen the three shadows were already sitting at the table.

Kitty's rampage with the strap yesterday had marked the end of a period of relative harmony in the Sullivan household, three whole days when their sustenance had taken on an almost intoxicating variety of flavours. There had been the cockles and mussels; deliciously sweet, soft and meaty to chew, there had even been the dark, heady acorn drink for Kitty. Mamo had necessarily become proficient at tempering her daughter-in-law's volatile nature and as soon as Michael had returned with the pocketfuls of nuts, she had set about boiling and shelling them, smashing them into tiny pieces and roasting them in a pan before taking a stone and grinding them into a fine powder. Nancy liked the sweet smell of the powder but not the bitterness when she tasted it. Still, for her mother, it was an obvious pleasure that seemed to help settle her agitation. That had been a good afternoon's work on mamo's part for all of them but now after three days, the temporary calm had begun to fracture as the dulse ran down and the cornmeal was finally reduced to dust. Their fragile fortunes were turning again and their small crop of potatoes was failing although no one dared utter the words. She had seen her father on his knees, nose to the red earth, studying the black marks that had appeared on the tips of leaves that had begun to shrivel. With so much rain the previous week, the ground had become more bog than soil and she knew that wasn't a good thing, and as he had crawled the lines hopeful that he could stop the march of the blight that would mean no potatoes to take them through the winter, her mother had watched him too, bitter like the acorn drink, at his continuing failure as a provider.

A half-filled bowl of pale, runny liquid, more thin soup than porridge, would have to suffice for breakfast and Nancy knew that at best, it would be dulse for supper and perhaps a few poreens if anything edible could be unearthed from amongst the failing potatoes. She predicted that tomorrow would bring another trip to the bay with her father if the weather was fine but for now they would all have to navigate the growing storm of Kitty's foul temper and do their best to stay out of her way. As she came in her mother gave her a cold look. 'Dawdlin' again girl? Set yerself down an' be quick 'bout it.' Throughout breakfast Nancy stayed quiet and watchful of her mother like mamo told her to. Nothing else passed between them after that and still no one mentioned Issy's name – and she knew not to speak it herself - except to Faerie who understood her loss.

To everyone's relief, Kitty went back to her bed straight after breakfast, bringing a welcome, although depressing calm to the cottage. Nancy and mamo were careful to work quietly and keep their voices low as they swept the floor and boiled water for the laundry, not wanting to disturb her and hoping to keep her in bed as long as possible. Now as her mother's greying, stained stockings and petticoat flapped in the wind, strung up on a line between two trees, Nancy was happy with their morning's work. She and mamo had used ash for the worst stains and got the water as hot as mamo's hands could suffer before scrubbing the clothes as hard as they would stand without falling apart, but mamo always talked about how she would love to have some soap, like it was something magical. Nancy had helped mamo count out four of their ten clothes pegs and then pinned her mother's underclothes up on the line, both of them hoping that Kitty would be pleased by their waving at her like almost-white flags of surrender. Now, just as she picked a final stem of frothing Meadowsweet to decorate their table,

Faerie stood up on his hind legs alerting her that someone was approaching them. She looked up and in the distance saw a man she didn't recognise. It couldn't be her father, she knew his uneven gait, the hang of his head, his stoop. Even Fairie stood his ground for now. No, this was a stranger, so she must make ready to run. She looked back towards the open door of the cottage but curiosity held on to her and she didn't move. Could it be Dark Wings? The man kept coming, striding with purpose, growing bigger and finally recognisable to her as he got closer. It could not be. It **was** her father but not as she had ever seen him. He was grinning and the strange sight of it frightened her. She turned and ran inside the cottage, almost knocking her mother off her feet in her hurry to reach mamo, then stood behind her grandmother's chair for protection from the demon that had taken over her father.

'What is it chile? Mamo reached round and pulled Nancy forward until she was standing in front of her. 'What's the matter?

'Me da!'

'What 'bout him?'

Nancy just stared at her grandmother.

'Spake when yer told girl.' Sleep had done nothing to improve Kitty's mood and she moved to grab Nancy and shake an answer out of her just as her husband appeared in the doorway 'Kitty me love; you'll be lured stiff wi' me news.'

Nancy and mamo looked at each other, something was wrong, he never spoke pretty words like that, they didn't know they were anywhere in him to be found. The devil definitely had him. Kitty looked equally perplexed at his words searching his face for some understanding of what was at play.

'Sit. A'll tell yuz the story o' me day.'

Kitty hesitated for a moment but sat down on the bench never taking her eyes off her husband.

'C'mon, you too Nancy.' He had used her name and in an instant she was elevated to a person not just a thing. Encouraged with a gentle shove from mamo, she climbed up onto the end of the bench, nearest the door, just in case. Then they waited. Satisfied that he had created sufficient anticipation for what he was about to tell them, Michael sat at the end of the table, all the while shaking his head incredulously, smiling to himself. His eyes were shining pink and Nancy couldn't tell if he was about to laugh or cry, either way, she was frightened.

'A wur out at the ridge, breakin' me back cuttin' peat, mindin' me own business, when a stranger approached me.'

'Whar's the peat?' Kitty interjected looking at the empty bag he had dropped by the door on his way in.

'Whisht woman, ferget the peat, it don't matter.' Kitty was about to protest but curiosity stopped her from stalling his story any further. He was going to take his time, make the most of the tale. 'As A wur tellin' yuz, a stranger approached me. Well A says a stranger, but he's a Collins, from the big house.' Now he had everyone's attention.

'A thought he wur after tryin' t'stop me tekin' what's any man's right t'tek an' A wur ready fer him, but he wurn't minded t'no such thing. He asked me if A knew o' any hard-workin', trustworthy fella lookin' fer work. A says, *he stands in front o' you sir,* an' he says, *well A cannot fathom it, this is indeed a most for-tous meetin', A cannot believe me luck.'* Michael grinned as he looked around the table to make sure everyone was listening, so wide and enthusiastic the crack in his face, that Nancy could see for the first time he had all his teeth.

'Thems after startin' work on a new spring house the morra - such a fine house requires more than one be all accounts – s'need the services o' a fine fella like meself t'help build it.' Kitty looked at her husband, he hadn't been drinking, she knew the signs, besides, he did not have the wit or intelligence to successfully convince any man to give him a free drink and there was simply no money to honestly acquire it.

'Tis a week's work at least an' A'll be paid handsome an' reckon we'll have enough t'live well fer a month or more.' He waited for his applause.

Kitty thought there must be a catch. 'Didn't you think it strange **you** wur approached husband, the big house must have a lob o' men wantin' the work, why you?'

Michael was irritated; it was not the response he craved. 'Thar be more t'tell.' He went on quickly, eager to impress. 'He gev me an advance on me wages.'

'Show me.' Kitty stretched out her hand.

Michael reached into his pocket and took out a disc of gold. Placing it on the table he kept his grubby fingers on its edge, fixing it to the surface, warning off anyone who ventured to touch it. A sovereign; two hundred and forty pennies right there in that tiny circle of gold no bigger than a pebble. Kitty gasped. 'Whar you 'bout? Havvy brought trouble t'this house?'

In his frustration, he quickly slid the coin back along the table and then closed his fist around it. 'Twas honestly got fer the promise o' me gud services an' thar be another when the work's finished.'

Kitty sat back stunned into silence. Good fortune did not come their way, so why had it now?

'A starts first thing the morra an' wur promised a measure o' butter an' cream every day an' fresh-baked bread too.' The abundance of his words was almost too intoxicating for Kitty and as her head began to swim she thought she was going to faint.

'If he's pleased wi' me, reckon thar be more work t'be had, imagine that.'

Kitty was imagining that and Nancy now watched her parents exchange a look between them that she had never seen before.

'Thar be one more thing, the girl's t'come wi' me every day.' He was looking down at the coin, turning it over in his palm, trying to pass his words off as if they were nothing, but his mother picked them up before they were discarded and lost.

'Why's he needin' Nancy thar? How'd he know o' her, diddy offer her t'him?'

'What kind o' man d'you think A'm? He already knows o' her, isn't that right girl?' All eyes turned in Nancy's direction.

'D'you know him chile?' Mamo searched her face.

Nancy hesitated, it felt like she was about to break a promise, an unspoken understanding between her and Dark Wings. 'Well?' Mamo persisted and went to rise from her chair stirring Nancy to respond.

A met him on the beach when da an' me went t'the bay. A didn't mean t'spake wi' him mamo. A don't know him an' A don't want t'go t'the big house. Don't mek me.'

Her father interjected before his mother could answer. 'You'll go. A've already settled it wi' him. Thar be n'harm in it, he only wants comp'ny fer his young nephews.'

Kitty said nothing but mamo protested 'An' you tek his word fer it? Tisn't proper. She'll be under yer protection Michael an' God fergive you if anythin' happens t'her.'

Michael rolled his eyes and sat back in his chair contentedly, he had done very well, and he would give no mind to his mother's warning.

CHAPTER 6

The Room of Sunshine

It was dark when her father shook her from her sleep the next morning. Beside her, mamo stirred and opened her eyes giving her son one final accusatory look, but it landed without impact and nothing more was said. 'C'mon be quick girl thar's a long walk ahead, still, A'm promised a fine breakfast when we get thar!' He laughed and slapped his stomach.

Not quite fully awake when they set off on their usual silent journey, her father walked ahead of her as always - but more upright than normal she thought – and although she did her best to keep pace with him he was moving at a lick today and she struggled with her boots, having to almost run, counting at least four paces to his one now. Her father had fastened the laces so tightly that it felt like her toes weren't there, even when she wiggled them inside the boots, while the coarse leather rubbed the skin of her ankles raw.

The dim light of the woods seemed to go on

endlessly until finally a tunnel of light opened up and they stepped out into bright sunshine by the black wrought iron gates of Cole Hall. Waiting there, as Michael had been instructed to, Nancy looked through the metal railings to the rainbow walled garden beyond. At its edges, roses of every colour and shape climbed the walls, heads nodding heavily under their weight, while lavender created a sea of blue and lilac where bees sailed like drunken mariners with their precious cargo onboard. Long rows of leaves pushed up through the soil, the darkest and brightest of greens, red-veined, big, small, fat, thin, crinkled, smooth, growing in perfect lines, springing up from roots below the earth that she had never seen let alone tasted. The crown at the centre of it all, a colourful arc of fruit trees – apple, pear, cherry – and to each side, bushes laden with blackcurrants and raspberries. Beyond it all, the back of the house rose up towards the sky like a shining white mountain.

Holding the bars of the gate, her face pushed through their gap, Nancy saw a stern looking woman walking towards them.

'Sullivan?'

Nancy let go of the bars and stepped back as her father straightened himself up and took off his hat, smoothing down his unruly greasy hair. 'Aye, A'm Michael Sullivan, howya?'

She ignored his inappropriate greeting and

didn't return it. 'And this is the child?'

'Tis me daughter, Nancy.'

Nancy looked up at the woman through the railings. She was fat with a round, pink face and blue eyes that didn't look out straight at you, instead one pointing towards the other. Her tight grey dress drew strained lines around a thick waist that no corset could contain and an ample bosom that rose up and down like a bellows with each breath. Attached to her belt was a shiny silver chain that disappeared down into her pocket making it bulge out from her skirt.

'Very well, I will take you to Mr Hamilton and he will put you about your work.'

Michael nodded his understanding and the woman pulled at the chain revealing at its end a heavy bunch of keys. Sorting through them until she came to the biggest, she slipped it into the lock and opened the gate to let them in. As it swung open, Nancy's father propelled her forward 'Move girl. Don't be after keepin' the lady waitin'.'

As they walked the gravel path around the edge of the garden towards the house, no one spoke, there was just the crunching sound of the stones under their feet. Then, as they approached a big oak door at the side of the house a tall, unsmiling man carrying a shotgun that hung down like a chicken with a broken neck, came out to meet them. 'Mr. Hamilton, here is the man the young master said to expect.'

The man looked them both up and down slowly with obvious disinterest.

'Ah well, you are the man the young master thinks we need to help with the spring house.' He said it like he was thinking it but didn't mean to say it out loud. 'Better follow me then.'

'Child, you will come with me, the young master is waiting in the summer drawing room.' Nancy didn't know what that meant, summer was passing but the days were still bright and perhaps it was a place where the sun shone brightest. Michael gave over his child to the stranger with an empty look and walked away from her, tailing the man out through a second gate and out of sight. She looked after him but he didn't turn around.

Pushing open the heavy oak door the woman took hold of Nancy's sleeve and pulled her into a huge kitchen, at the creaking of the hinges, the cook turning and staring at them as she stopped chopping the vegetables that were piled up in front of her. 'Wipe your feet girl, this is not a barn.' Nancy looked up at the woman but wasn't sure what to do. 'On the mat, clean your boots on the mat!' She watched the woman shuffle her feet backwards and forwards on the hairy mat and copied her. The cook just kept staring, eyes following Nancy as she was marched past her without a word, out through a door at the other end of the kitchen where they turned left down a narrow low passageway and then up steep, wooden stairs which opened onto another dark corridor. It felt like they were walking around the edges of the house rather than in it. Keeping her fat fingers on Nancy's back, the woman pushed her along for what felt like the longest time as they turned right and right again until finally she stopped pushing and they came to a sudden stop. Then she leant against what looked like a panel in the wall, but it was a door and opened up to bright light, on the other side, a different kind of space. Here, a corridor of pale green walls hung with gold-framed paintings, rose up to a canopy of faintly coloured flowers and birds ghosted against a white plaster sky, under their feet, a wool rug stretching ahead the full length of the corridor, its border of ivy leaves lightly meandering along its edges like the daisy chains she made for Issy. It was as green as grass in colour with splashes of blue and orange and Nancy found herself looking down at her feet, measuring her steps against the repeating square pattern that ran down its centre. After counting ten squares and eight they stopped outside a cream-coloured door and the woman knocked. As they waited, the woman looked down at Nancy with disdain, one eye meeting hers, the other looking somewhere else. 'Stand up straight girl.'

'Come in.' A voice came from inside.

She pushed open the door and putting her hand on Nancy's shoulder, firmly ushered her into the room.

'Ah. How nice to see you Miss Sullivan.'

The woman was embarrassed by the way he addressed the wretched child. 'Will there be anything else sir?'

'Yes I think some tea with sugar would be nice for our guest. Would you like that Miss Sullivan?'

Nancy nodded dumbly.

'Very well. I think too some bread and marmalade would be in order Miss Boyle. Please be sure the bread is warm and bring plenty of butter for our guest.' The woman seemed to bristle at the request. 'Yes sir.' Then she left shutting the door noisily behind her.

The room was not yellow like sunshine but cool blue and white with paintings of animals and flowers hung around the walls. A painting of a black pig caught Nancy's eye, its body was far too big for its head and she thought it looked more like a big fat beetle. Two blue sofas faced each other with a low table between them and a pair of velvet-covered chairs flanked the fireplace each with its own footstool. On the other side of the room was a large round table with chairs that matched its legs and left and right of the door were twin console tables, every silver and china trinket upon them identically paired, like a mirror stood between them. There were no other children there.

'Brigid' he said smiling at her. Then her eyes followed his as he looked down at her feet where she saw that her dirty brown boots had trampled on two white roses woven into the rug. She was in trouble. 'We must do something about those boots. Come sit here by the window with me.' Without touching her he guided her towards one of the large blue sofas by the window. 'Sit, sit, little one, you will find it most comfortable.' Nancy eyed the sofa, as big as a carriage with plump cushions and carved wooden feet instead of wheels, it was too high for her so she would have to climb up, but before she was able to make her ascent, he whisked her up into the air and set her down on the springy cushions.

'There, is that not comfortable?'

It was, but she didn't say so.

Then the man got down on his knees in front of her and tapping the toe of one of her boots said. 'Give me your foot.' She straightened her knee as he took the heel of her boot in one hand while untying the laces with the other before dropping the boot to the floor. 'Now the other one.' Again he freed her from the boot then taking a foot in each hand he squeezed her blackened toes. 'Your feet are cold little one, we shall warm them.' Then he looked down at the raw, red rings around her ankles and lightly ran a finger along their raised lines. Staring up into her face his look darkened and she thought he looked angry. 'Wrong, wrong, wrong!' The words burst out of him as he sprang up and turned his back on her, looking out of the window to the view beyond, his wings dropped.

As he stood there framed by the window, the light poured in on him illuminating his hair and clothes with glowing gold and she imagined his feet floating away from the floor and the angel flying out across the carpet of green and the billow of tree tops all the way to the calm waters of the lough beyond. She stayed quiet and still, like she could be invisible if she didn't move or make a sound, but the mantle clock striking the quarter hour broke the silence and made her jump as Dark Wings took a deep breath and stirred back into life. He turned to face her, the anger gone from his face. 'I should like it if you would let me read to you, would that be acceptable to you Brigid?'

Nancy hesitated but the warmth of the room and the comfort of the sofa were working their spell on her and she found herself nodding.

'Excellent. I have a book which I very much hope you will enjoy.' Mamo had a book, a bible, and she had looked at it but never heard its words, being as mamo couldn't read.

'You know Brigid, when we read we can go to places that we will never visit, discover lands far away with no need to travel there. We can love and care for people we will never know or put them away for their unloveliness.' She looked up at him as he paced up and down in front of her, hands dancing in the air like he was trying to catch butterflies. 'We can dream impossible dreams, enter into danger and mystery, stand as the arbiters of what is right and wrong while justice is served although it is not always, we can rage of course, but will have no voice when injustices come. We can cry but will not be heard when hearts break. We can seek, learn, question, hope. Climb and fall, travel through time and be there when great deeds are done and history writes another page. We can come back time and again for compass, for comfort or to revisit the shelf to find a truth.' He suddenly stopped pacing and looked down into her confused face. 'We fall in love with the words and their unique order and design, their plan to carry us along on a new journey, when we open a book Brigid. We fall into it all willingly and fall out only because the words run out.' Nancy had no idea what it all meant but his eyes were shining brighter than candles on a moonless night and she thought he must be saying something very important.

Just then the door knocked as the tea and the warm bread with marmalade arrived. A maid set the tray down silently on the table but didn't look at her, then bobbing awkwardly, almost ran out of the room as if she was being chased by Pooka! Nancy looked at the wondrous things set out before her and her stomach jumped at the smell of the bread. The cups reminded her of mamo's except the painted flowers were yellow not blue and there were no chips on the edges. In a small glass pot was something shiny and the colour of a fire lily and she found herself staring at it. Nathaniel caught her eye. 'Marmalade. This is marmalade Brigid.' And he took a spoon and dipped it into the pot before giving it to her to hold. 'Try it. It is delicious.'

Nancy hesitated. It was a strange colour and not like anything she had eaten before. 'Eat it Brigid. You cannot come all this way and not experience the delights of marmalade.'

She brought the spoon to her mouth and let her lips touch the shiny, orange thing called marmalade. Then as her tongue touched her lip, she tasted it. Its sweetness, its spiciness, its glory. It was fresh and vibrant and unlike anything she had ever tasted before as the flavour travelled around her mouth, up into her nose and finally down into her throat. It was as delicious in its sweetness and spiciness as dulce was disgusting in its fishy, saltiness.

He was watching her face. 'You see, I knew you would like it.' And for the first time since they had met, Nancy dared to smile at him.

'Ah the sun comes out when you smile bright one.' He spread butter and marmalade on the bread and handed her the plate before sitting down beside her on the sofa and opening the book. 'Sit close, you can look at the words while I read to you.' She shuffled up to sit closer to him but didn't touch him, she was sure you shouldn't touch an angel. As he opened the book, on the first page there was a picture of a girl looking out at the sea her long hair blown by the wind, she looked familiar, like her. Then he laid the book open in his lap and began to read, following the words with his finger line by line as the shapes became sounds to her. She settled easily into the pleasing sound of his voice, never taking her eyes from the book so she wouldn't miss a word, except when he skipped over some of the pages. Then after hundreds of sweet sentences, she fell asleep, only waking at the sound of knocking at the door. Through the fog of sleep, she heard Nathaniel say. 'We have roast chicken and potatoes for lunch Brigid.' The maid set the tray down on the table but again didn't look at her or Nathaniel and left quickly.

All the afternoon he read to her until closing the book he said, 'I think we will have to stop there for today Brigid but we will continue again tomorrow if you would like. Did you begin to recognise some of the words, many are often repeated are they not?' She nodded, they were - *and, he, she, you, we, the* - she could see pictures of these words in her head and hear the sound of them. 'That is very good Brigid, I think you to be very clever.' Her father said she was stupid. Nathaniel looked down at her feet and then at the boots on the floor 'Now what to do about these...' Picking up two linen napkins from the table he knelt down in front of her and then wrapped one carefully around each foot before putting her boots back on and fastening them up. 'There, that should be more comfortable for you Brigid until we can do something about these cruel boots. Be sure to tell your parents that I expect my napkins to return with you tomorrow in your boots otherwise I will consider them stolen.' She nodded her understanding of his stern warning.

As they walked down through the kitchen garden and approached the gate, Nancy could see that Miss Boyle and her father already stood awkwardly waiting for her, so she took her chance and gently tugged at the angel's coat. 'What's yer name?' she whispered.

Nathaniel stopped and bent down nearer to her.

'What did you say little one?'

'What's yer name?'

'Nathaniel.'

Lower than a whisper she said. 'See you the morra Nathaniel.'

'Until tomorrow fair Brigid.' He gave a little bow and then turned back to the house, hands in his pockets, wings spread.

Walking away from Cole Hall her father looked

back over his shoulder at Nathaniel. 'Strange fella but tisn't fer us t'care. Wur on t'a gud thing girl. See here.' He untied the bundle in his hands to reveal bread, cheese and butter. 'N'cream though, A'll be sure t'remind him o' his promise the morra.'

Should she tell him her secret, that she had eaten marmalade? She wouldn't, he would want some of that too and it was too special, its taste too precious to be wasted on him.

'A've a better idea, you can remind him 'bout the cream girl. Get us some vegetables an' fruit from that garden too eh? Thems plenty t'share. Ask him the morra.'

'A don't want to.'

'You'll do as A says.'

She said no more and her father didn't speak again.

That evening after the excitement of the food and her father's tall tales of his hard labouring and skilful work, mamo had asked her about the man. What did they do all day? What did he say to her? Were there other children there?

'Wurry alone wi' him chile?'

'Thar lobs o' people in the big house mamo. A saw a garden man an' a cook an' a maid…'

'A'm sure chile, but wurry alone in a room wi' him?'

'Leave her be. She be in one piece; nothin' fer you t'be fussin' over.'

'Tisn't proper an' whar wur the chiles he toldy 'bout? That wur surely a lie. Tisn't natural fer a grown man t'want t'spend time alone wi' a chile.'

'Leave it be! We g'back the morra an' the gentleman can do as he pleases s'long as he remembers the cream this time, A can't abide a man that don't keep his word.'

Frances cursed him under her breath.

When night fell and the candles were blown out, lying beside mamo in the darkness Nancy whispered. 'A'm not afeared mamo. A think he likes me.'

'Chile, thar be things you don't understand. You must tell me everythin' 'bout what he says an' does an' tell him that yer goin' t'tell me o' it all. Thar shud be n'secrets kept between yuz an' he shudn't want it so iffy be a gentleman. Promise you'll tell me everythin'!'

'A will mamo. Canny sing t'me?'

'Aye, if ye promise t'go t'sleep now.

'A promise.'

'Shall it be *Blow the Candle Out* t'night me darlin?'

'A love it the best.'

'A knows chile.' And she stroked her hair as she began to sing,

...The moon was shinin' brightly,
The stars wur twinklin' clear
When he went t'his love's winda

T'ease her o' her pain
An' she quickly rose an' let him in
An' went t'bed again.

Me father an' me mother
In yonder room do lay
Thar embracin' one another
An' so may you an' A
Thar embracin' one another
Wi'out a fear or doubt
Sayin' tek me in yer arms, me love,
An' blow the candle out

...Sayin' tek me in yer arms, me love,
An' blow the candle out.

Nancy was asleep before mamo reached the end of the third verse.

The next day, Miss Boyle met them at the gate just like before, key in the lock, up the gravel path, into the kitchen, along the dark passageways, through the secret door, down the bright corridor to the cream-coloured door and the room of sunshine.

Miss Boyle knocked.

'Come in.'

'Good morning Miss Sullivan.'

'Mornin' Nathaniel.'

Miss Boyle cuffed her ear knocking out of her the happy feeling she had at seeing Nathaniel again. 'How dare you address the master so, it is

Mr. Collins to you girl, know your place in this house.'

Nathaniel stepped forward until his face was inches from Miss Boyle's and her crooked eyes. 'You will never strike this child again and you will never speak ill to her or mistreat her in any way. Do you understand me?'

Nancy looked up at Miss Boyle's face which looked like a juicy fat raspberry about to explode.

'Sir, I only...'

'I do not want to hear your protestations; there is nothing you can say that will right your wrong so my advice would be that you say nothing more and heed my words. My father relies on me while he is away in Spain, and I shall be sure to update him on all that has gone on during his absence, do you understand?'

'Yes sir.'

'Very well. Now please bring Miss Sullivan and I warm bread and marmalade. Also, arrange for a bowl of hot water and a towel to be brought in. Oh, and a measuring tape.'

'A measuring tape?'

'Yes, a measuring tape. You know what that is I presume?'

'Yes of course sir.'

'Well then, what is your question?'

Her eyes stared in different directions looking for an answer. 'I shall bring one directly.'

'Thank you Miss Boyle. That is all.'

Ada Boyle turned and left, careful to close the door softly behind her so as not to give away her fury.

'I am sorry bright one, she thinks too much of herself. Come and sit and let us take off those awful boots.' As he knelt down and carefully unfastened them, she stared at the top of his head. His hair was the colour of corn and swirled in soft circles from the centre like the ripples she made when she dropped a pebble into the stream, it made her want to trace her fingers along its strands, but she knew she mustn't touch him and kept her hands by her sides.

'There! You are released!' He smiled up at her as he unwrapped the napkin around each foot just as the door knocked and the maid and another man she hadn't seen before entered the room. The maid put the tea tray down on the table like before and the man brought in a jug and bowl and had a white towel draped over his arm which he set down carefully on the table too. Then the maid reached into her pocket and handed Nathaniel what looked like a fat, round pebble. 'Miss Boyle said you required a measuring tape sir.'

'Yes. Thank you. That will be all.'

A bob and a bow and they were alone again.

'Let us have breakfast and then we have much to do.'

Nancy ate the bread and marmalade with a new sensation at the pleasure of the taste and feel of it but not the desperation of hunger for it to fill her hollowness. For the first time ín her life, she ate slowly and chewed thoroughly, taking the time for the glorious taste to leave her mouth and enter her belly. When they had finished, Nathaniel set aside the tray and picked up the large bowl placing it on the floor beneath her dangling feet. Then he picked up the jug of water and the towel.

'Hold this.' He gave her the towel. Then he lifted the jug and began to pour the warm water over her feet, cupping his hands around her toes and her heels, smoothing the water across her skin washing it clean. Then he lifted her from the sofa so that she was standing in the bowl on the floor. 'Wash between your toes bright one.' Clutching the towel against her, she reached down with her other hand and wove her fingers between her toes releasing all the dirt that had gathered there as the warm water turned a cloudy brown colour. Then he lifted her back up onto the sofa. Without him asking, she handed him the towel and he dried her feet, until they were the same colour as Issy's.

'That's much better. Now let's see.' He picked up the brown pebble that the maid had brought in and holding it in one hand, with the other he took hold of a small brass ring that was sticking out of it, then pulling it, a white ribbon with black shapes printed on it emerged as he stretched it out. He wrapped the tape around her ankle; four and three-quarter inches. Then he stretched the tape along the sole of her foot; ten and a half inches. Finally he passed the tape around the width of it; four and a half inches. He reached into his pocket and took out a pencil and then went to a small bureau by the door, opened a drawer and took out a piece of paper. 'Four and three-quarter inches, ten and a half inches, four and a half inches.' He said out loud as he wrote the measurements down.

'Come stand here by the door Brigid.' She slipped down off the sofa and went over to him. 'Stand with your back against the door post.' He helped manoeuvre her round. 'As straight as you can.' With the pencil he marked a line on the wood just above her head then as she stepped away he put the measuring tape up against it and ran the other end down to the floor, checked the number and wrote it down before winding in the tape like a fishing line.

The rest of the day passed blissfully in the room of sunshine. He read to her for hours and seemed happy and content, but when the time came for her to leave, she knew she had to carry out her father's instruction and ask for the cream or she would get the strap.

'Me da telled me t'asky fer somethin'.'

'Did he now. What might that be?'

She hesitated and he could see she was

uncomfortable, drawing herself in smaller. 'He be after gettin' some cream please.'

'Cream? Yes I think he was promised cream. I shall arrange it but tell your father that I will expect him to ask me himself in future for anything he thinks is due to him and not to have you do his work for him. I believe he will understand my meaning. Can you do that for me Brigid, exactly as I say?'

'A can Nathaniel.'

Later when she repeated his words to her father, she thought she saw the colour leave his face. There must have been power in what she said because he gave her a nervous smile and simply answered. 'A understand.'

CHAPTER 7

B is for Brigid

At the start of the fourth day of Nancy's visits to Cole Hall, Ellen Collins stood looking out across the kitchen garden. The sun was only just up but she had risen early in order to station herself at the window to observe the arrival of the mysterious child. At half past seven exactly she saw a man and a young girl appear at the garden gate and Miss Boyle walking down to meet them. As the gate was opened to them, she focussed her eyes, expecting to see something remarkable or of some note but they were ordinary, ragged like any poor wretches she might pass on the road in her carriage. The child was probably about six years old she thought, perhaps a little younger or just small for her age. Her smudged face was pretty enough and she had waves of auburn hair that caught the light as it moved over her shoulders, but there was nothing else to set her apart. As she had expected, the child's father looked like a criminal, and she was sure the man had no merits at all. As the three walked up the gravel path towards the back of the house, the child looked up and smiled at her, waving, hopeful of a return of it but instead Ellen Collins stepped back into the shadows.

Miss Boyle hadn't wanted to alarm her but had come to her yesterday afternoon concerned about the young master spending so much time alone with the child. Locked away all day except if they walked around the kitchen garden looking at the flowers and vegetables. You would wonder whether the family had some hold over him, why else would he entertain such low-living people, have the child sit on their fine furniture and eat their food? She was at pains not to speak out of turn, but something surely was amiss with the young master and she felt it her duty to inform the mistress of it. Ellen Collins relied on Ada Boyle's crooked eyes and would speak with her son this evening after the girl had left.

This morning, Nancy again took the familiar walk with Miss Boyle along the dark passageway, around the edges of the house and through the secret door. Then down the bright corridor with pale green walls and birds flying overhead, along the wool rug of grass green, blues, and oranges with its border of winding ivy leaves, counting ten squares and eight until they reached the cream-coloured door to the room of sunshine.

Miss Boyle knocked. They entered. Miss Boyle

left.

'Good morning fair Brigid, how are you today?'

'Grand, thanky Nathaniel.'

'Grand are you?' He smiled at her words. 'Come sit. I have something for you.' Lifting her up onto the sofa as he had done every morning, he removed her boots and unwrapped the napkins, but then he stood up and brought a brown paper parcel to her that was tied with string, placing it in her lap. 'A present for you,' she had never been given anything, 'open it.' He was smiling as he helped her untie the string, freeing the paper so she was able to see what was inside; a pair of boots of shiny, soft brown leather with stitching so fine she thought it must have been done by faeries.

'Do you like them?'

'Thems fer me?'

'Of course they are for you, they definitely won't fit my feet Brigid!' He laughed at her. 'Mr. Hamilton's uncle is a fine shoemaker and I have had him make these for you specially. There is not another pair like them in the world. See here.' And he took one of the boots from her lap and turned it around, on the back a 'B' was stitched at the heel. 'And feel inside.' He took her hand and guided it inside the boot. 'Lined with the softest kid leather Brigid, you shall walk on clouds from now on.'

Suddenly, something she didn't recognise rose

up inside her and she began to cry.

'What tears are these bright one? This is a happy thing; it was not my intention to make you cry. I think perhaps you feel something unfamiliar and altogether different to the misery that has taken root inside you and you don't recognise this new visitor as happiness. Always be open to happiness Brigid.'

She kept running her fingers around the inside of the boot, it was the softest thing she had ever felt, except the precious feel of Issy's skin.

'Let's try them on for size shall we?'

He loosened the boot laces and she pushed one foot and then the other inside. Then he gently pulled the laces tying each into a bow. 'There, now stand up and let us see how they look.' He stood back. 'Brigid! You look like a fine lady! Walk up and down a little, how do they feel?'

Nancy looked down at her booted feet which for the first time in her life looked like the feet of a child. As she began to walk she lifted her knees high as if she were marching as she over-compensated for the weight of the old heavy boots, these were light and yielding and perfect.

'Thems soft. Thanky.'

Nathaniel smiled and took a little bow.

'I will teach you how to tie the laces then only you Brigid will be the one to decide when they feel comfortable. Now come and sit with me there is something I would like to speak with you about.'

He lifted her up onto the sofa and sat down beside her. She couldn't take her eyes off her boots and stared at them, as if, were she to take her eyes from them, they might disappear.

'I have very much enjoyed our time together this week but it is coming to an end.'

Nancy stopped staring at her boots and looked into his face.

'You and I are not so different Brigid. We both seek a life better than the one we have been dealt so that we can feel free and alive. I want to help you Brigid but I can do little to change your future if you stay in Kinlough. Your life here will move on but its shape won't change, poverty will contain it and keep it small and wretched, but there is a way. You can sail away to a new life and leave behind what you were born to.' She thought of a faerie queen sailing in Donegal Bay. 'You can grow up in a place where there are opportunities and perhaps claim your own future one day. I can arrange it Brigid.'

Nancy listened and thought about leaving behind Faerie and Issy.

'Tomorrow I will speak with your father. He will be a necessary, if undeserving, beneficiary of my plans and I predict he will not refuse my offer as such an opportunity will likely never present itself again. Although I know him to be ignorant, he is not stupid. I shall arrange it all Brigid.'

She watched his face as he leant back and

closed his eyes.

'I too hope to find my freedom one day.' He almost said it like she wasn't there. 'But for now, I can perhaps share something of the liberty the birds I free from their cages experience. While they fly, I can feel a little free too.' He opened his eyes and turned his face towards her. 'Do you understand?'

She didn't, but she nodded because she thought that was what he wanted her to do and she wanted to please him.

'One life Brigid, that is what we are given, we must grasp it and make the best of it. I want you to remember that kindness, compassion and generosity will always be the masters over wealth and power or the privilege of social position. You have it in you to make a success of your life Brigid, never let anyone take that away from you. If you take help when it comes and always return it in full measure, the circle will be complete, and all may happily reap what they sow.'

She nodded again at his pretty words.

As they walked down the gravel path again that evening her father and Miss Boyle were already waiting looking even more impatient than usual. 'Mr. Sullivan. I should like to speak with you first thing in the morning. Miss Boyle, you should bring Mr. Sullivan to me directly and tell Mr. Hamilton that he will be along as soon as we have concluded our business.'

'Yes sir, as you wish.'

'Nancy has new boots.' Nathaniel placed his hand on Nancy's shoulder and smiled down at her. Michael had already registered them as his daughter had walked light-footed towards him. 'They are a gift, not to be sold and not to be withheld from her. Please carry the old ones home.' Nancy offered mamo's boots up to her father, laces tied together, two instruments of torture now discarded. Michael took the boots and hung them over his shoulder.

'You have been given the cream you were promised I hope.'

Michael looked embarrassed. 'Aye sir, wur gretful t'you.'

'I am sure you are. I very much hope Nancy will enjoy the taste of it... Until tomorrow then Mr. Sullivan. Goodbye Nancy.' He smiled as he backed in through the gate, never taking his eyes from her, while the pink and flustered looking Miss Boyle hurriedly turned the key in the lock before dropping the bunch back into her pocket. As they turned to walk back towards the house, the pressing, and inevitable exchange, took place between them. 'Your mother asks to speak with you in the blue drawing room sir.' Nathaniel stopped and turned to look at Miss Boyle. 'You appear a very enthusiastic messenger Miss Boyle, I suspect if I were to venture to ask, you would know exactly what my mother wishes to speak to me about.'

'It is not my business sir.'

'I suspect you have made this and indeed many other things that are not your concern, your very particular business over the years. I am not blind to your meddling Miss Boyle and you should not overestimate your value in this house. I know my father to also see you for what you are but it appears to suit my mother to keep you so he and I shall tolerate it for now.' He let the significance of his words settle on her before speaking again. 'Thank you for passing on her message, I will of course heed my mother's request and go to her straight away, your work is done Miss Boyle.' With the final slap of his words, he set off at pace towards the house, leaving Ada Boyle shaken and alone on the gravel path.

He found his mother sitting stiffly in a chair, a kettle that had been boiling over for hours, her agitation clear to see.

'You wished to speak with me mother?'

She stood up and walked towards the window, keeping her back to him.

'Close the door.'

He could guess her expression even if he couldn't see her face. He had never liked her; she was a thin excuse for a mother and seemed to him to offer nothing of any merit as a human being. She was just there, almost industrious in being pointless every minute of the day, more concerned with what people thought of her than who she actually was.

Without facing him she began her interrogation. 'What business do you have with the child?'

'What business? She is a child.'

Turning now she tried to soften her voice to keep him from bolting like he usually did. 'Precisely. You lock yourself away with her and there is talk.'

'Yes I see. Indeed I understand that there are those in this house who would consider foul behaviour might be at play.'

'Why do you spend time with her alone and why bring her father to this house? Mr. Hamilton did not require him nor does he give any merit to his skills.'

'True, true. I too can bear no testament to the man's virtues and suspect him to be feckless and quite useless.'

She threw her hands in the air in frustration. 'Well then, what is this about?'

'He is the child's father and he brings her to the house.'

'Then I ask again, what is your interest in the child?'

'To me, *the child* as you call her, is every innocent child who suffers misery and hardship, none of which is of their bidding or making. I believe I can play a part in changing her future.'

'What does that mean?'

'It is in our power mother to lift up those who are born lowly. What else would be the point of having money and influence?'

'Your father would not approve of you associating with such people.'

'My father is not here.'

'Do not be impertinent. You shame him, shame us all, with your wild behaviour and associations with such undesirable people. Do you intentionally seek to bring trouble to this house?'

'No mother, I seek to honour my family by showing compassion and generosity, *blessed are the poor, for theirs is the kingdom of God.*'

'Do not quote scripture at me.' She seemed breathless and was becoming more and more agitated.

He had to change tack or his plans would be ruined. 'Mother, I do not wish to cause you distress. Let us not argue.' He went and stood next to her by the window and laid his hand gently on her arm to calm her. 'You are right, I have been foolish, I will send the child and her father away.'

Ellen Collins gave her son a dubious sideways look. 'You will?'

'I will. Tomorrow I shall send them both away for good. You will never see them again and I shall devote my attention to managing the estate in my father's absence.'

She had been ready for a fight but he had given in too easily and she was suspicious. 'You promise this?'

'I do. I shall explain to the child and her father tomorrow that they should not come to the house again. Does that satisfy you mother?'

'Well, yes... I am sure you understand my concern and why I had to speak with you on the matter.'

'Of course, I completely understand your disquiet mother and it was never my intention to give you cause to worry. Tomorrow, all will be resolved happily for you I am sure.'

'Very well then. I shall see you at dinner?'

'I look forward to it mother.'

She searched his face but couldn't read it.

'Is there anything else mother?'

'No, I take you at your word Nathaniel that you will do as you say.'

'Very well, then I shall take my leave of you.' And closing the door quietly behind him, he left her to wrestle with her confusion. Ellen stared at the closed door. She wanted to trust him but he had proved too many times to her that his words of contrition did not lead to a change of heart or deed and yet, she sought concord with her son and his love and respect over Henry's, over everyone's. Henry, the son that said everything you wanted to hear, did everything you wanted him to do, but who never cared about any of it.

CHAPTER 8

America Bound

Nancy sat at one end of the huge table, delivered to the kitchen this morning by Miss Boyle with instructions to Cook that she should feed her while the young master met with the girl's father, she would come back for her later and was to take no nonsense. Cook didn't like Miss Boyle with her air of self-importance at the best of times so was more than irritated by her orders this morning, she was busy with no time to mind a child. Now, standing over Nancy with her hands on her hips, she asked. 'Will it be marmalade for Miss again this morning?' She feigned interest in what Nancy might actually want. 'A'd like it wi' warm bread please.' She repeated the words as Nathaniel had to Miss Boyle each morning. 'Warm bread, yes of course, you should expect no less than warm bread.' Cook didn't seem to mean what she was saying and when Nancy's breakfast arrived, the marmalade and bread came down heavily on the table with a thud, when the tea came, she set it down so hard it made the cup clatter enough to break.

'Will there be anything else?'

Nancy looked at the banquet set out in front of her. 'Tis grand, thanky.'

Cook turned away from her muttering something under her breath, going back to the plucked, limp chicken she had been preparing at the other end of the table, hacking at it noisily, like she was chopping wood or Miss Boyle's head.

Nancy thought her father had been even quieter than usual on their walk to the big house this morning and seemed nervous when Miss Boyle took him away to see Nathaniel. She had seen him rubbing his palms together, like he was trying to wipe away something that afflicted him, cast it off before it took hold. She wondered if they were in the room of sunshine. They were, and while Nancy sat in the kitchen eating her breakfast, the two men sat facing each other on the blue sofas. 'I wish to speak with you about Nancy.' Michael Sullivan looked nervous at what might be coming next but said nothing. 'It is clear that the prospects for your family are poor and that you have had little work these past months.'

'A've suffered very bad luck sir tis true.'

'It is indeed bad luck that you have been unable to control your drinking and gambling and your family have had to suffer for it. I already know your story Mr. Sullivan.'

Michael swallowed his anger at such foul criticism, he would have knocked him flat, but there was too much to gain from him and he caught the sniff of an opportunity coming his way.

'You live in your mother's cottage.' He wasn't asking, he already knew.

'We do. This last year.'

'You understand the terms of the cottage's tenancy and that the land, poor as it is, will be reclaimed by the estate when your mother dies, it will not pass to you.'

Michael knew it but chose to ignore what the future held. He nodded reluctantly.

'What provision will you make then for your family, for Nancy?'

'A'll labour sir if any decent man gives me the work.'

'I fear there is little unskilled work for men such as you and you can predict a lean future if you depend on it. I think perhaps more drastic action is needed if you wish to change your family's prospects.'

'A've nothin' t'offer other than the labour o' me hands but A hope fer a change o' fertune, twud be fair.'

'Your circumstances are set Mr. Sullivan. Life for those on this island, who have no money or power, gets worse with every passing month, there will be no reprieve for any poor soul who finds themselves in your position unless they turn to dishonest means - thieving and poaching for instance and that will lead to a bad end.' He looked into Michael Sullivan's face, here was such a man, he knew he would not hesitate to steal what was never rightfully his. 'There are opportunities beyond these shores perhaps that might cast a different light on the future.'

'England?'

'Perhaps, or America. Have you considered it?'

'Whar wud A get the money?'

'My question is not one of finances but of the desire to make a new life. Let us set the money apart for now. Do you think you could make a good life there for your family?'

'A hear America is full o' gold. Twud offer me a better life t'be sure sir.' Michael was visibly excited at the prospect.

'What kind of life would that be?'

Michael hesitated, he wasn't sure he understood what was required as an answer, he wanted to get it right. 'Roof over me head, decent food on the table, mebby a business o' me own rather than fillin' some other fella's pockets.'

'I ask about your family. What about Nancy? What do you see for her future?'

'Reckon she'll marry, bring me some grandchildren.'

'What of her education?'

'Learnin'? Why wud she need learnin'?'

'So that she need not live such a small, meagre life as you Mr. Sullivan. She has a desire to read and I already know from the little time I have spent with her that she has a quick mind and an appetite for learning as you put it. It would be wrong to starve her of it. I would insist on it if you were to take up my offer.'

Here it came and he was ready. 'What offer wud that be?'

'I can arrange your safe passage to America, to Boston, with enough money to secure you a place to live until you can find employment. Would that interest you?'

Michael's mouth slackened until it fell wide open. 'Go t'America? T'be sure A'd mek the best o' it sir.'

'You understand my terms regarding Nancy?'

'Aye, you wish her t'be in school.'

'In school and not put to work to fund your vices, that is non-negotiable, you would have to agree to this.'

'She can go t'school. Meks n'difference t'me or her mother s'long as her schoolin' costs me nothin'.'

'It is heartening to see how much you value your child's education Mr. Sullivan.'

Michael was confused, Nathaniel's sarcasm lost on him, he didn't care a bit whether she could read or not. He hadn't learnt to read or do numbers and it had done him no dis-service. 'If you be requirin' that, twill be done.'

'Very well then, I think we understand each other, but remember an ocean will not stand in my way if you go back on your word. There is a ship that sails in these next three days from Sligo and I can secure safe passage for you and your family to Boston by way of Liverpool. Ten sovereigns shall be yours to secure lodgings and to get yourself set up.'

Michael nodded but shifted anxiously in his chair, so much was almost within his grasp and he must not let it slip away, but why was he helping them? Maybe he was mad. He looked sane enough but who could tell the frailties of the mind. 'How can A trust all you say be true?'

Nathaniel smiled. 'Well I suspect you are not weighed down with other such generous offers Mr. Sullivan, so it is up to you to decide whether you wish to trust my word in this matter. There is no insistence on my part that you accept my terms and I will happily wish you good day if you choose to decline them.'

'A'm not declinin' nowt an' A'm most thankful, tis just un-spected is all.'

'Yes, I imagine it is. If you accept my offer then here is what I will arrange. A carriage will come for you on Monday morning at seven o'clock. Be ready with all your belongings packed. I expect it will not be difficult for you to travel lightly, but still, you should consider how much you take, space will be limited on your voyage. My man will take you on to Sligo from where you will sail for Liverpool and then onward from there to Boston. When he is satisfied that you are boarding the ship, you will receive the ten sovereigns. Can I take it that you are satisfied with these arrangements?'

'Aye, A'm happy.'

'Speak to no one about our agreement and do not visit this house again. If you do, my offer will be withdrawn. Do you understand?'

'A understand.'

'Good. Then I think we have concluded our business. You are in your daughter's debt Mr. Sullivan, if it were not for her, you would be destined to rot with your potatoes. Treat her well.' Nathaniel stood and held out his hand while Michael scrambled to his feet to take it. 'We shall not see each other again. I wish you God's speed Mr. Sullivan.' He rang the bell and when the maid came he instructed her to tell Miss Boyle and Mr. Hamilton that Mr. Sullivan and his daughter were being sent home and that they would not be returning to the house again. Miss Boyle received the news with visible delight, her talk with the mistress had done its work, her influence over her was intact.

CHAPTER 9

Faerie

Two days had passed since they were last at the big house and her father had hardly taken a breath from telling them of his cleverness in securing a new life for them all in America. The young Mr. Collins had taken a particular shine to him he said, seen his potential to make a successful life in a land full of gold. He strutted like a cockerel, crowing his brilliance, eyes brighter than Nancy had ever seen before.

Her mother on the other hand had received the news with muted enthusiasm and a full measure of suspicion, not convinced by his story, not certain by any means that a carriage would arrive on Monday let alone that any ship would take them to America. She had asked question after question. 'Don't mek sense. Whar's the benefit t'Collins? This cottage isn't worth anythin' t'them an' the land is cropped out.' Her father had twisted and turned to try and bring sense to it, to convince himself not just Kitty, but he steadily tied himself in ever-increasing knots until he was further away from reason than when he began. As Kitty went through the physical motions of washing clothes and packing their life in Kinlough away, she dared to believe that it might be true, although the hope in her of a life that might be worth living, had been lost years ago.

Mamo had been subdued at the news, sitting quietly listening to all that Michael had to say, considering the enormity of how life was going to change. Could she travel halfway across the world to start a new life in a foreign country? Most days she journeyed only from the bed to her chair and back again apart from visits to the privy or to sit outside the cottage door on fine days. Her legs didn't work so well and she didn't trust them to carry her far away from a table or a chair for guidance and support. Too many cold winters, and every other of the seasons of wet and damp, brought aches to her bones that hummed their painful tune inside her constantly now. She didn't fear it, but she was approaching the end of her days and could feel the invisible thread of her ancestors tugging at her, pulling her towards the sweet earth of Kinlough as a feeling of belonging overwhelmed her.

There was little for her to pack, she only had one dress other than the grey wool one she mostly wore, lighter in weight and cooler against her skin, but much less suited to Kinlough weather.

She would leave the cottage wearing the green and brown tartan wool shawl that she never took off but the other - pale blue and pink worn on her wedding day but now more like lace than wool as moths devoured it - would be left behind. All her pretty china was gone, sold long ago to put bread on their table, even her wedding ring was lost to her, the indentation of over thirty years of encircling her finger finally filled out and faded like it had never been there. Her bible, a small blotchy mirror, a hairbrush, two pairs of threadbare soleless stockings, two sets of undergarments and an empty bottle that once contained perfume - now with only the echo of the scent of roses and lavender - were all she would take. There wasn't space for the quilt her mother had lovingly stitched for her as a wedding present, those colourful soft squares that had warmed and comforted her through the hardest of times, would be left behind and grow damp and mouldy, decaying with the cottage. She had hope for the child though. A chance that she could have a future not blighted like the potatoes. Michael said she would be going to school; have the learning that she herself had craved. There would be books, Nancy would learn to count beyond ten and have need of it, be able to make some claim over her life and its direction. In all the stir of their preparations, she had watched a quiet settle on Nancy as she took in what was said without resistance or protest, but then at night as they lay in bed together, they had spoken in whispers about it. Mamo had always been the catcher of her worries and now that fear was leaving everything she had ever known to make a new home in a place called Boston while Issy and Faerie would stay behind. Her grandmother's art was to turn her fears into the most wonderful story of a magical land across the sea that shone like a jewel, so that when she closed her eyes, it came to life as a place of bright colours that flashed and danced in her head dispelling the darkness.

Standing in the cottage doorway, Nancy looked out on her world, around her everyone seemingly lost in their own and paying no mind to her, except mamo, whose eyes seemed to rest on her almost constantly even when her hands were busy at something. She would do it now, tell Faerie that she would be going away tomorrow. Heading out towards the stream Faerie came to meet her as soon as she was a safe distance from the cottage like he always did. Keeping in step with her, he stayed very close, until they reached the bank of the stream where she dropped down into the long grass so they couldn't be seen. Speaking slowly to him, she pulled the terrible news out of herself, trying to explain it all, but he just stared up at her seemingly unmoved by her news.

'A'll miss you every day Faerie but you can't

come wi' me on the ship.' She picked at the grass throwing tufts of it into the water while Faerie watched her intently. Glancing back towards the cottage she continued. 'Remember, you must stay away from the cottage 'til we leave, or me da'll kill you. Understand?' She wagged her finger at him but it was useless, he wasn't listening, he just stood up on his back legs and looked at her. 'You need t'go away from here Faerie.' The thought of their parting made her cry.

She had to get him far away from the cottage, she had to. They would go further up the stream, much further than she was supposed to go alone. Standing up she began walking along the bank with Faerie following her closely until the cottage was out of sight and she found herself in unfamiliar surroundings. As she looked around her, despite the dark shadows cast by the mountains, the colours seemed brighter and more vibrant here, even the grass shining greener in its wetness. No one walked this way and here everything belonged to the earth and sky, drawn perfectly, undisturbed and untainted.

'You must g'that way Faerie.' She pointed into the distance to where grey mist hung over the dark mountain tops but he didn't move and just stared up at her. 'Go that way!' Faerie seemed nervous, recoiling, his body stiffening as she raised her voice in desperation 'You must, you must, please Faerie.'

She walked on a little further, weaving her steps like she might be able to lose him if she didn't walk in a straight line, but with every change of direction the thread followed the bobbin and he was right at her heels. Then suddenly, to catch him out, she turned and began running back in the direction of the cottage as fast as she could. Still he followed her. She stopped and wagged her finger at him. 'Go back, don't follow me.' She ran on a little further but still he pursued her, the thread lengthening out, as he kept a little distance now. 'A'm not playin' a game wi' you Faerie.' She shouted over her shoulder at him. Then, in her desperation, she stopped and picked up a small stone, throwing it and hitting him hard on his back, flattening him to the ground. She began to cry again. 'Sorry Faerie.' Still he crept closer to her moving hesitantly and keeping his body low. She picked up another stone, this time her aim missed him but he froze from the fright of it and made a strange squealing noise she'd never heard before. 'Stay thar!' Turning away from him she began to run again; he must not follow her.

As the cottage came into view, she could see her father was outside digging over the stunted potatoes, looking for any that could be salvaged to add to a bountiful last supper. There was no sound in the air just the earth giving up the rhythmic thump of her soft boots as she tried to outrun her friend but then, as if someone had tapped him on the shoulder, her father looked up and she knew how it would end and her heart began to break for a second time. Faerie was right behind her and her father had spotted him. She watched with horror as he wrenched his shovel out of the ground and began running towards them. 'Run away Faerie, run!' Crying out she raced at her father trying to block him, but the back of his hand hit her full in the face as he swatted her away, knocking her to the ground. Then, as her friend tried to reach her, she saw the shovel come down and it was over.

'Stop yer snivellin' girl, 'bout time that vermin had what wur comin' t'it. Count yerself lucky thar be plenty o' food fer the table t'night an' we won't be needin' yer friend – me da always said a rat's readier mate than a runnin' hare!' Her father laughed as he scooped Faerie up and pulling back the shovel, threw him away like a rotten potato, like he had been nothing at all. A silent scream that went on and on emptied her lungs and she didn't speak after that, not even to mamo, but scratched her skin until it bled to take on the anger and pain of her loss.

CHAPTER 10

Farewell to Kinlough

They woke before the breaking of the darkness to a damp, chill day, and a heavy mist so thick you could swallow it. Rest and longed-for unconsciousness had teased each of them through the long hours of the night but none had found sleep, escaping them all for different reasons. Everything in the room was displaced except mamo's chair, a stool and the table with its benches that centred the room like a mighty oak left standing while all around it has been felled. Now, for the last time as Nancy put her hand on the bench to climb up, her gaze was held for a moment by the ancient, furrowed grains in the wood. She ran her fingers along one of the lines, it had always been here, it was still solidly here, but she was not.

'Be quick girl, don't be dallyin'.' Her father prodded her stirring her into action as she joined her family at the table for their final Kinlough breakfast, but although her body wakened at the jabbing of his finger, there was no power in her and her heavy head hung down, chin resting on her chest as she stared at her hands twisting in her lap. It broke mamo's heart to see the grey shadows under her eyes. 'You shud ate somethin' chile, thar be a long journey ahead an' you need yer strength.' She tried to encourage her but eating was such a trivial thing now. In her own fashion, Kitty tried too. 'If yer not after atin' this, thar be nowt fer you later.' She pushed a thick slice of bread slicked with butter at her. Nancy didn't take it and her eyes didn't even flicker away from her lap. 'Suit yerself girl…' Her father leaned over and took the bread and butter stuffing it into his mouth greedily. She didn't care if the murderer choked.

'Now stop yer daydreamin' an' clear the plates, we need t'wash an' pack everythin'; the carriage'll be here within the quarter hour.' Kitty gave Nancy a shove but it was gentler than usual.

'C'mon chile, we'll do it t'gether.' Mamo cast her an encouraging smile but it didn't reach her.

The last plate was wiped and packed and with nothing left to do, Kitty and Michael stood facing each other awkwardly, both wondering if they would turn out to be fools for believing Collins. Then the unfamiliar sound of carriage wheels broke into their silence saving their pride, and Michael went to the door, opening it as a shiny red carriage came to a stop outside. Two men dressed almost identically from head to toe in black, with scarves pulled up around their faces against the cold, were only separated from each other by height and the shiny brass buttons on the shorter man's coat. Steadying the horse, they climbed down from the carriage as Michael went out to meet them, the taller of the two men stepping forward. 'Michael Sullivan?'

'Aye, A'm Michael Sullivan.'

'Donald Ryan. Nathaniel Collins sends us to take you and your family to Sligo, are you ready?'

'Wur packed an' ready. Come in.'

The two men followed Michael into the dismally lit cottage where an elderly woman sat by the fire staring into the flames and a tall, younger woman looked at them with suspicious dark eyes. In the darkest corner, a small child sat silently on a stool, brown-booted-feet dangling lifelessly. Looking around the barren cottage, they imagined its lack of any merit to be easy to leave behind with not even modest comforts to cling to now, those just amounted to a pathetic pile of belongings heaped on the floor by the door waiting for collection. Donald Ryan had been into many such cottages over the years, but they seemed to him only to corral misery and compound its effects, rather than offer any measure of refuge to their inhabitants. Still, it was true that life inside brought with it a chance of survival, outside and abandoned to the elements, there was none. So poor souls clutched at any dark, vile dwelling as if clinging to life itself. 'I will help the women and the child into the carriage; you assist my man here with loading the luggage.' He gave Michael and the other man a nod as a sign to pick up the sacks from the floor but then put out his hand and stopped Michael in his tracks. 'First, put out the fire.'

Michael picked up a bucket and approaching the fire, raised it to douse the flames.

'Stop! A'm not leavin'.' He slowly lowered the bucket as all eyes turned on Frances sitting by the fire.

Kitty was the first to respond to her outburst. 'What d'you mean auld woman?'

'A'm stayin' here in the cottage.'

'You can't be stayin' here, A've gev it up.' Michael stared at his mother, lips clamped tight, willing her to do the same and shut her mouth.

'It wurn't yers t'gev up.' She said flatly.

Michael's anger flared, he would not have her embarrass him in front of the two men and moving towards his mother, he raised his hand as if he might strike her, but she looked directly into his face daring him to try it and the coward dropped his hand without a blow.

In the stand-off, Donald Ryan looked across at the other man and then stepped forward, ignoring Michael and speaking directly to Frances. 'The master expects you to leave this place Mrs. Sullivan, that was the agreement and you will appreciate this is an unexpected turn of events.'

'A wish t'die in this cottage; A belong t'the soil o' Kinlough.'

The man hesitated. 'You understand that I cannot vouch for what will become of you if you decide to stay? It will be hard for a woman here alone.'

Frances smiled up at him and then turned her face away looking into the flames. 'A wonder if you knew auld man Collins? Mr. Edward Collins.'

'No, I did not.'

'Ah well, by me reckonin' he wur a fair an' decent man fevoured t'mek auld bones an' die peacefully in his sleep because me husband seved his life.' She turned and looked directly into his face pausing to let her words settle. 'T'be sure me husband wur a brave man an' put himself in harm's way wi' no thought fer the wife an' baby waitin' fer him at home; put the master's life 'bove his own he did. When Edward Collins promised him this cud remain our home til we took our last breath, we took him at his word wi' no need fer contract. Gud men don't always live a long life an' me husband an' all his gudness wur teken long back, God rest his soul, an' now A'm not long fer this life meself, A'm after finishin' me days in the shadows o' the Dartry mountains an' A hope wi' the shelter o' this cottage unless A'm put out o' it. A'm not after endin' this life in a foreign land whar A've no claim t'the air or the soil beneath me feet.' She spoke slowly and deliberately so that he would not miss the weight of her words and the promise that was made to her.

'We will not force you but you understand that I cannot speak of the consequences if you stay.'

'A'll tek me chances. A live only now t' breathe the sem air o' me first breath in this world; Kinlough wur me cradle an' twill be me grave.'

Donald Ryan hesitated and again looked in the direction of the man with the brass buttons who said nothing but made the smallest gesture with his hand like he was swatting a fly away. 'Very well, then we will leave you, but we must be on our way or time will be against us.'

Michael put down the bucket and picked up the smallest of the four sacks, dropping it down next to his mother's chair.

'We'll not be comin' back; you'll be on yer own.'

'Don't worry, Annie'll tek care o' me ending.'

Michael caught the full meaning of her words; that Annie would do for her what a son should. He reached inside his coat taking out coins that were mostly the colour of mud, greedily slipping all but three of the silver ones back into his pocket. 'Tis the best A can do.' Frances took in the sum of the meagre offering in her son's outstretched hand and then looked up at him. 'Twill suffice, A'm not after atin' much these days an' when A can no longer fetch water, me days'll be done.'

Michael glanced at the depleted pile of peat turves stacked up by the fire, enough for a week, two at most. He knew once they ran out she would be done for. 'Gudbye. We'll not see each other again.' His hand twitched as if he would reach out to place it on her shoulder, or touch her cheek as some measure of intimacy, but he did nothing except turn and pick up one of the sacks on his way out of the cottage.

The two men followed, picking up the remaining sacks.

Kitty had been standing near the door watching it all. 'Well, gudbye then.' Frances looked into the cold, empty face of her daughter-in-law. 'God's speed Kitty. Tek care o' Nancy, she'll need you.'

Mamo's shocking announcement had wrought a third brutal blow, and as the words had dropped from her grandmother's lips, Nancy's six-year-old world completely fell away. Mamo was lost to her now too, just like Issy and Faerie, and as the weight of their separation crashed down on her, it felt like the cottage was collapsing in on her too. She held her breath until she thought she would suffocate, but when she finally gasped for air, there was nothing. No feeling, no pain, no sensation.

'Come here chile.' Mamo could see her distress

and in the gentlest voice beckoned her over.

You must do what your elders tell you to do, so she got down off the stool, walked around the table and stood in front of her, but as she stared at her grandmother, what she saw began to change shape in front of her eyes, she was just a decaying old woman who had abandoned her and meant nothing to her now, she was not her mamo.

'Nancy darlin' listen t'me. A'll never ferget you an' A'll always keep you here in me heart.' And she laid her hand on her chest, patting it softly, 'We'll always be t'gether.'

Nancy heard her speaking but only the shadow of her words came to her now, her mamo was gone, and all that she had thought true had shown itself as a lie.

'Shally kiss yer mamo gudbye me love?'

No she wouldn't and without replying, she turned away, walked past her mother and out of the cottage. No need to say goodbye to a shadow. Mamo's desperate voice followed her out into the cold air. 'A love you Nancy darlin'.' Kitty looked at the pathetic old woman but it stirred nothing in her and taking one final look around the dismal cottage, with relief she turned and left, closing the door behind her for the final time.

Outside Donald Ryan was holding the horse while the other man was passing their luggage up to her father who was stowing it in the well between the seats. Seeing Kitty Sullivan and her daughter approach, the man threw up the final sack to Michael before walking towards them. 'Let me help you up into your seat Mrs. Sullivan.' He took her hand to steady her as Kitty put her foot on the step and pushed up into the carriage just as Michael climbed over the backrest of the seat and dropped himself in beside her. 'Come this way child.' The shorter man waved Nancy towards him and they walked around to the other side of the carriage. Then he took hold of her around the waist and swung her up, setting her down on the seat gently, before climbing up to sit beside her.

'Are we ready for off?' Donald Ryan called over his shoulder as he got up into the driver's seat.

'We are ready.' The man with the brass buttons turned to look at Nancy. 'Try not to worry about your grandmother child, there is something to be done I am sure.' Nancy didn't care about her and didn't answer, she just stared down at his brass buttons and the two wild, hairy dogs that reared up on them. Just as the horse was being pulled around, the cottage door flew open and a desperate mamo appeared in the doorway, but there would be no crying, no hearts beating against each other, no final kiss. Holding on to the doorframe with one hand, she waved with the other. 'Gudbye! Gudbye!' Michael and Kitty briefly raised a hand in acknowledgement before easily resettling their eyes on the road to their life ahead but Nancy didn't lift her head as the carriage rumbled into motion and mamo stepped back into the shadows of the cottage and closed the door.

Nancy's lowered eyes traced along the edges of the stream as the carriage followed its line for a few minutes, then as the road took them away from it she raised them looking back over her shoulder, but the cottage had already disappeared from sight. To their left the tall, sheer pillar of Eagle's Rock rose up from the lush green of the valley like a broken shard of glass, its point disappearing into the mist, then as the haze cleared, Benwisken grew large, looming over her like a giant. For more than four hours, the carriage shook and rattled, as the wheels bumped over rocks and fell into ditches, bouncing them in their seats and violently rocking them from side to side until a strange sliding sensation in Nancy's head signalled their descent into Sligo as the road began to fall away from them.

Donald Ryan twisted around in his seat to update his passengers on their progress. 'I expect we will arrive in Sligo within the quarter hour.' They were the first words anyone had uttered during the whole journey and it roused them all from their thoughts. As he turned his eyes back to the road, the wind carried his voice to them again. 'You sail on the tide today but there will be time enough to take some rest and refreshments at an inn before you depart.' After that, he didn't speak again until the carriage rattled over the bridge, the hollow sound of the horse's hooves beating out their rhythm, before giving way on the other side to the discordant percussion of clattering, thumping sounds and the thin sharp thread of people's shouts rising up through the dense drone of a thousand murmuring voices. As they made their way down to the quayside, the awful din grew louder and Nancy put her hands over her ears to shut it out, trying to stop the spinning sensation in her head.

As wheels and hooves slipped on the wet cobbles, the horse tried to hold back against the narrow sloping streets, as they were shunted from left to right in their jerking progress along the street of terraced buildings that curved along the Garavogue. Nancy's stomach was empty but still it felt as if something was boiling up inside her ready to spill over and then it did as she leaned forward and was sick over the side, just missing her dress, spattering her boots.

'You will feel better now.' The man with the brass buttons took a handkerchief from his pocket and passed it to her. 'Wipe your face. Take heart, we are nearly there and I promise you will be standing on steady ground soon.' Arriving on the quayside, the smell of fish overwhelmed her and she thought she would be sick again, but she held on to her stomach and pressed the handkerchief against her face holding it in.

Donald Ryan steadied the horse bringing the carriage to a stop as the man with the brass buttons jumped down. 'Mr. Sullivan, come with me please.' Her father climbed down, straightening himself up like he might make himself look more respectable, before heading off with the man through the crowd of people.

'They go to the ship's office to make sure your tickets are in order and you're signed to the ship. I expect they will not be gone long. Then we shall find somewhere to take some food and rest.'

Nancy raised her eyes to take in the scene. Barefoot women in scarlet skirts, aprons stained with fish guts and grease, carried baskets of fish on their heads or sat on boxes gutting the fish, creating streams of watery red entrails that filled the gaps between the grid of cobbles, spilling over and then moving on to fill the next line. A woman was talking to a man selling trinkets and crosses from a lidded wooden box strung around his neck, holding up a looking glass for her, as she held a string of tiny pink threaded shells to her neck. He seemed to be doing good business as other women gathered around looking for the pleasure of an adornment or a good luck token for their voyage. Blackened men loaded and unloaded sacks of corn, sugar, and salt shouting words unfamiliar to her but which others seemed to understand. Heaving boxes of tea and other treasures and rolling barrels, they rumbled and weaved in and out in the congested space with ease, while man and beast mingled together as men with sticks corralled disorientated cattle that veered left and right, correcting them with a sharp tap.

Then her eyes were drawn to a smartly dressed man who was waving his arms in the air as he approached a group of children who were climbing on a shiny black capstan then jumping off it and screaming excitedly as they landed. 'Get off, devils!' They scattered, laughing at him and pulling faces. 'Look out!' Another man shouted as one of the boys ran in front of his horse and cart bringing it to a sudden halt. The mother grabbed her child from behind and cuffed him dragging him away by the collar. 'Jayzus woman, keep hold o' yer wain!' The shaken man called after the woman before moving on.

They found an inn but despite encouragement from the two men, she didn't eat and fell asleep at the table, leaving her parents to make the most of the free refreshments and beer on offer. As the last glass was drained Donald Ryan checked his watch 'It's four o'clock, time we were away, you sail in an hour.' They left the man with the brass buttons behind at the Star Inn to settle their bill and headed through the crowds on the quayside to board the ship. A winding line of passengers had already formed as boarding passes were checked and one by one, people were making their way up the gangplank. Donald Ryan walked with them as they joined the queue and stayed alongside them as they made their way up the line to where a man was checking papers, then reaching into his pocket, he handed Michael a heavy black pouch. 'I am instructed by Mr. Collins to give you this.' Michael immediately began to untie its cord. 'You can be assured it contains the ten sovereigns you were promised, there is no need to count it.' Kitty immediately whipped the pouch out of his hand and pushed it down inside her bodice folding her green shawl and arms tightly across herself to be sure it was safe.

When they finally reached the front of the queue, Michael handed the man his papers and Donald Ryan stepped back. 'Goodbye Mr. & Mrs. Sullivan.' And with that he was gone.

'Sullivan?' The officious man said in a flat voice.

'Aye, A'm Michael Sullivan an' thems me wife Catherine an' me daughter Nancy.'

The man looked from one to the other dispassionately. 'Berths 41 and 42.' And he waved them on. Kitty had been sure they would be turned away but it was real, they were on the list, they were going to America.

Three ships would sail on the tide including theirs, and to the unsettling accompaniment of the murmured prayers from women standing nearby, Nancy looked down on the people milling around the quayside, watching the two men looking up at the ship. They stood apart, Donald Ryan talking to a man who was trying to sell him something in a small wooden box, sending him off, each time the man coming back for another try. While the man with the brass buttons was bending down talking to a small raggedy-looking child of about her own age who was sitting on the ground crying. Then he put his hands in his pockets and the angel spread his wings. Nathaniel.

PART II: BOSTON 1858

CHAPTER 11

A Boston Greeting

As they made ready for arrival, the general talk amongst the crew was of a straightforward voyage and the ship's log would record their crossing as one of fair weather and without incident of injury or fatality, the never-ending lurching of the ship and vile food may have caused sickness amongst the uninitiated it was true, but that was to be expected and was not a point of record. With the first sight of land, Nancy's stomach flipped over again and she vomited a foul, watery mess. For ten days her head and lungs had been constantly filled with the dusty smell of coal and a saltwater cold meant she had been sick every day, her head swimming like a fish lost to the power of the currents. The confines of their cramped, airless cabin made things worse and whenever it had been possible for them to be up on deck, she had focused on the grey line of the sea to help steady the motion below her feet and in her head. Now, as she leaned against her father's leg, she struggled to stand, not just because of the constant lurching of the ship but because she was weak from the putrid food that went down and then back up again leaving no nourishment in her. Her father looked down at her and flicked his leg. 'Pull yerself up girl, thems'll be after pokin' an' proddin' us all if thems think you've the sickness, see you don't delay us.' Nancy straightened up and held on to the rail to steady herself.

As the ship began to slow the excitable shouting of the crew grew louder bringing pandemonium to the deck as they scrambled to organise disorientated passengers and their luggage for disembarking. 'To be sure thems lost thar minds t'the sniff o' a jar an' some skirt. 'Fastest thems moved the whole time.' And her father had clicked his tongue and winked at her.

Despite the growing chaos boiling up around them, the Sullivans stood perfectly still, transfixed by the alien shapes of Boston that stretched out ahead; hard artificial lines drawn by man - houses, church spires, the imposing dome of the state house crowning the hill - each of them longing for the familiar skyline of Kinlough and the grandeur of the Dartry mountains that dominated you and reminded you of your place in the world. Then the boards beneath their feet tilted as a packet ship with a curving wooden hull and intricate rigging threaded like silk on lace bobbins, was towed into harbour alongside them, the white lady at her bow leaning forward gracefully and eagerly towards the harbour, while passing them on their other side on its way out of harbour, a gleaming white steamer with wisps of grey smoke rising up and fading against a blue sky, reminded Nancy of the cottage's smoking chimney. All around them rippling circles of clippers, barks and brigs moved silently and gracefully like gliding swans, or rocked gently from side to side on anchor like baby's cradles, their Boston welcome party.

The world had grown bigger since they had left Ireland. Sligo had dwarfed Kinlough, Liverpool had dwarfed Sligo and now Boston spread itself out far and wide, bigger than anything mamo had prepared her for, but as the imagining of this far away land became real, she wanted to close her eyes to shut it out.

Like ants emerging from their nest to scout for food, passengers continued to swarm up onto the deck from their cabins below, while a tall man in uniform with a leg that didn't bend, limped the deck shouting out instructions to have papers ready for inspection, the clay pipe hanging in the corner of his mouth bobbing up and down as he spoke.

Keeping a tight grip on the rail, Nancy looked up at the dropped sails as the engines quietened, slowing them as they clunked and creaked their way into harbour, but when the gang finally went down, no one moved, each waiting for another brave soul to go first. The man with the pipe was impatient. 'C'mon folks, get moving please, we don't have all day.' He cupped his hand around the elbow of the woman standing nearest to him with a child in her arms. 'Madam, perhaps you would be kind enough to lead the way.' She looked hesitantly at her husband and then stepped forward onto the plank as the other passengers began to fall in behind her, the seething mass quickly turning into a single file procession going down off the ship. Nancy held on to the hem of her father's coat as they made slow progress with small shuffling steps until they reached the man at the end of the gang who was checking tickets. He glanced at their papers and simply nodded them through without a word. Michael and Kitty looked at each other. 'Whar we s'posed t'do now?' Michael asked the man who was already dealing with the next disembarking passenger behind them. The man looked at them blankly. 'It's no business of mine what you do now. You'll be going in search of those streets of gold like every other dreamer I'm sure!' He laughed, and calling after them as they were carried along by the crowd, shouted. 'Just watch out for the catchers!' When Nancy's feet finally touched solid ground her head felt like it was still moving and she had the sensation of falling as did every other poor soul in this drunken, chaotic mess as they pushed and grabbed from all sides trying to steady themselves.

'This way.' Her father snatched at her hand and began dragging her through the sea of legs and skirts to where the crowd thinned out at its edges and there was space to breathe. Jeering and angry shouting was coming from the harbour entrance to their left and Nancy could see men in long blue coats with stars on their chests pushing back a crowd who were waving their fists in the air and shouting what sounded like 'No more Irish! Go back to where you came from!' The police raised their batons high and brought them down hard on backs and shoulders as they tried to shut them up but brutality only fuelled the crowd's fury. As their protestations grew louder, more scuffles broke out and in the pushing and shoving a woman screamed as she was knocked to the floor and trampled underfoot. 'Get back! Get back! Or you'll all be headed for a seven by three in *the Charlestown.*'

Then a close voice cut through the cacophony of noise. 'Friends!' A man appeared in front of them from nowhere, not expensively dressed, but rakish in his appearance and far too familiar for a stranger. He stood too close to Kitty, and grinning at her tipped his hat, replacing it on his head at a jaunty angle. Smelling of beer, and a pungent sourness that wafted towards them as he waved his hands about enthusiastically, he was lazily chewing on something that blackened his teeth and lips. 'Welcome to the great city of Boston, I'm sure you are in need of someone to show you around, get you fixed up.' He spoke in a strange way, drawing out his words like a cat meowing. 'Who're you?' Kitty asked. 'John Deary at your service madam.' And he tipped his hat again.

'What's yer business Mr. Deary?' Michael stepped forward, positioning himself between the man and Kitty, forcing him to take a step backwards.

'I'm here to be of service to you. I know many people in the city and it would be my pleasure to help you with finding a comfortable room for the night and your first good meal on land.'

'A'm sure we can do wi'out yer services.'

'Ah well, there are places to be had but there are also many seeking to prey on a stranger who may, might we say, not be used to the ways of the city. Not everyone in Boston will be a friend to you.'

'Wur happy t'tek our chances, thanky.'

'I strongly suggest that you do not, especially where it concerns your pretty wife and child, who I am sure will be a great attraction, to shall we say, the less decent element in the city.' He pulled a face like he had a toothache.

'Wur not afeared.'

'Then I think I fail to convey the seriousness of the risk you take. Tomorrow the city will be yours to command I am sure, but tonight, a safe place to stay would be advisable, then you can learn the ways of the city. Mr?...'

'Sullivan. Michael Sullivan an' this be me wife Kitty.'

'Pleased to meet you I'm sure. I know a respectable inn where you can sleep without fear of being murdered in your beds. Only yesterday a poor fella and his wife were found with their throats cut, cleared out they were, only been in Boston for two days. Terrible, terrible shame. Why not come with me? If you don't like what's on offer, we can part as friends, how's that?'

'Tis gettin' late an' it'd serve us well t'fix a room fer t'night Kitty, the morra we'll look fer ourselves. What d'you say?'

Kitty nodded her reluctant agreement.

'Good. That's settled then. Follow me, it's not far. Madam, let me help you with your luggage.' Picking up Kitty's sack and throwing it over his shoulder he set off, pushing his way through the crowd as they followed on behind, Nancy holding on to her father's coat trawled through a dark sea of skirts and legs. The man took them up a narrow street, shadowed by tall buildings on each side where people stood in doorways looking out at them suspiciously as they passed by. Then around a corner, along a wider street where a butcher washed the sidewalk of the day's spilt blood, and an old woman sat outside at a small table selling meat pies. Walking on a little further, they came to an alleyway and looking down it could see steps up to a narrow black door and hear the sound of laughing and shouting coming from beyond it. 'Here we are.' Climbing the steps and pushing open the door, they fell into a dark, smoke-filled room where men and women sat at small round tables eating and drinking. All stopped and missed the same one beat as they turned to look at the strangers as they entered.

'Maggie! Maggie!' John Deary waved his arm in the air and beckoned over a woman who was draping herself across a man as she poured him beer from a jug. Giving them a wide smile she lumbered towards them.

'Well who might these fine folk be and such a sweet little girl.' She smiled down at Nancy and picked up a strand of her hair like she was feeling a ribbon she might want to buy.

'These are my friends Michael and Kitty Sullivan, just come ashore and new to the city.'

'Pleased to make your acquaintance. Any friend of Mr. Deary's is a friend of mine.' And she stared at them all, the wide smile still fixed on her face.

'Maggie, I want you to give my friends the best room in the house and a fine dinner with as much as they can drink.' The man slapped Michael on the back.

'It will be my pleasure. We have a fine

reputation Mr. Sullivan and you won't find a warmer welcome or a more delicious roast chicken in the whole of Boston for such a reasonable price.'

'Whar yer rates?'

'Oh ,very, very reasonable. For our best room and as much as you can eat and drink tonight with breakfast too of course, I require just one dollar from you this evening. You won't find cheaper.'

'Wur just landed wi' only sovereigns.'

'Oh, a sovereign is fine, that's no problem at all.' Michael was relieved and thought he had struck himself a good deal into the bargain. 'I shall require the sovereign now you understand. You are fine people I'm sure but there are some not so honest as you, so I make it a rule to take a payment in advance.'

Michael looked at Kitty and nodded. Making a half turn away from them, Kitty loosened her shawl and reached down into her bodice, careful to only take out one coin from the pouch so as not to reveal the entirety of their stash, then handing the woman the money, she watched as she slowly turned it over in the palm of her hand, feeling the weight of it before dropping it into her pocket. 'Let's get you something to eat, the child looks like she might fall down on her feet. Come, come, I have a quiet table for you away from the noise. Mr. Deary will take your luggage up to your room.'

They followed the woman across the sticky floor to a small table in the corner.

The chicken, if it was chicken, was tough and was boiled not roasted with a grey gravy that tasted fishy. There were potatoes though, plenty of them, and they filled their bellies. By the time they had finished eating Mr. Deary had disappeared but Maggie asked a young lad to show them up to their room which was up three flights of stairs at the very top of the building. On each landing there were four doors, all closed. The top floor just had two doors leading to the rooms in the eaves. The boy opened the one on the right. It was even more bare than the cottage, just a bed, a chair, and a small table with a candle. The sacks containing their belongings had been dumped on the bed. In the dim light, it was hard to tell what colour the walls were but looking up it seemed like there were dark clouds on the ceiling made by water that had found its way in. Michael was about to take issue with the boy about *the best room in the house*, but he had already gone.

'Twill do t'lay our heads. A don't care 'bout any o' it or what we had t'pay; A just want t' sleep.' The beer had made Kitty light-headed and her legs gave way as she slumped down on the bed. The linen was soiled and smelled of oily hair and sweat but it didn't deter her, as she listed sideways from where she was sitting and then didn't move. Michael shut the door, took their luggage from the bed, removed Kitty's shoes and lifted her feet up. As he took off his own boots he pulled the laces on Nancy's. 'Tek off yer boots girl.' Then he pulled the covers from under Kitty to free them and lifted Nancy onto the bed before climbing in himself beside his already snoring wife. There were no curtains on the window and a full moon cast its thin silvery line across the floor just like it did in Kinlough. She didn't feel sad, she didn't feel anything really, not even sick anymore. She touched her mother's hair; it was soft and smooth and she rubbed the silk of it between her fingers as she listened to the strange sounds of the night and the excitable voices coming in through the window as drunken singers tried to outdo each other in their tunelessness. All the while the far away rumble of carts and doors slamming brought an eery percussion to the night, she would fall asleep to a different kind of lullaby.

'Seven o'clock! Seven o'clock!' Loud knocking and a child's voice coming from the other side of their door shook them from their sleep. Staring up at the cloudy ceiling, they listened as he moved on to the next room, then clattered down the stairs two at a time, the assault of his shrill voice rising up from the floor below as he woke the whole building. Michael got up without speaking, stretched his crackling joints and then went to the corner to relieve himself in the pot. 'Tis time you wur both up.' Kitty didn't move and just gave him an empty look. 'C'mon, A've a hunger on me an' A'll need me strength; thar things t'be done the day.' Kitty pulled herself up in the bed and rested her head against the filthy wall, but she was not for rushing.

Michael sat down on the chair and put on his boots before looking over at his wife and child still limp and full of sleep. 'A'll go down an' leave you both then but don't be slackin'.' And with that he was gone, heavy footsteps clunking down the stairs. 'Good morning Mr. Sullivan, you slept well I hope.' Maggie Bates stepped out in front of him before he even reached the bottom step. 'Well enough A s'pose.' He was going to complain about the room but decided it would not serve him well to cause trouble before breakfast as she may serve him short on what he was due. 'Where are your good lady wife and daughter?' She glanced up the stairs. 'Thems followin' me down but A didn't want t'dally over me breakfast.'

'Of course, of course, we shall feed you up no trouble. Come with me.' She took him to the same table they had dined at the night before, unwiped, still with the ring marks from their beer glasses stamped across it. 'You look like a man with a healthy appetite, we have some fine bacon or I can bring you boiled ham and as much bread and butter as you would like of course.'

'Bacon wud be grand, sem fer me wife an' the

child.' Maggie nodded and disappeared through a door which he assumed led to the kitchen. As he looked around him, people at the other tables were already eating, tearing at the bread and meats greedily, their eyes constantly scanning like they feared someone might try to steal it from them. They drank coffee as black as tar or supped beer like there had been no interruption to their drinking from the night before. Ten minutes later Kitty and Nancy came down the stairs and Michael waved them over just as a young girl who was no more than about ten years old appeared at the table carrying a heavy tray stacked with their breakfast. She dropped everything noisily onto the table, plates almost slipping from her right hand, as her left hand struggled with the uneven balance of the tray as she unloaded it. She didn't speak as she concentrated on not spilling anything. 'Whar's the tay?' Michael complained.

'The tay sir?'

'Aye, the tay! A've a thirst on me an' needs a drink.'

The girl looked at him nervously. 'Mrs. Bates is bringing you coffee.'

'Coffee? Whar you 'bout, A want tay!' She began to panic, glancing towards the kitchen door just as Maggie appeared. 'Here we are Mr. Sullivan, your coffee.' She slapped a heavy metal pot down on the table, Kitty leaning forward to breathe it in as a smell like roasted acorns steamed out of the spout and into the air, she wanted it. 'Will you be wanting beer too?' Michael would take it all. 'T'be sure, bring beer too, me wife'll tek the coffee.' Maggie gave him a thin smile and went off.

She came back with the jug of beer and glasses slotting them into a space on the cramped table. 'Well if that is everything, it's time to settle your bill Mr. Sullivan.'

'A paid last night, you've already a sovereign o' mine.'

'Yes of course, you paid me one sovereign on account but it is a dollar for each of you, or a sovereign as you have no dollars. You had our best room, fresh linen and the best food in Boston.' She stood smiling confidently, hands on her hips.

'If that wur yer best room the gud Lord's seved us from yer worst an' as fer the linen, A swear the sheets haven't seen washin' these last twelve months t'bear such stains an' stench!'

'You are very unappreciative of me taking you in at short notice especially you being an Irish and all.' She wasn't smiling now and Nancy thought she looked like a trout with her dead eyes and drooping mouth.

Michael would not be so foully insulted and was not for backing down. 'You cheat me. You never said it wur a dollar fer each o' us an' one o' us only a child. We wudn't have stayed here if you'd told us plain. A'll not be payin' any more.'

'You will not pay? And there was I thinking you such a gentleman. I am afraid you will have to pay.'

'Yer a thief madam!'

'Be careful what you say Mr. Sullivan.'

Just then John Deary appeared at their table. 'Trouble Maggie?'

'Our fine Mr. Sullivan refuses to pay what is due.'

'Friend, you are new in the city but I see you do not heed my words, it would be best not to make enemies on your very first day. You must of course pay what you owe.' He looked over at Maggie and Michael caught the look between them.

'A see it now. Yer in on it t'gether.'

'I helped you out and this is how you repay me.' John Deary tutted and shook his head. 'I would not want to have to persuade you, if you understand my meaning?' He slowly pulled something from his coat pocket and Michael could just make out the handle of a knife followed by the silver flash of its blade. 'How much does he owe Maggie?'

'Two dollars, but I will accept two sovereigns as he doesn't have the necessary.'

'That is good of you Maggie. So Mr. Sullivan, two sovereigns are owed if you wish to leave this place. I think Mrs. Sullivan keeps the money in the softest of places and I am sure she would rather give it over herself than have me take it from her, although I'm happy to oblige of course, unwrap that charming shawl with its pretty pink fringe.'

Michael's anger flared. 'The police'll hear o' it.'

John Deary laughed. 'They will probably hear of it in here! Maggie is this not almost a second home to the officers of the Boston Police Department and are you not the most admired and respected of landladies?'

'Mr. Deary, you make me blush but I cannot deny it.' And she gave him a coquettish smile ill-suited to a faded woman of such mature years.

'Tis no use Michael; we must pay her the money.' Kitty wanted to bring their increasingly threatening exchange to an end.

'You are married to a very wise woman Mr. Sullivan, that's for sure. You and I will collect the luggage from your room while your wife settles up with Maggie.' As he said it, he made a small jabbing motion with the knife keeping it close to his body so nobody else would see it.

Within the quarter hour they were out on the street; fresh from a mugging with only seven sovereigns stashed in Kitty's bodice and not a friend in the city.

CHAPTER 12

In the Vestry

The Reverend Paul Wing entered Elm Street's vestry with a heavy heart. A stiff and unwelcome atmosphere greeted him with James Toogood already seated waiting for him; it was going to be a difficult conversation.

'I am sorry if I have kept you waiting James.'

'Not at all Pastor, I was a little early but I have used the time well to study scripture.'

'Ah well, time spent with God's word is never wasted.' He took off his hat and coat and hung them on the back of the door taking his time in order to steel himself for the conversation ahead. Then taking the nearest seat facing his opponent, he sat, folded his hands in his lap and readied himself for the onslaught.

'Pastor, I think you are aware of the Elders' concerns about your association with the young Irish girl, you know to whom I refer?'

'Yes of course, Miss Eliza Green.'

'There is growing concern about her regular

visits and how much time you spend alone with her.'

'Alas, Miss Green's need is great. Her mind is fragile and she seeks the comfort of prayer and spiritual guidance which I am bound to offer to any poor soul.'

'She is very...' he paused 'young, Pastor.'

'Seventeen.'

'Yes indeed. There is also rumour that there is a child.'

Reverend Wing hesitated, not to withhold the truth but to give his growing anger a few moments to fade before speaking. 'There is a child, a girl, reluctantly given up for adoption.'

'The father?'

'Gone. She was abandoned by him.'

'They were married?'

'They were not. It is clear to me that he took advantage of an innocent girl and had no intention of marrying her.'

James' disquiet deepened with every truthful answer the Pastor gave him. 'Catholic is she not?'

'She is but has not been raised to practice it. Like all poor lost souls she simply seeks direction for her life and the forgiveness of God for her transgressions. I fear her delicate mind was near broken by her troubles James, but despite it, she asks many questions and is bright and inquisitive. I believe she has a good heart that wishes to serve God. She craves guidance and instruction on how to live a good Christian life and who are we to deny it to her?'

'We would all seek to bring a lost lamb into the fold Pastor although it would seem that any instruction you might offer on the importance of exercising self-control is come too late for her.'

'You do not appear to judge the man so harshly James.' He fully understood the risk of his sharp response. 'I consider her to have been badly treated, he gained her trust, won her over and then took advantage of her when she was barely more than a child. I cannot lay all the sin at her door nor see the poor mite she bore as the wages of that sin James, the more one reads God's word, the more we should marvel at His grace and forgiveness, it is beyond my comprehension but He sees it all. I am reminded of Galatians 3:28, we are all one in Christ Jesus.'

James was not for giving up. 'We must still consider whether she has truly repented of her sins. She cannot be washed clean simply because of her desire to live a more virtuous life; it cannot be so easy.'

'I leave all that is divine to the Lord. If she is truly sorry then forgiveness is already hers. It is not for us to judge the depths of God's grace nor is it ours to give. It does not pass through our hands like some gift we can hand out to those we choose. Perhaps you consider her undeserving of God's favour and forgiveness, I do not.'

'That is not what I suggest Pastor, still there are reasons to be concerned about your association with Miss Green, how it might be seen by some. It is the Elders' view that you should leave it to the women of the church to help straighten out her path in life if there be a path for her to be found. Besides, there are those who would welcome such close attention and instruction themselves from their Pastor.'

'Worthier recipients like Mrs. Dantry or Mrs. Lowell perhaps? Ladies whose tongues trip over themselves in their haste to say the right words to ensure their salvation while their hearts play no part in it at all. They do not seek my guidance and instruction, rather they would wish to be seen to be receiving it. You can pour nothing into a jar that already considers itself full as they do. I take it they have expressed a view on the matter to those who will listen?'

James bristled at his words. 'Both are well-respected and influential members of this church.'

'They are rich and I fear that is where any respect for them takes root.' Reverend Wing stopped; his anger was spilling and he had said too much.

'Both are most generous to this church Pastor...'

'You are right James, I am sorry, I spoke in frustration not in fairness. They are of course very good to this church and we are grateful for all they enable. Still, where Miss Green is concerned, I simply cannot deny that which God stirs in my heart. She is a poor wretched soul with no one to care for her in this world and I will do no less than serve the poorest and most lowly just as our good Lord did. James, she has relied on the precarious fortunes of an elderly aunt, but she is to be put out of her home for the non-payment of rent. The Overseers will most likely see them both sent off to Deer Island and I fear for the girl's delicate state of mind if she finds herself in the almshouse.'

'We cannot take in every waif or Irish that comes to our door. They take advantage, they see what is to be gained and seek to turn us over in favour of their own agenda. We must not be shaped by their discourse.'

'Ah the terrible echo of the *Know Nothings* sounds loud still. Men who professed to know the mind of God and take it into their own hands to defend a nebulous threat of papacy that would subvert our religious freedoms. Much noise, no substance of any worth. They sought to take us backwards, sow fear, divide people with their lies.'

Now it was James who tried to cover his anger. 'They sought to protect us against those who would denigrate our religious and political values.'

'Our great city is home to brothers and sisters

from so many other lands and I am convicted that we must continue to open our hearts to those who give up all that is dear to them simply to make a decent life for themselves and their children. The good Lord would not turn them away in their hour of need…' He stood up to bring their futile conversation to an end.

James cleared his throat and then stood too. 'I fear the Elders will be most dissatisfied with my report of our discussion Pastor.'

'Ah well then, I must pray for my greater understanding of your disquiet and theirs regarding this matter James. We are called to be put to work in ways that may not always feel convenient or without price to the delicacies of our nature, I believe the Lord delights in disturbing our equilibrium in order to do His good works.'

James listened but made no eye contact, instead staring down at the floor. 'I shall leave you then Pastor.' And he left closing the vestry door a little too firmly behind him.

Reverend Wing slumped back down in his chair. He was tired all the time and felt every one of his forty-six years these days, as the growing burden of the impossible task he faced weighed more and more heavily on him. No longer the young man, alight with a burning faith and the energy and desire of youth to bring salvation to anyone who had ears to listen, but a weary old man, beaten and dismayed by the lack of charity that abounded and yet the overwhelming need for it. As the years passed, the more he learned, the more the mystery of God seemed to grow, his heart aching constantly at the wonder and beauty of it all whether he understood it or not. He picked up his bible but did not open it, instead leaning back in his chair and laying it on his heart, as all it required, and promised, soaked into him.

CHAPTER 13

Wings on Elm Street

Nancy looked down at her feet, partly to avoid touching the lines between the flaggs, mostly so that she could keep her footing on the undulating surface that constantly had her on the verge of stumbling. They had walked street after street, turned away from every dismal hovel that might have offered them shelter with a curse or a spit or a *can't you read the sign?* They couldn't read the signs but learnt quickly that heavy black letters spelt out NO IRISH. 'Whar the folks in this city wi' some charity in thar hearts?' Michael spat out as yet another door was slammed in their faces.

The sun was beginning to dip in the sky as they turned another corner onto a street that looked just the same as the last. At the end of it, the spire of Elm Street Church rose up in front of them like a long grey finger pointing to heaven and they could see that a man dressed in black was outside locking the front doors. 'Thar be a gud church fella who'll tek pity on us. Hurry, afore we loses sight o' him.' The man began to make his way down the alleyway at the side of the church and would be gone from them if they didn't make haste. 'Wait! Hey wait!' Michael called out, his shrill voice easily stretching down the street and into the alleyway where the man stopped and turned around to see three wretched creatures, one a small child, barrelling up the street towards him. He walked back up the alleyway and waited.

'Thanky.' Michael gasped breathlessly as they came to an untidy stop in front of the man. 'To be sure tis hard t'find any friend in this city.'

'How can I help you? Are you in trouble?'

'Oh we've done nothin' wrong, all the wrong has come upon us.'

'I see, I am sorry to learn that.' The man of God looked down at the child who looked dazed and vacant, *suffer little children...* 'I am Reverend Wing.' He spoke softly as he placed his hand gently on Michael's shoulder.

Michael stared at the spotless white cravat around the man's neck before turning his head slowly to study the clean hand that had never seen dirty work, resting on him, pink nails raggedly bitten to the quip. Looking back up into the man's face he said. 'A'm Michael Sullivan an' thems me wife Kitty an' me daughter Nancy, wur just arrived in the city yesterday.' Nancy stirring from her stupor at the mention of her name, looked up at Reverend Wing, who had no wings.

'Welcome to Boston, I hope it will prosper you and your family.'

'S'far it steals from us, we've been turned over gud an' proper.' Michael paused for effect but Reverend Wing said nothing so he pushed on. 'Wur honest, hard-working folk who just seeks a chance t'live proper but it seems things are turned 'gainst us afore we've even begun. Turned away from every measly room we've been wi' n'reason 'cept wur Irish. A've the sem needs as any other man o' flesh an' blood. Cruel tis fer people t'be s'cold when we've done no ill to any livin' soul.'

'Indeed we are all equal in the eyes of God Mr. Sullivan, all his children.'

'Right you be 'bout that yer reverence s'A'm hopin' God'll tek care o' us when wur in such terrible need.' He looked directly into the Reverend's face like he was challenging him.

'I will pray for you and your family Mr. Sullivan, that God will stay close to you as you make your way in this new life. That your difficulties will be overcome and that he will prosper you in your desire to create a decent life for your family here in Boston. I pray things will change in the future, but for now, it is indeed a hard road for the Irish. You must be determined and not let your spirit be dimmed by such adversity.' Michael didn't understand what he was talking about but smiled back at the Reverend expectantly anyway. 'I may be able to help you with finding accommodation but it is late and nothing will be possible for tonight. You must find an inn.'

'Twas at an inn down by the docks that thieves got us an' held the sharp point o' a knife to me belly. Twudn't be sef fer me wife an' child.' He patted Nancy on the head, putting on the face of a concerned father.

Reverend Wing eyed the woman who stared back at him strangely. Probably no more than a score and some in age, she wore the look of a much older woman, set hard by life's trials and disappointments perhaps and yet, the look she gave him invited something softer that he didn't understand, the call of something he didn't recognise and wouldn't answer.

'I'm sorry, there simply isn't anywhere possible tonight. Come again tomorrow morning at eight and we will see about finding you a place.'

'What 'bout here?' Michael turned his head towards the church.

'In the church? No that is not possible I'm afraid.'

'A thought it wur God's house; wud he turn away a poor woman an' child? A don't ask fer meself o' course, but thems cud be murdered in thar sleep, or somethin' other, out on the streets at night.'

Reverend Wing followed Michael's gaze

towards the church and then, despite all that had been said between him and James earlier, found himself saying, 'I suppose one night in the vestry would do no harm providing you are on your way to somewhere else first thing in the morning.'

Michael enthusiastically grabbed one of the Reverend's hands clamping both of his around it and shaking it up and down vigorously. 'Grand, grand, God blessy.'

Reverend Wing looked up and down the street, it was quiet with no one about. 'Follow me.' He almost bundled them down the alleyway until they were standing outside the vestry door. Turning the key in the lock he opened the door to a modest but warm room that smelt of liberally polished wood. Once inside, they all stood awkwardly for a moment as Michael and Kitty surveyed what would be their shelter for the night, Reverend Wing considering the folly of his hasty decision. Too late now. 'Well then, let's get you settled in.' He went to the door at the back of the vestry and unlocked it. 'Wait here, I will fetch you blankets.' And he disappeared.

'Fertune is turnin' in our fevour Kitty; A can feel it.'

'You get ahead o' yerself Michael Sullivan, he promises us only one night away from the streets an' the morra he may turn us out t'tek our chances.'

'Didn't yer man say he'd help us find somewhar

proper?'

'What man ever does what he says? Thar be only one thing that's certain 'bout what a man wants an' he don't even have eyes fer that!' Kitty had worked out that her attractiveness held no sway with Reverend Wing and she had nothing else to use. 'What's in it fer him?'

'He's a man o' God; he'll keep his word.' But he said it with lessening conviction as Kitty began to chip away at the edges of his confidence. 'Don't worry, A'll see t'it he keeps his word.'

'An' how'll you do that? You've n'power over him, the great an' mighty Michael Sullivan, yer a right brawl! Hah!' She laughed at him and rolled her eyes. 'Yer a poor excuse fer a man, on that you never disappoint.'

'Shut yer clab woman or you'll be sorry.'

Kitty drew herself up to her full height and stepped forward until her face was so close to his that he could taste her foul breath in his mouth. 'How'll A be sorry?'

'Don't push me Kitty.'

'See you've nothin,' pah! Pathetic!'

Michael raised his hand but Kitty's reactions were quick and she grabbed his wrist. 'Strike me an' A swear A'll kill you, church or no church.' Quick as lightning she saw the fear strike in his eyes so she loosened her grip letting his hand drop lifeless and unused. Nancy was oblivious to the show her parents were putting on and just stood quietly willing time to pass until she could sleep, all the time picking at the scabs on her arm drawing blood, reminding herself she was alive.

Just then the door opened and Reverend Wing came in carrying a grey woollen blanket and something red with a gold-coloured fringe. Transferring the bundle to one arm, with the other he turned and locked the door behind him. 'I can only find one blanket I'm afraid, but this old curtain is heavy and will provide you with warmth. I'm sorry but it is the best I can do for tonight.'

'Wur gretful yer reverence.' Michael was at his most charming.

'I ask you to touch nothing. No money is kept here or anything of any value and my desk is locked.' He put weight on the word *locked* to make sure they understood not to pry. 'There is oil in the lamp and water in the jug if you are thirsty but I am afraid I can offer you no other comforts tonight except the good book.' From their blank faces he concluded they couldn't read. 'Very well, I will be back at 7 o'clock, we must be away early before…'

Michael jumped in. 'A'm sure we won't be seen yer reverence if yer afeared o' that.'

'It would be better if you were not.'

Michael nodded his understanding as he took the blanket and curtain from Reverend Wing. 'We'll be as quiet as church mice yer reverence.'

'Very well, until tomorrow then. I hope you sleep well. God bless you.' As he went out through the door, he cast a look over his shoulder, scanning the room like he was securing the position of everything in his mind. Then they heard the key turn in the lock and they were alone. Kitty grabbed the blanket from Michael's hands. 'Nancy an' me'll tek the blanket.' She had already eyed the thick woollen rug on the floor, that would be theirs too to lie on. 'Don't be comin' near me t'night, you can sleep in a chair.' Michael was ready to protest but it was useless, so as Kitty laid out the blanket and took a cushion from a chair for her head, Michael pulled two together until they faced each other, then sat in one, putting his feet up on the other. He was irritated and affronted by their fight and fussed noisily with the curtain that wasn't big enough to cover his legs and his chest at the same time. With no thought for his discomfort, Kitty was already asleep, Michael cursing his wife under his breath as a final amen.

CHAPTER 14

Under the Roof at Pine Street

True to his word, the pastor's key turned in the vestry door's lock at precisely seven o'clock. Holding his breath against the sour stench of their bodies Reverend Wing closed the door behind him and greeted them kindly. 'Good morning Mr. and Mrs. Sullivan and little Nancy, I hope you were not too uncomfortable.' Michael shot a look at Kitty but said nothing. 'I have brought bread and cheese.' And he went to his desk and set down a small bundle, carefully unknotting and then unfolding the linen napkin that gave way to a thick chunk of bread and a generous wedge of cheese. Tearing the bread into three pieces he reached into his pocket and took out a small knife, flicking open the blade and cutting off lumps of the cheese. Starting with the child, one by one, he placed the simple breakfast into their hands with so much reverence, it was like he was sharing the Eucharist with them, then sitting down at his desk he eyed the pathetic trio as they noisily devoured his offering. He would give them ten minutes and then they would be on their way to the South End, away before anyone was about.

'Pastor, are you in thar?' There was the gentle tapping of knuckles on wood as a woman's voice came from the other side of the door. 'Pastor, Paul, A saw you, A knows yer in thar. Please let me in.' Her voice was soft and its lilt familiar.

Michael and Kitty looked at the Pastor waiting for him to call out a response but he seemed stricken by the interruption and sat motionless until in a whisper he said. 'Please stay quiet, no one must know you are here.' And he got up and went to the door, opening it to just a crack, his face pushed into the space between the door and its frame. 'How can I help you child?' Michael and Kitty listened but the woman didn't answer immediately.

'You've someone wi' you Pastor?'

'I am about the Lord's work.' Again there was a hesitant silence from the other side of the door.

'Can A come in? Me heart is full wi' the things we talked 'bout yesterday an' A must spake wi' ye t'put things straight in me head an' heart.'

'Come back after noon. I will be very happy to see you then.'

'But Paul, tis yer Eliza, don't you care fer me n'more? All that's been said between us, wur it false?'

Reverend Wing cleared his throat 'Do not upset yourself child, I see that you are tired, go and rest and then come back later, this is not a convenient time for us to speak. Go now.'

'But Pastor...'

'Please go. God bless you.'

The woman didn't answer and Reverend Wing closed the door softly leaving his hand on the doorknob like he would open it again, but he let go, went back to his desk and sat down.

'Friend o' yers Reverend?'

'One of my flock.'

'Sounded like a lovely young girl, reckon she might be pretty too,' and he winked at Reverend Wing, 'seemed very friendly...'

Reverend Wing was a kind and gracious man but not stupid. He had met men like Michael Sullivan before who saw the dark side to everything good, who sought to diminish everyone down to his low level of thinking for his own comfort, who looked at you for what he could get, not what he could give. He would pray for his soul like any other man.

'We must be on our way. Please gather up your things.' He spoke slowly, distracted, then picked up the pace like his words were beginning to catch up with his thoughts. 'I have contacts in the South End area who have helped me before to find accommodation for those in difficulty shall we say. You will pay for your accommodation but it is fair and there are landlords who do not seek to profit handsomely from people's misery. You have money for the rent I assume?'

'Aye, we've some.' Michael wouldn't give away how much, better for the Pastor to think they needed as much favour as possible in that respect.

'In these circumstances, I stand as a personal guarantor of your good character which is why decent men are willing to take a chance on a stranger, so please do not let me down. Your rent must be paid on time, if it is not, you will be put out. Do you understand?'

'A understand yer reverence, A'm an honest man, you've n'reason t'be afeared.'

'Very good. I can also make introductions that will help you find a job perhaps at the iron works, the pay is fair and the war ensures constant demand, there is often work to be found at the docks too for those who are not afraid of hard work.' Michael's disinterested expression gave away the truth, that he would be avoiding hard work if he could. 'Will the child be put into school?'

Michael and Kitty looked at each other and then at Nancy. 'Her mother an' me are agreed she'll have learnin'. Tek care o' us in our auld age eh yer reverence?'

Reverend Wing looked at the child and hoped she would be open to learning and the small possibilities it might bring her but everything about her seemed shut off and distant like she wasn't fully there. 'Would you like to go to school Nancy?' He asked gently.

Nancy just stared back at him, eyes glassy, like they might spill over.

'She don't spake much these days yer reverence.' Kitty gave Nancy a shove. 'Answer Reverend Wing when he spakes t'you.'

'Don't press the child.' He crouched down to be eye to eye with her. 'I am sorry Nancy; I did not mean to upset you. Everyone feels a little scared sometimes but you will make lots of new friends I am sure of it, and before you know it, Boston will feel like home.' He smiled kindly at her but she turned her face away from him. 'Now, we must be away, we have a bit of a walk ahead of us although I am sure it will be worth it to you.' He stood and waited patiently as Kitty and Michael folded their makeshift bedding and gathered up their belongings. 'One more thing, it would be better if we were not seen together so I ask that you follow me at a distance, keep me in sight but do not make any sign that we are together, that way we can avoid any difficult questions.'

Michael nodded. 'Whatever fevours yer reverence.'

'Very well then, let's be off.' Reverend Wing went to the door and opened it slowly looking out into the alleyway like he expected someone to be there. Satisfied that there was no one about, he opened the door fully and waved them through into the alleyway. Then locking the door behind them he gave them a quick, nervous smile and was off, black coat tails flying in his haste as he made his way up the alleyway and onto the street. When they were satisfied he had made safe distance, Michael and Kitty followed, Nancy trailing behind as they wove their way through dim streets not yet fully lit by the sun, careful not to make eye contact with anyone they came across. After nearly half an hour and just as Michael was about to call out to complain about the distance they were being asked to walk, Reverend Wing came to a stop ahead of them, turning and holding his hand up as a signal to stay where they were. Then he disappeared down a side street.

'A'll not be after waitin' all day fer him, he better hurry.' Michael dropped his sack and leaned back against a wall folding his arms in petulant protest, kicking the sidewalk with the toe of his boot because his irritation would not stay still. Kitty angled her body away from him trying to ignore his sulking presence and looked around aimlessly at the tall buildings lining the street. It was still early but she could see life was beginning to stir as windows were thrown open to the new day, then her eyes drifted to the second-floor window of a house on the opposite side of the street where a man stood looking out - yawning as he ran his fingers through his hair – and she caught the moment he noticed her. Straightening up, he lifted the window to get a better look at her. Kitty took a quick sideways glance at Michael who was as stupid and unobservant as usual and hadn't noticed the man but was staring down the street to where Reverend Wing had vanished from sight willing him to reappear. Tracing her eyes back again to where the man stood, she saw he was leaning forward now, hands resting on the windowsill and she knew he hadn't taken his eyes off her for a second. He began mouthing something she couldn't understand and then slowly tapped his finger against his lips. Now she understood.

'At last!' Michael's shrill voice beside her made her jump. 'Let's be away. A reckon the God fella has gud news fer us.' Reverend Wing had reappeared on the street and was beckoning them to join him. As Kitty picked up her sack and followed Michael, she looked back over her shoulder to where the man stood smiling at her, eyes tracking her progress down the street. She was sure they would meet again.

'What news yer reverence?'

'Good news Mr. Sullivan. I believe I have been able to secure you a room on very reasonable terms. Your accommodation will be modest but it is dry and clean and the landlord is a fair man with a good Christian heart, still, he offers no wild favours and you must pay what is due, when it is due. Follow me.' He took them down a narrow side street, past the repeating black doors of identical facades until they came to the last on the corner where a dour looking man with an ashen pallor and clothes to match was waiting outside for them.

'Mr. Dyer, here are Mr. and Mrs. Sullivan and their daughter Nancy.'

Jacob Dyer nodded acknowledgement but didn't offer any welcome. 'This way. It's on the third floor.' He took them up the creaking wooden staircase and as they turned on the first landing Nancy counted three doors before the next flight of stairs. On the next landing another three doors and on the third, two shorter doors flanked the landing. Opening the one on the left Jacob Dyer led the way into their attic room which at first sight seemed both cluttered and bare at the same time. A rectangular table and two chairs were placed near the window, facing them on the other side of the room, the ceiling sloped down over a narrow, wrought iron bedstead with a thin lumpy mattress that had no linen and would be a tight squeeze for them all. The room was L-shaped, the ceiling sloping into a cramped space where a washstand was wedged into the corner and a bucket hung from a hook on the wall. A Small stove would have to suffice for all their warmth and cooking needs and there was a single shelf on the wall awaiting their belongings. Even in the centre of the room, at its highest point, the ceiling was low and Kitty found herself stooping despite it clearing her head by at least four inches. The furniture having claimed its territory around the edges, they were left standing in a space of no more than six feet square, definitely too close for comfort for the Sullivans.

Standing in awkward silence they waited while Jacob Dyer caught his breath from climbing the stairs. 'Now then, the privies and the water tap are in the yard directly below.' And he went to the open window, leant over the table, and pointed down. 'There are lines for your washing down there too but you'll need to take your turn. I expect my tenants to sweep the landings and the stairwells and keep the hall clean and tidy. You share with another family on this floor and I leave it to you to work out a rota that suits you both. Mark my words, I run a respectable house and no alcohol is to be consumed nor any gambling to take place or any other thing of an immoral nature.' Michael didn't blink, feigning the wide, open look of an innocent man. 'I make no judgement about the origins, colour or religion of my tenants but they must all behave civilised. I see all the comings and goings in this house and I will act swiftly if its rules are not followed.' Michael nodded as Jacob Dyer droned on while Kitty looked on impassively simply waiting for him to stop speaking.

'I am sure Mr. and Mrs. Sullivan understand what is required of them and God bless you Mr. Dyer for giving shelter to strangers when so many have turned them away.'

'It is only what the good Lord requires of me Pastor.'

The rent, to be settled every Wednesday, was agreed and a deposit paid to Jacob Dyer who pointed out the difference in value between a dollar and a sovereign so as not to cheat them. Warning them about unscrupulous moneychangers; he told them they should go to Anderson's General Store on the corner of the block, ask for Mr. Anderson himself, he would see them right, give them a fair exchange. Michael listened to his advice but quietly cursed the thieving Maggie Bates and John Deary who had tricked him out of a small fortune. 'I shall leave you to settle in then. Goodbye Pastor.' And Jacob Dyer left them to unpack.

'I must be going too; I have pressing church work to attend to.'

'Aye, yer reverence mustn't be late fer yer meetin' wi' the lovely Irish girl...'

Reverend Wing met Michael's mischievous eye but ignored the comment. 'I very much hope you will be able to find work at the iron works Mr. Sullivan, it is hard but steady employment and would serve you well in providing for your family.' Reaching into his pocket he took out a white envelope and handed it to Michael. 'Take this to Elmer Davis at the works office on Iron Street and do yourself credit by presenting yourself smartly to him. I know Mr. Davis well and I believe my commendation will encourage him to look upon you favourably for work.' Then he looked down at Nancy. 'God bless you little Nancy, I hope you enjoy school and learn many wonderful new things.'And he laid his hand gently on the top of her head like he was bringing a blessing down on her.

'I am sure the school on South Street will be very happy to have Nancy as a student, Alice Perkins is a fine teacher and takes great pride in the advancement of all the children in her class, I believe Nancy will flourish there. The new semester has begun and I would encourage you to speak with Miss Perkins at the earliest opportunity. It's only a few minutes from here; it will be easy for her to walk to school.'

Michael and Kitty both gave Reverend Wing a completely disinterested look so he wished the Sullivans well and left them to survey their new home. As soon as he had gone, Michael slapped the envelope down on the table. 'Men the likes o' me can do better than the hellish furnaces o' an iron works, thar be gold t'be had out thar an' A'm goin' after it.' The bluster of his words faded though with the cold look Kitty gave him. 'Don't tek airs on yerself, the streets out thar be dirty, how'll we live if you don't find yer gold mister high an' mighty? By me reckonin' half the money is near spent already, runs through yer fingers like water from a leakin' bucket!'

'Wur it not me clever workins on Reverend Wing that got us this place?'

'This place? Tis too small an' we'll be too hot in the summer an' freezin' cold in the winter up here in the roof.' Kitty paced out the six-foot square. 'An' how's we all 'spected t'sleep in that bed?'

'You'd think you'd lived in the queen's palace or somethin' the way yer carryin' on.'

'Sure, A never felt trussed-up like a chicken in Kinlough, this place is goin' t'choke me.'

'Ah, you'll get used t'it s'stop yer sim-samin' yer doin' me head in wi' it woman. Don't be after vexing yerself, A can mek a bed fer the child on the floor an' you'll feel better when we've wood fer the stove an' food on the shelf. How's 'bout I buys you some o' that thar coffee wudn't that be nice?'

'It'll tek more than coffee t'put right all yer wrongs Michael Sullivan...'

Still, an industrious two hours saw the stove lit, bread and cheese on the table, a sack of cornmeal in the corner, a small pat of lard, potatoes, turnips, a blood pudding, a kettle of water boiling for the coffee and even the luxury of a small sugar loaf cone to sweeten it. Michael had also been able to secure two discarded fruit boxes from Mr. Anderson and knocking out one end of each, placed the two boxes together to fashion a cot for Nancy which he stowed under the table so as not to take up valuable floor space. He was pleased with his handiwork. 'Unpack yer blanket girl s'we can fix up yer cot fer the night an' then stash yer other things under the bed.' Nancy opened the sack that had travelled all the way from mamo's cottage and reached inside her fingers touching something strange and unfamiliar. Reaching in further, she pulled out a squashed brown paper package that had once been neatly folded and tied with string. 'What's that? Let me see it.' Nancy reluctantly handed the package to her father who pulled the tangled string away tearing at the paper as a book fell out onto the floor. 'Eh? Whar'd this come from?' He picked it up turning it over in his hand with no idea what he was looking at, then shoved it into Nancy's hands. 'An' what's this in here?' Something as blue as a stormy ocean with a scattering of tiny white flowers was folded inside the brown paper and as he pulled it free it fell into the shape of the prettiest dress she had ever seen. It had a square scooped neck, its edge traced with a line of white lace, and long sleeves puffed out with blue ribbon bows gathering the cuffs at the wrists. The full skirt had side pockets also edged with lace and a row of four pearl buttons fastened it at the back. Nancy stared at it in wonder.

Kitty piped up now. 'C'mon. Whar'd you get it?'

Nancy finally found her voice 'A've not seen it afore.'

'How'd it get in thar then? Faeries A s'pose?'

Nancy thought it must have been a faerie, it looked like a faerie dress, and it was hers. 'Can A keep it?'

'What use d'you have fer a dress like that? 'Sides it'll mek a pretty penny.'

'Fer when A go t'school.'

Kitty looked across at Michael. 'We'll be seein' 'bout school.'

Michael remembered Nathaniel Collins' words. 'It wur promised t'her Kitty, it wur promised t'Mr. Collins.'

'He isn't t'know.'

'He told me he knows people, has eyes here in the city.'

'An' you believe him? He don't know anyone livin' in places the likes o' this, he wur gamin' wi' you.'

'A gev him me word.'

'You gev him yer word? Ah well that's grand then, yer word is yer word.' And she tutted, clicking her tongue loudly.

'Can A go da?'

'We'll see 'bout it. Now unpack yer things an' mek up yer cot.' He rolled up the dress and shoved it back into the paper. 'An' put this under the bed.' Handing her the package she held it tightly just for the feel of something that was hers then emptied the rest of the sack and stowed everything under the bed as she was told except the book which she wrapped inside her blanket before placing it in the makeshift cot. Tonight under a dark wooden sky in her own little boat that would sail to nowhere, she would touch the cover and the pages and imagine the words that would become hers when she learned to read.

CHAPTER 15

Met by Grace

Kitty forced the envelope into Michael's hand. 'Tek it.'

'A'm not after tekin' the rotten job, thar be the sovereigns Collins gev us, tis enough t'set somethin' up meself, mek us lob o' money A bet.'

'Gamble wi' it you mean.'

'A'm not after gamblin' wi' it, A'll get meself set up proper wi' me own business.'

'Doin' what?'

'Thar be plenty A cud turn me hand to.'

'Like what?'

'Stop pushin' me woman, A needs time t'think is all.'

'Ah stop yer bladderin' you don't know what yer talkin' 'bout, s'while yer thinkin' 'bout yer great plans, A'm holdin' on t'the money.' She folded her arms across herself to make her point.

He would easily get his hands on the sovereigns, but looking into his wife's determined face, he could see she was set on him taking the work and he would not risk crossing her anymore today, he would save his chances for another time when there was more at stake. So he would go; take the stinking job if it was offered to him, but alongside it he would make other plans. No need to share them with Kitty, she would just try to dissuade him from taking risks, getting above himself. She was not quick and smart like him, she was just a woman.

'Well, A've had n'breakfast.'

'Some other fella might get ahead o' you if yer lingerin' wi' a leisurely breakfast.' As always, Kitty was a step ahead and had already cut bread and cheese to take with him. Scooping it up from the table she pushed it into his hand 'Here, tek it A tell you an' don't be after givin' me yer lip!'

'Don't be orderin' me 'bout woman, A'll be goin' 'cause A chooses to.' He went to the door and pulled away the chair he had wedged against it *to keep out devilish thieves during the night* and went out, slamming it behind him. Kitty listened to the protest of his heavy footsteps as he lumbered noisily down every wooden step until the last. Always happier at his going out than his coming in, she dropped down into a chair and savoured the silence, smiling to herself as her mind drifted to the man at the window. Nancy was still lying in her cot one hand on her book under the blanket. 'Time you wur out o' yer bed girl, thar be chores t'be done. First you can fetch the water.' Nancy was already well versed in collecting it and had made four trips down to the yard yesterday for her mother, making her slow progress back up the three flights of stairs, resting the half-filled bucket on each step as she went so as not to spill anything. This new day would offer up no respite and ten minutes later she felt Jacob Dyer's unseen eyes on her as she passed his door which he left open just enough to spy on his tenants as they came in and went out.

She needed to relieve herself first so walked across the yard to the row of four wooden privies but as she opened the first of the doors, there was a man sitting doing his business, trousers dropped round his ankles. 'Don't ya know someone's in here if the doors shut? Stupid brat, get out!' She slammed the door shut and moved along to the next privy where the door was slightly ajar, peering in through the gap she saw that it was empty and went inside, setting the bucket down on the only dry patch on the floor before closing the door behind her. In the dim light she could just see the sheets of newspaper threaded on string that hung from a hook beside the wooden seat and a fat spider that scrabbled in the corner and balled itself up small as the vibration of her steps alerted it to danger. She kept her eye on it as she held her breath, lifted her skirt and got herself up onto the seat making sure never to look down the hole at the filthy mess below. Instead she looked at the newspaper hanging up beside her running her eyes along the big letters which shrank to a smaller size further down the page. Imagining Nathaniel's finger running along the lines of words as he read to her, she realised she recognised some of the shapes as sounds in her head *a, be, it, the...* Then she tore off the sheet with all the beautiful words printed on it, used it, and got out of the privy as quickly as she could.

Outside a woman in a blue dress, holding a baby in one arm while hanging washing with the other, smiled at her as she went to the tap for the water. 'New here are you?' Nancy wasn't supposed to speak to strangers but the woman had a nice face so she put down the bucket and nodded back at her. 'What floor?'

'Under the roof.'

'Top floor. Same as us eh Maude?' and she jiggled the fat baby on her hip.

Nancy thought that this must be the screaming brat that her father had complained cried all through the night and kept him from his sleep.

'Pleased to meet you neighbour. What's your name?'

'Again Nancy hesitated but it felt safe and she wanted to hear her own name so said it. 'Nancy Sullivan.'

'Such a pretty name ay Maude?' The practically

toothless baby smiled her ignorant agreement simply because her mother was smiling at her.

'I'm Grace Thompson.'

Nancy found herself blurting out, 'A'm goin' t'school.'

'Well, well, isn't that something. You ever need any help with your reading or numbers, you just knock on my door.' She smiled at Nancy again. 'Those are pretty boots you're wearing.'

Nancy looked down at them and then said, 'A've a new blue dress too.'

'Well how lovely. Blue is my favourite colour.' And she pinched her skirt between her fingers and swished it backwards and forwards.

Nancy felt emboldened by Grace's voice which felt gentle and close, not brutal and far away like all the others. 'That'd be grand.'

'Grand ay?' She laughed kindly at the child's words that were beyond her years. 'I think we shall be great friends Nancy.' Then she looked at the empty bucket. 'Who waits for the water?'

Nancy jumped at her words. 'Ma!'

Grace saw her sudden distress. 'Will you be in trouble for dawdling? Fill it quick and I will carry it up for you. Hurry.'

Grace climbed the stairs easily despite the plump Maude on her hip and the bucket in her other hand. Tip-toeing up the last flight, on reaching the top, she put down the bucket quietly and whispered 'That's my door.' And pointed to the one directly opposite the Sullivan's own. 'I will be seeing you Nancy…' and with a smile, she disappeared into her room, leaving Nancy alone on the landing.

Struggling to pick up the over-filled bucket, she half lifted, half pulled it along the floor and pushed open the door to where her mother was sitting at the table peeling potatoes. 'At last!' She eyed the full bucket suspiciously 'How'd you carry that?'

Nancy looked down at the bucket too but said nothing.

'Well set you down an' help me wi' these potatoes.' Nancy climbed up onto the chair and taking the knife from her mother began cutting out the black eyes and rotten bits then, settling into the rhythm of the work, her eyes drifted towards the window. Looking down into the yard Grace Thompson's washing waved at her as it flapped in the wind and the stripped hare thought she might feel a little bit happy.

CHAPTER 16

On Iron Street

By the time Michael Sullivan stepped onto the bridge at Dover Street the sun was rising over the city casting a burning orange light on the glassy surface of the water. It was early and the bridge was quiet but below him boats already bobbed in the water, knocking against the piles, heavy with their night's haul, while up through the gaps in the wooden planks under his feet came the smell of fish and human waste, mingling like ugly bedfellows, the putrid stench burning his nostrils. He lifted his nose higher into the air in the hope he could catch a sweeter smell but the city seemed to bring only foulness from every direction. As he reached the midway point of the bridge, the grey silhouette of the foundry loomed large ahead of him dominating the horizon, furnace stacks industriously belching their acrid smoke into the sky. With all her ordering him about Kitty had put him in a bad mood this morning but it darkened even further as he looked across the water and realised he had traded the Dartry mountains for brick chimneys, the clear fresh loughs for stinking rivers clouded by man's filth.

Kitty had pushed him out too early and he waited nearly an hour at the foundry office to see Elmer Davis who greeted him with silent suspicion as he took the envelope from his outstretched hand. Taking the letter out he read it then folded it and stuffed it back into the envelope. 'Reverend Wing commends you as honest and hard-working but I know him to be a generous man who is perhaps too enthusiastic about seeing the good in men like you Mr. Sullivan.'

Michael was sorely affronted but clamped his mouth shut for fear of saying something he would regret.

'You have no other references I take it?'

'No sir. A've worked the land. Been me own man.'

Elmer Davis gave him a disinterested look. 'Hmmm. Are you prepared then to become an indoor man? I warn you; fresh air and blue sky will seem a distant memory when you stand at the furnaces day after day.'

'You've no outdoor work fer me? A'd fevour it.'

Davis turned from him and went to the fire to warm his hands, rubbing them together, speaking slowly and deliberately. 'Beggars can't be choosers Mr. Sullivan. I can take you on charging the furnaces, but I have nothing else to offer you. Eight to eight shifts, six dollars a week Monday to Saturday; Sundays will be your own and I am sure Reverend Wing will be pleased to see you in church.' As he turned to face Michael he was smiling. 'Up to you, take it or leave it.'

With every fibre of his body Michael wanted to leave it, he could do better for himself but he didn't have a better plan in place yet, so found himself saying 'A'll tek it.'

'Very well. Come here to the office tomorrow morning at eight o'clock. You can give the clerk your details then. If you prove to be unreliable Mr. Sullivan, no commendation from the Reverend will stand in your favour and you will be let go, I'm sure you understand. Until tomorrow then.' He almost marched Michael to the door and that was it, he had the job.

Walking back down Iron Street towards the bridge he met himself coming the other way as he passed lines of shuffling grey men, heads hung down, on their way to light their faces at the furnaces of hell, depressing his spirits as the reality of it all fully settled on him. He wouldn't hurry home, hah! he'd keep Kitty guessing, make her stew. By the time he reached their door he would make sure he was wearing the expression of a man who had been sent away empty handed, make her wait, think he'd been unsuccessful, that would teach her to try pushing him about.

As he came through the door, Kitty was waiting.

'Whar you been? What news havvy?'

'Get me some tay an' A'll tell you.'

'What're you 'bout Michael Sullivan? Tell me now an' don't be givin' out t'me.'

Sighing loudly, Michael pulled out a chair and sat down, spreading his hands out on the table. 'A went all the way thar, gev him the letter like A was told, but he said thems no jobs fer me.'

'Why wud Reverend Wing send you if he knew thar wur no jobs? Meks no sense.'

Michael shrugged his shoulders.

'What did yer man say?'

'That he wished twer different, but thar wur nothin' he cud do 'bout it, is all.'

'Yer lyin'!'

Nancy knew to make herself small and quiet in her cot under the table as the storm between her parents brewed.

'Thems no jobs A tell you, but Mr. Davis wur sorely impressed wi' me, s'med a place fer me even though thar wurn't one t'be had. He's no fool, he knows a gud thing when he sees it.'

'Stop gamin' wi' me. Diddy tek the job or not?'

'A did. A start the morra morn.'

'Well then, that's gud news, you shudn't have med me think different. How much do it pay?'

'Six dollars a week.'

'What? That's not enough, the rent's as much.'

'Thar's the sovereigns an' a few little investments shud see us right.'

'A told you, yer not gettin' yer hands on them.'

'Well, you'll need t'be after findin' work yerself woman, plenty o' ways you can bring somethin' home. The girl'll be in school s'she's no gud t'us an' thar be no money fer you t'sit 'round suppin' tay an' gettin' fat on sweetmates an' puddins.' He would play with her, have a bit of fun.

'Devil!' Kitty's anger burst now as she picked up a spoon and threw it at her husband, hitting him above his left eye, a thin red line giving way to a trickle of blood.

He'd show her this time. 'Bitch!' Kicking his chair away he grabbed a knife from the table and lunged at her holding the blade up close to her face. 'Mark me words, yer days o' lazin' 'round are over, tis not enough t'just look pretty an' that's not even true no more. Pah! yer bloom is almost over girl, thar be fresher, sweeter fruits t'be tasted on just 'bout every street corner o' Boston.'

'Look in the mirror yerself, you'd lose t'a pig's arse in a beauty parade.' Kitty hit back defiantly, but his words had wounded her, losing her beauty was inevitable but it was too soon, she wasn't finished with it yet.

'A'd rather look like the pig's arse than **be** the pig's arse wi' all the stinkin' shite that comes out o' it!'

Both and neither won as they each seemed to run out of spite at the same time. Well matched in their contempt for each other, equally they knew when enough had been said to last a month of Sundays. Michael put down the knife and sat back down at the table, wiping his sleeve across his forehead sweeping away the blood, while Kitty drew herself up to her full height and made a point of stepping daintily to the stove, like a fine lady, to pour the tea. It would be quiet now that the dam of their fury had burst.

From her cot Nancy looked up at her father's legs, still now, no longer twitching with anger, his fists unfurled and relaxed in his lap. In the relative calm after the storm she crawled out from under the table and sat on the chair opposite him. He tried to ignore her staring at him. 'What're you gawkin' at?'

She didn't know she was staring but she sorely wanted to ask him about school. She longed to go more than anything. 'Can A go t'school the morra da?'

Michael looked over at Kitty. 'Yer mother'll see t'it.'

Nancy wasn't convinced. Her mother had never given her anything she wanted. She was mean and only thought about herself. 'Can A ma?'

'Stop yer chunterin', we'll see 'bout it.' She stirred the tea but kept her back to them. 'Twud get you out from under me feet but you wud still need t'do yer chores. Understand?'

'A will ma.'

'A s'pose we cud go visit this Miss, Miss…'

'Alice Perkins!' The name exploded out of Nancy's mouth like a firecracker going off.

Kitty turned slowly and looked at her daughter with a cold, dull expression intended to muzzle her enthusiasm. 'If that be her name we'll go this afternoon.'

'A'm goin' t'school.' Nancy whispered to herself, as if by saying it out loud, someone might steal it away from her.

No part of Kitty wanted Nancy to have an education and what was the point anyway? Still, she would go along with it for now, coming and going more freely away from the girl's sight, seeing who she fancied when she fancied. Yes, it suited her.

The school stood square on the corner of South Street and Lincoln. A low wall surrounded a neat patch of green where an apple tree dipped its laden branches dappling the light on the path under their feet. It was painted white with four tall, blue-shuttered windows and a blue door which Kitty pushed open without knocking. They stepped into a large room with white walls and a polished wooden floor that had a centre aisle formed by two rows of wooden desks - boys on the left, girls on the right – running all the way up to a large fireplace at the front. To each side of it, wide blackboards stretched across the wall into each corner and in front of one stood the teacher, chalk suspended in mid- air.

'Good day madam. Can I help you?'

'A want t'see 'bout schoolin' fer me girl.'

Alice Perkins was irritated by the interruption and the disturbance to the smooth running of her classroom. All the children had turned around to eye the strangers and their concentration had been broken. She put down the chalk. 'We are in the middle of a lesson Mrs...?'

'Sullivan.'

'Mrs. Sullivan. You must wait until class is over. Wait there by the door please. Children stop your gawking and face the front.' Nancy watched in wonderment as the teacher picked up the chalk again and white words appeared on the blackboard as she wrote them, then spoke them, wrote them, then spoke them. Finding herself silently repeating the words in her head she knew this was learning. Twenty minutes later the class was dismissed and the children filed out of the classroom in two noisy but orderly lines. 'Shush! Don't be making such a racket, it's enough to shake the bones of the dead.' And at their teacher's command, their noise dimmed, fading to nothing as the last child left, closing the blue door behind them.

'Come, come.' Alice Perkins waved them forward to her desk. There were no chairs in front of it and so Kitty stood awkwardly looking down on the teacher feeling the smaller of the two of them despite her stature. 'Who sent you to me?'

'Reverend Wing.'

'Ah Reverend Wing, he is prolific in his good works.' She shook her head very slightly from side to side but was smiling to herself. 'What's the child's name?'

'Nancy.'

'And how old is she?'

Kitty hesitated; she thought there might have been six summers since the child was born but it could be seven. She couldn't remember the date or how long had passed since, but she vividly remembered the night she nearly died. Waves of excruciating pain had woken her in the middle of the night, it had been too soon, but this baby was ready to come feet first. One leg out and one in, Frances had reached inside her to grab a foot and twist the baby around to heave it out and it had felt to Kitty like she was losing all her insides as finally a baby in shades of blue and red entered the world silently. Frances had taken the cord from around the baby's neck, rubbed her back, shaken her until finally a small stuttering cry emerged and she began to blossom pink. A small weak cry had become a shrieking wail of protest when the baby was placed in Kitty's arms. Then, as now, she felt nothing for this scrap of a being, except resentment for what it had put her through.

'You know how old your child is I take it?' Again she waited for a response.

'Six, A think.'

'Well when was she born?'

'Winter. December twur.' Alice Perkins wrote it down.

'Does the child have any ailments? We cannot take her if she is not in good health.'

'She's sturdy an' never sick 'cept if she's on a ship or in a carriage.'

The teacher gave Kitty a confused look then turned her attention to Nancy. 'And do you want to be in school Nancy?'

Nancy almost jumped over the desk in her excitement 'A want t'read an' write Miss. A have a book!'

Alice Perkins looked into the earnest bright eyes of the child. 'Very well Mrs. Sullivan, I am happy to take Nancy but she must be here every day at eight o'clock sharp. If you keep her away she will lose her place here at the school and there will be no coming back. Is that clear?'

Kitty nodded.

Alice Perkins opened her desk drawer and took out a sheet of paper, pushing it across to Kitty. 'Please fill this in for the school register.'

Kitty stared down at the piece of paper blankly and then back at the teacher.

'I see, you need help.' Alice Perkins took

back the piece of paper and wrote down all their details. When she was finished she stood up, subconsciously straightening her skirt and pushing back a stray lock of hair as if standing in front of a mirror, the reflection of two dishevelled wretches staring back at her. 'We are grateful to have a very generous benefactor who provides milk and a piece of fruit for each child every day but Nancy must bring her own lunch or go home for it, nothing else will be provided. I expect her to be presented clean and tidy every day and if she becomes infested with lice you must keep her away until she is clear of it. This school has an excellent reputation and I expect all my students to live up to its high standards. Is that clear Mrs. Sullivan?'

Kitty bit her lip and nodded again.

'Do you have any questions?'

Kitty tried to think of something clever, anything at all to show she wasn't stupid, but she had nothing. 'Nothin' comes t'me mind.'

'Very well, I will see you tomorrow at eight o'clock.' And with that they were dismissed as the teacher stood up and turned away from them to wipe the words from the blackboard.

Kitty was furious and complained all the way back to Pine Street. 'What's she 'bout talkin' t'me like A'm nothin' an' diddy ever see a woman s'plain? An auld maid wi' no man t'pay any eye t'her A'll bet. Dried up auld bitch.' Nancy listened to the string of insults as they sailed above her head but didn't care, she was going to school.

CHAPTER 17

The Blue Dress

Sitting at her desk she took in the strange new vista. From her seat at the end of the front row she could almost reach out and touch Miss Perkin's blue and cream checkered skirt as she paced up and down in front of them animated and quite splendid. To her right was a girl with blond hair wearing a green dress, a bit older than her. She had a cross face like she was thinking something bad or had a toothache and didn't look at Nancy or speak to her. It felt odd to sit beside another child and she wasn't sure what you were supposed to do or whether there were any rules. To her left across the aisle, a boy with frothing marmalade hair and freckles leant on his hands like sitting up was just too much effort and as she looked at him, he turned and stuck a fat, pink tongue out at her. She would keep her eyes fixed straight ahead like they had been told to by Miss Perkins, it was safer that way, anyway she was too afraid to turn around in her seat to look at the three rows of strangers behind who would be staring back at her.

'Good morning class.'

'Good morning Miss Perkins.' Nancy just about caught the tail end of their droning ensemble as she realised they were supposed to repeat the greeting.

'We have a new student joining us today and I want you to make her feel welcome. Nancy Sullivan, please stand up.'

Nancy was stuck to her seat.

'Stand up, come on now, be quick about it.'

Mortified that everyone was looking at her, Nancy climbed down off the bench. She should have been wearing her new blue dress; they might have thought she belonged here if she had been wearing it but without its armour, she was still just the stripped hare that stood naked and small in front of unkind strangers, chin almost resting on the top of her desk despite pulling herself up to her full height. Her mother was mean for not letting her wear it, forcing her to wear her old brown dress, she was just jealous that she didn't have anything so pretty or fine herself.

'Class please say welcome to Nancy.'

'Welcome Nancy.' Came a stuttering chorus of unenthusiastic voices.

Nancy kept her eyes fixed on the fireplace, rigid, afraid to catch anyone's eye.

'You can sit down now Nancy.' Miss Perkins

returned to her own seat and from her desk, began calling out names, each child in turn putting their hand in the air saying, 'Here Miss Perkins' as she ticked them off her list. The register complete, she slipped it into her desk drawer and stood up, sweeping her eyes around the silent classroom. 'Joseph Hall and Myrtle Wilson, please help me to handout the slates.' The two pressed recruits got up and went to their teacher's desk where she handed them something that looked like a stack of square wooden plates. Nancy was the first to receive hers from the hand of Myrtle Wilson and looked down at the mysterious object. It was about the size of mamo's bible with a wooden frame that surrounded a black centre dusty with the ghosts of erased shapes that she couldn't quite make out. The frame was printed with shapes on each of its four sides – a square, a circle, something that looked like a sugar cane cone - and other strange objects with lines and curves and angles that she traced her finger along. Turning it over, the black slate was striped with horizontal white lines waiting for words to sit upon them and along the top of the wooden frame the alphabet was printed in perfectly even curling letters, while along the bottom; numbers counted themselves from one to twenty.

Miss Perkins followed around behind her two helpers placing a piece of chalk in each desk well and when the last had been deposited, she went back to her desk and picked up a book opening it at about its mid-point, leafing through the pages until she came to a stop. 'Howard Clark, please come out to the front and read to the class.' An older boy, who was taller than her father, unenthusiastically made his way to her desk. Handing him the book she said 'Start reading at chapter six on page eighty-three headed *Massachusetts Bay Colony*.' Then pointing at the book and running her finger down the page she said 'Then read the first one, two, three, four, five, six paragraphs but be ready to pause when I tell you.'

The boy began to read haltingly in a deep monotonous voice. '*The Puritans of England, still subjected to various restrictions, continued to seek an asylum in the new world. A grant having been obtained from the Plymouth Company of a tract bordering on Massachusetts Bay, John Endicott was sent out in 1628 with one hundred followers. After exploring the neighbourhood Endicott's party finally settled at a place whose Indian name Naum-ke-ag, they changed to Salem.*'

'Stop there please Howard.' Miss Perkins picked up her chalk and wrote *Salem* on the board as she spelt it out slowly for the class to follow S-a-l-e-m. 'Class please write it down on your slates.' She waited until the gentle clicking of chalk on slate quietened down all except Nancy who was still trying to control the wobbling lines of the snaking S.

'Please continue Howard.'

'Two hundred more soon followed, some of whom joined the Salem colony, while others founded Charlestown.'

'Stop please.' And she raised her hand to halt his reading as she wrote *Charlestown* on the blackboard, again spelling it out for the class. Nancy stared at the letters that seemed to go on and on but again the class had moved on before she had copied down anything legible.

Howard Clark continued reading going on to reference Dorchester, Roxbury, Cambridge, Watertown and finally Boston, all written down, all a calamity of unguided and incomplete shapes on Nancy's slate. Then, to her horror, she realised that Miss Perkins was going to review their work, and being nearest her desk, hers would be the first to be checked. She kept her eyes down and fixed on her slate willing the letters to take better shapes as Miss Perkins studied it. 'Your Cs and the D are very well-formed Nancy; I am very encouraged by your first attempt.' Nancy couldn't believe her ears. 'Next time, I would like you to just write the first letter of each word, let's practice at getting those right.' Then she moved on to the unsmiling girl in the green dress and on down the line to the end before weaving back up the next row offering encouragement and criticism in almost equal measure.

At the end of the day when she fell into line with the other children, she felt part of something new and exciting and didn't even avoid the lines on the sidewalk on her way home, stepping confidently with her head up. She had been left to find her way back to Pine Street and this morning had tried to memorise the buildings and stores on her way to school so she could retrace her steps. As Anderson's came into view she knew she'd done it and was nearly home. Mr. Anderson's two store windows were cleverly and thoughtfully presented to entice customers in off the street. In the window on the left, three carefully constructed pyramids presented a colourful array of cans, packets of coffee and spices, soaps and hair dressings but it was the window on the right that drew Nancy in. Pretty dishes and cups stacked and propped to show them to their best effect, rainbow bolts of colourful cloth, boots and shoes on wooden stands that tipped the toes daintily as if a delicate ankle suspended them, bonnets and shawls folded neatly on display shelves, dresses, blue with a scattering of white flowers, lace, bows, her dress! She stood, nose almost touching the glass and willing it not to be true, then went in to claim her property.

For two minutes or more, the assistant manager Herbert Thomas, stayed put behind the counter trying to ignore her, but there were no other customers inside the store and the child began to unsettle him as she continued to stare up at him silently.

'What is it girl? I have nothing to give you if you look for handouts.'

'A want me dress.'

'What dress?'

'Me blue dress.'

'There's nothing of yours here, everything in this store is the property of George Anderson.' He looked over his glasses at her, waving her away with his hand.

Nancy was not going to be put off and stepped closer to the counter. 'Tis mine, A want it back.'

'Go away I tell you.' The man came round from behind the counter picking up a broom on the way, pushing it at her feet as if trying to brush dirt but she was not for moving and dropped down on the floor, spreading herself out so that she was impossible to sweep away. 'You're in for trouble child, that's for sure. Mr. Anderson! Mr. Anderson!' Nancy didn't know why he was calling out, there was no one else there, then she saw a door behind the counter open and the top of a shiny bald head emerging from the back room.

'What's all the hollering about Mr. Thomas?'

'This child is causing trouble Mr. Anderson and will not leave the store.'

'What child?'

'This child.' Herbert Thomas pointed down to where Nancy was lying.

The elderly man leant forward over the counter and looked down into the face of the child lying prostrate on his floor. 'What is it child? Are you unwell?'

'A want me dress back.'

'What dress?'

'That dress, over thar.' And from where she was lying she pointed towards the window where her property hung from a hanger.

His baggy eyes followed the direction of her finger 'I bought that dress this morning and gave the lady a very fair price for it. It is my property young miss.'

Her mother had sold it. She was jealous of something so pretty and she had sold it. 'A never even wore it.' The words came out of her like a sigh.

'Oh I see.' Mr. Anderson came around the counter and crouched down beside her, floorboards and knees creaking in unison. 'Seems to me you've had a nasty surprise young lady but you cannot have it back unless you have two dollars to give me. Do you? Do you have two dollars?'

Nancy looked up into his crinkly face slowly rocking her head from side to side.

'I thought not. Very well then, I think we have concluded our business, it is time for you to leave now. Up you come, you'll get splinters down there on the floor!' He smiled and offered a bony hand which she took as he lifted her to her feet. 'Wait there.' Moved by the hopelessness of the child who had seemingly lost the little she had, he went to the counter and lifting the lid of a large glass jar, took out a stick of candy. 'Here. Take this.' She looked at the candy he held out to her and on a different day she would have grabbed its delicious sweetness with enthusiasm but now she just stared at it. 'It's for you, take it.' And he lifted one of her hands and placed the candy into it. 'Now off with you.' Eyes still fixed on the dress, she didn't move, so George Anderson gently ushered her towards the door and onto the street. 'Go home child.' And he went back inside.

Nancy didn't go home but stayed on the sidewalk looking in through the window at her dress clutching the candy until it became sticky and glued itself to her hand. 'She's still out there Mr. Anderson.' Herbert Thomas adjusted the spectacles that had slipped down his greasy nose to get a better look at her. 'Would you like me to chase her away?' He lifted the broom that was leaning against the counter where he'd left it. 'We don't want her putting our customers off.'

George Anderson grabbed the broom, wrenching it from his hand. 'Leave her be. The poor child is learning a hard lesson about her lot in life, we will not add to her misery by being unkind Mr. Thomas. Please get back to your work and leave me to worry about our customers. Call me if you need me.' And with one final sympathetic glance towards the child he went into the back office and closed the door. Herbert Thomas had learnt to hold his tongue and bide his time. Old man Anderson was past it and too soft-hearted by far, he had lost sight of making sound profits, it would be different when he took over as store manager.

When later Nancy protested to her mother about her dress being sold Kitty threw her hands in the air. 'Sellin' it fer two dollars eh? He only gev me one dollar. That man does gud business at me expense.' Unmoved by her daughter's distress, her only beef was that she could have got a better deal. 'Sure he's a right gombeen, everyone's fer tekin' advantage these days.' She kicked at the table leg in exasperation. Then she eyed the door before looking at Nancy and spitting out. 'A'll see you later an' be sure t'get yer chores done.' She went out, slamming the door behind her, hammering down the stairs. Satisfied that her mother was gone and unable to give her any more orders, Nancy picked up the bucket and headed down to the yard for the third time that day.

'Hey neighbour, how are you doing?' Grace was coming up the stairs as she was going down. A crying Maude was chewing her fist like it was a chunk of cheese so Grace bounced her harder and harder to try and calm her. 'She has more teeth coming don't you my love. How was school? Do you like it?

'A like it.'

'And your teacher? Is she nice?'

'She's Miss Perkins.'

'Well I am sure Miss Perkins is very nice indeed. Would you like to come up for some lemonade when you have finished your chores, that's if your mother is happy to spare you for a little while.'

'She's not here.'

'You're alone?'

'Ma said *see you later* but A don't know whar she's gone.'

Grace eyed the child with sadness. 'Fetch the water and then come to my room and stay a while until your mother returns. You can help me to settle Maude and tell me about what you have learnt in school. How does that sound?'

Nancy nodded and edging past Grace went on down the stairs to fetch the water picking up her pace as usual as she passed Mr. Dyer's part-opened door on her way out. She half-filled the bucket and then heaved it back up the stairs one step at a time until she reached the landing. Grace had left her door ajar and called out to her from inside. 'Come in Nancy.'

Nancy put down the bucket and then crossed the landing, pushing open Grace's door. 'See we have a visitor Maude.' The Thompsons' room was the mirror of her own except that it looked friendly and made you want to go inside. The bed was in the same position but smaller than her parents' and was covered with a colourful patchwork quilt that reminded her of mamo's. Alongside it was baby Maude's crib where Grace stood leaning over trying to stop her grizzling. 'Will you pass me that spoon on the table please Nancy.' Taking it from her, she placed it against Maude's lips who grabbed the handle and began sucking hard on the bowl. 'There that's better isn't it?'

'Sit yourself down and I'll get us some lemonade.' Nancy sat at the table by the window and looked around as Grace poured the cloudy liquid into glasses. The room was the same shape as hers and had all the same furniture really, except for a threadbare tapestry armchair that would have been pretty once, and a strange object at the foot of the bed that stood on a small wooden table. Behind it two bolts of cotton fabric, one white, one pale blue, leant against the wall.

'Ah, I see you have spotted my sewing machine.'

Nancy had never seen one. 'What's it fer?'

'For making petticoats, all manner of things. Would you like to see how it works? Stay there and I'll show you.' She pulled a chair across to the machine and opened a small drawer in the table taking out a scrap of white material and laying it on the black shiny surface of the machine. Then with her left hand she fed the edge of the material in under a silver needle that pointed down into a hole in a brass plate, with her right hand she took hold of a small handle and began to turn it as cogs circled and the needle chuntered up and down pecking noisily like a chicken eating corn. As she turned the handle and the needle rose and fell, white cotton thread pulled at the reel on top making it dance a lop-sided jig as it unravelled itself. 'See here.' Grace cut the threads and brought the scrap of material to Nancy to inspect. 'See how quickly it stitches a line. It must be ten times faster than sewing by hand.'

Nancy ran her finger along the even line of stitches and then smiled up at Grace.

'Very clever isn't it? I make petticoats for T. H. Middleton's, they sell corsets, camisoles, skirt hoops and the like. There's many a fine lady in Boston who wears a petticoat made by Grace under her dress.' She winked at Nancy. 'I rent it from Middleton's but one day I hope to own one myself, perhaps start up my own business. Would you like to have a go at stitching a line?'

'Can A?'

'Sure you can. Come and sit at the machine with me.' Grace sat down at the worktable lifting Nancy up onto her lap. She could feel Grace's breath in her hair as she rested her chin on the top of her head, and although it felt strange and a bit too close, Nancy thought she liked it. 'Now, put your right hand on the wheel and when I tell you, start turning it away from you. Then put your left hand on the cloth to guide it, although you must keep your fingers well away from the needle. Don't worry, I will help you. Ready?' Nancy was ready and as the wheel turned and the needle pecked she watched in wonder as she produced perfectly even stitches on the cloth just as Grace had done.

'See how well you do, I better watch out, you'll be after my job!'

'Ma sold me dress.' Nancy stared ahead at the sewing machine.

'Your blue dress?' Nancy couldn't see Grace's face but she was sure that if she could it would look just as sad as her voice sounded in her ear.

Nancy nodded.

'That's such a shame, still, I am sure you will have another one day.'

Then Maude began to fret again and Nancy knew she had lost Grace's attention as she slipped her off her lap and set her back down on the floor. 'Go and sit at the table Nancy dear.' Going over to pick up the baby, Grace brought her to the table to comfort her and Nancy watched a mother gently rock her child and smooth her bald head until peace was restored and Grace was able to come back to her.

'A like it here.'

Grace smiled. 'Well Maude and I are very happy to have you in our home, aren't we my love?'

Nancy didn't know what Maude had to do with anything.

'A wish A cud live here.'

Grace looked uncomfortable. 'Ah I think you'd be fed up with Maude's crying and my sewing machine going day and night, besides, what about your mother and father?' She didn't know what else to say.

'Thems don't want me.'

'I'm sure that's not true.'

'Thems loved me brother best.'

'You had a brother?'

'Issy is wi' the angels.'

'I'm so sorry Nancy.'

Nancy didn't feel the need to push on with proving the most truthful thing in the world. Her parents had no love to give, if there had ever been any crumb of it, it had gone with Issy. In her desperation Grace scrambled for something to cheer her and change the direction of their conversation. 'Hmmm, let me see, perhaps I could make you a dress. It would be from scraps but I can make it pretty I'm sure. How would that be?'

It worked. Nancy smiled. 'Thanky.'

'Consider it done.'

Just as they were finishing their lemonade they heard the sound of footsteps on the stairs and then one final shuffling step up onto the landing.

'Tis ma come back.' Nancy looked stricken.

'Quick, you'd better be going, she'll take a fright if you're not home.'

Grace jumped up and opened the door onto the landing coming face to face with Kitty. 'Mrs. Sullivan?'

'Who're you?' Then she saw Nancy at her skirt hovering in the doorway. 'An' whar you doin' wi' me daughter?' It was clear to Grace that she was an unwelcome presence at Kitty's homecoming; she seemed cagey, pulling her shawl tightly around her, folding her arms across herself like she needed to block something or hide it from sight.

'I'm Grace Thompson. Nancy just came in for some lemonade.'

'Humph! Well thanky fer bein' neighbourly but she's n'need o' yer lemonade an' shudn't be after troublin' you.'

'Oh she's no trouble at all Mrs. Sullivan, I invited her in.'

Kitty just stared back at her blankly then stepped forward taking hold of Nancy's sleeve, pulling her out onto the landing. 'C'mon girl, time you wur home. G'wan, get yerself inside.'

Grace took it all in, the look of her, alcohol on her breath and then as Kitty turned away from her she caught the scent of something else, a thick and heavy smell not borne of a woman. Closing the door, she went to the crying Maude's crib and looked down at her daughter, the sadness she felt for Nancy overwhelming her as she began to cry too.

Later, when Maude was finally asleep, she pulled up her chair and sat at her machine. Reaching down into her bodice she pulled at a velvet cord around her neck and fishing it out, caught hold of the key it held, then turning it in the drawer lock she opened it taking out a roll of lace and a measuring tape. Carefully unwinding it, she measured what was needed for four petticoats, cut the lace, re-wound the roll and stowed it safely back in the drawer locking it and dropping the key back down into her bodice. If the baby slept, she could make four petticoats hemmed with lace tonight, earn them a dollar sixty. Twenty petticoats a week and she could eat and keep up with the rent for the room. She knew Mr. Dyer showed her more favour than his other tenants and was more patient with her if ever the rent was late but it made her feel uneasy, like there was an unspoken, inevitable consequence if she were to fall behind too far. Twenty-five petticoats a week and she could afford ham and butter and sugar treats.

The light was already beginning to fail as she folded the first of the completed petticoats and laid it out on a sheet of brown paper on the bed, then as she was about to light the lamp, she heard heavy footsteps on the stairs and the sound of the Sullivans' door slamming shut. There was shouting and cursing, banging around, someone from the floor below called, 'Shut up!' banging on their ceiling in protest but it went on and on. She couldn't get it out of her head so hummed to herself and focussed on the clattering sound of the sewing machine in the hope of blocking out the ugliness.

At just before midnight, she finally tipped into her bed exhausted, Maude breathing lightly and steadily beside her. There was no noise coming from the Sullivans' room now but the dead silence somehow disturbed her more than the terrible racket they had been making. Getting out of bed, she opened her door and stepped onto the landing, tiptoeing across to the Sullivans' door. She put her ear to it. Nothing, but then what did she expect? Whispering, 'God bless you little Nancy' she went back to bed.

The next day Nancy made her way to school on the other side of the street to avoid Anderson's window, no point wishing for the dress now, it was gone and she didn't have two dollars. As her school came into sight, she felt shut out of things as she saw the other children arriving, already established in their groups moving in twos and threes filing in through the door. Reaching the gate, with her usual sense of otherness in tow, she spotted another solitary student in the distance. He was the colour of a peat turve, with hair like wild Irish moss and long dark limbs with the bend and sway of a sapling blown in the wind. His long strides seemed to hesitate as he approached the school gate and saw her looking at him, but he kept coming towards her, as she stood motionless and transfixed by him.

Then the vision spoke. 'Good morning. Reckon by the look you're giving me you've never met a boy my colour before.'

She looked into his face, he was clean, but he was black.

'Lost your tongue?'

She still said nothing and just kept staring at him.

'I'm Samuel Marshall, pleased to meet you properly Nancy Sullivan.' He had a wide smile and big white teeth and seemed friendly. 'How was your first day in school?'

'Miss Perkins is nice.' The words stumbled out of her mouth.

'Miss Perkins is fine and good and always slow with the switch; I think she suffers for it more than we do. She's fair to me and the others in the back row too.' The significance of his words was lost on her.

'Shall we go in? Miss Perkins is not quite so nice if you're late for her class.' He swept out his arm to show that she could go first, like she was a lady. As they walked in together, most of the class was already seated and Samuel peeled off to the left, sitting at a desk in the back row, joining two other boys as dark as him who were already sitting there. Keeping her head down she went to her own desk and ignored everyone staring at her. As she sat, eyes set straight ahead, she didn't know that she would remember the exact moment she met Samuel Marshall forever.

When the end of the day came, Samuel stayed at his desk until Nancy was almost level with it, and then stood up to join her so they could walk out of the schoolroom together. 'How did you get on in school today?'

'A like the readin' A want t'learn t'read.'

'You like books?'

'A've a book o' me own.'

'One book? A bible?'

'Not a bible, just a book.'

'Hmmm... my father has a whole shelf of books.'

'Canny read them?'

'Yes, I've read them all and more. I'm not a chosen reader in class of course, Miss Perkins would think the words spoiled by my delivering of them.' He said it as if it was of no consequence at all. Nancy didn't understand, he had a nice voice.

'I reckon you'll be a good reader Nancy Sullivan.'

His words made her feel so light and she thought of Nathaniel for the first time in weeks.

'Nice boots you're wearing.'

It was like he had read her mind.

'Me friend gev them t'me.'

'Nice friend to have! Where do you live?'

'Pine Street.'

'I know it. Can I walk with you? It's on my way home.'

She found herself nodding.

All the way back to her house he walked a little way apart from her on the edge of the sidewalk and didn't say a word. Nancy didn't speak either not knowing what to say to a black boy or any boy for that matter. When they reached the corner of her street she stopped and pointed towards her window 'A live thar. Under the roof.'

'Well, you're flying as high as a bird up there, that's for sure!' He smiled and then he was off, calling over his shoulder. 'See you tomorrow Nancy Sullivan.'

CHAPTER 18

The Spoilt Dress

The sun was coming up as a final button completed the row of five, and as she cut the thread, she hoped Nancy would be pleased with the dress. Using offcuts from the petticoats she had cleverly stitched the pieces together by hand, almost invisible to the eye where one section joined with the other, so it hardly looked patched at all. Mr. Anderson had been kind and, on asking, had given her the last piece of red and white gingham from a bolt in the store, too little to sell for anything other than patchworks. He remembered Nancy and shook his head sadly at the memory of the child's distress. It had a white collar and blue cuffs, the red gingham giving way to a band of pale blue around the waist that tied in a bow at the back, while the blue and white petticoat underneath was stitched in panels, striping it like a stick of candy from Anderson's store.

Two weeks had passed since Grace had

promised the dress to Nancy but she was so tired all the time and had struggled to keep up the supply of petticoats for Middleton's. Maude was waking most nights, sometimes because she was teething, other times because she wanted to play and because Grace was both mother and father to her, she gave twice as much of herself because of it. Nancy had two parents but Grace knew that the sum of the two of them came nowhere near equalling one good parent, in fact, things were doubly bad not just because they didn't care for Nancy but because they didn't seem to care for each other either.

She thought of her own dear parents, God rest their souls.

Holding up the dress, she shook it out and held it at arms-length to check her handiwork, she was happy with it and would give it to Nancy when she came home from school. Laying it across the back of a chair, the wakening Maude stretched in her cot and began to cry. 'Shush my love, mama's here.' And picking her up she showered her with kisses. 'Are you hungry little one? Would you like some porridge?' She put Maude down on the floor, crawling now, she moved fast and had a need to touch and taste everything whether in or out of reach, so while she heated the milk for the porridge Grace kept one watchful eye on her adventurous daughter.

When she finally heard Nancy's footsteps on

the stairs later that afternoon, she jumped up from her chair excited to give her the dress, going to the door to call her in. 'I know you will have chores to do for your mother but I wanted to give you a present first.'

'Me dress?'

'Yes your dress. Come in.'

Nancy watched excitedly as Grace went to the bed and carefully picked the dress up by its shoulders, she could already see how pretty it was, even before she brought it over and held it up for her to look at. But something was wrong, it was spoiled, a dirty looking grey shadow tracing its way down the front of the dress from its collar to its hem, ghosting its way like a winding river through the red and the blue. Nancy looked up at Grace blankly.

'Do you like it Nancy?'

'Tis dirty an' A haven't worn it yet.'

Grace was taken aback not by her disappointment but by her rudeness and obvious anger. 'There was a little accident I'm afraid, not Maude's fault, I should have put the dress away out of her reach. I've tried everything to get the ink stains out but it's the best I can do. You can hardly see it, and it will fade even more with time, but I'm sorry if you're disappointed.'

'Maude shudn't have touched it.'

'She's just a baby, she doesn't know any better.'

'She shudn't have. Tis nothin' t'do wi' her.'

'Well, why don't I hold it up to you.'

Nancy stood stiffly as Grace held the dress against her, not looking down at herself but staring all the while at the guilty Maude sitting in her cot, grinning to herself like an idiot.

'I think you look very pretty Nancy.'

'A've chores t'do fer me ma.'

'Oh alright, well, here you are then.' And Grace handed her the dress.

Nancy took it reluctantly, like she was being handed an overflowing, stinking po to empty, then went out and slammed the door behind her.

Grace stood staring at the door and felt uneasy.

When Kitty came home, she held up the dress to examine it. 'Wear it if you want, meks n'difference t'me. Thar be nothin' t'be med on it bein' tis stained s'bad.' There was frustration in her voice. 'Some gift t'give you, already dirty an' spoiled, A thought she liked you?' Kitty's spite was flowing freely; more salt being rubbed into Nancy's wounds of disappointment and betrayal with every word that came out of her mother's mouth. 'Thought she felt somethin' fer you eh? Ah, no one does nothin' fer nothin'. Fancies you t'do a few chores fer her A bet, look after that brat o' hers when she needs t'lie down fer a rest from all that bein' s'sweet an' perfect. A knows her sort well enough, sugar on the outside, vinegar on the inside.'

Her mother was right about Maude at least; the

brat was the cause of it all.

As she lay down in her cot that night, she resolved to wear her usual dress to school, put the blue and red one away out of sight, try and forget it. Then as she'd felt for her book under the covers, she realised it was gone too, her only treasure sold to Mr. Anderson she supposed for a few cents, someone else enjoying it now. In the darkness she pictured Maude spilling the ink on her dress and laughing at the fun of spoiling it, and all the while she pinched and scraped her skin, the pain of it her own with no one able to steal it from her.

CHAPTER 19

N is for Nancy

The passing of a little time did its job of blunting the sharp edges of Nancy's fury over the dress, so when on a warm Thursday afternoon two weeks later Grace invited her in for cookies and lemonade, she went. As she sat waiting at the table by the window she watched the stupid, fat Maude, stumbling around the room, grabbing a chair or table leg to pull herself up before dropping down heavily on the floor again with a look of stunned surprise on her face. Grace smiled over at her daughter as she poured the lemonade and put their cookies on a plate. 'You're going to be fast on your feet aren't you my love?' Maude grinned at her mother stupidly like she always did before trying to climb up on the chair beside Nancy.

'Be careful Maude. Nancy, don't let her fall.'

As soon as Grace turned away again, Nancy flicked Maude's fat little hands off the chair making her cry. She deserved it, she'd committed a crime, no good her trying to look all innocent about it.

'Oh dear, shall you sit on my lap my darling?' Grace set their glasses and the plate of cookies down on the table before scooping the crying Maude up in her arms and Nancy watched again in wonder as a mother's magic turned fretful tears into uncontrollable laughter in an instant. As Grace looked into her child's face, Nancy felt invisible.

'How was school today? Tell me what you learnt.' Grace and Maude both looked at her expectantly but she hadn't learnt much except writing some letters on their lines that didn't add up to words to her yet. She was cross that she didn't even have the crumb of a thing to boast about and so said nothing.

'Come on now. Let me see, can you write your name yet?'

Nancy shook her head. 'A can only write the N.'

'Well then, you're almost halfway there, that's very good indeed! Shall we practice it together?'

Nancy nodded.

Grace went to her worktable and fetched a pencil and a scrap of paper bringing them back to the table.

'So show me how you write the first letter of your name, the N.'

Nancy took the pencil but it seemed to have a life of its own and as it ran away from her forming an unruly grey shape on the paper she looked at Grace for reassurance. Grace tilted her head to one side. 'It has almost the right shape but I am sure we can make improvements.' She took the pencil from Nancy and drew two parallel horizontal lines across the paper. 'Now I want you to stay between the lines. The top of the N mustn't go any higher than this line, and the bottom of it no lower than this one.' She put the pencil in Nancy's hand and then folded hers around it. 'I will guide you to start with.' With Grace's hand on hers it was so simple and a perfect N emerged on the paper between the lines. 'Now you try without me.' Her second lone attempt was much better and recognisable as an N. 'Well done Nancy, I believe you shall have a fine hand.' She showed her how to write the other letters in her name, drawing them out first, and getting her to copy them.

Nancy was on the *right side of the door* when she was with Grace, like she had been when she spent time with Nathaniel reading and eating marmalade in the room of sunshine, not shut out and unseen. Here, Grace beside her, with the taste of the sweet lemonade and a gentle breeze coming in through the window, she was content as long as she didn't think about her spoiled dress or look into the face of the vandal that did it. The thought of it brewed a terrible storm in her that wanted to burst out and smash things.

Inevitably, after half an hour of not being the complete centre of Grace's world, Maude began to grizzle in protest. 'I think someone is getting tired and needs a sleep.' Grace tried to lay Maude in her cot but she would not be put down and screamed every time Grace let go of her. 'Is it your teeth my love?' But Maude just howled even louder, her face turning shiny and pink until she looked like a pig. 'Alright, alright.' And Grace gave in, picking her up and dropping down into the armchair so that she could rock her. Nancy stayed at the table and watched as the pair swayed backwards and forwards until eventually Maude fell asleep and so did Grace leaving Nancy feeling like an unwelcome guest in their dreams, unsure whether she should stay or go.

Getting down off her chair she went over to Grace's worktable, touching the fabrics, running her hand across the smooth, cool metal of the machine. Then she went to the bed dipping her head down to put her face against the softness of the quilt and so she could breathe in Grace's smell of roses and vanilla. While they slept she would stay invisible, so she climbed up on the bed and got under the heavy covers. It felt safe and as she began drifting into sleep, she imagined Grace lying in the bed beside her, singing to her like mamo used to. Then a terrible sound like the night scream of a vixen shook her back into the world but as she pulled the sheet down from her face, she could see Grace and Maude were still sleeping silently in the chair. It came again, louder this time, more urgent. She got out of the bed and went to the window, opening it wider to see if the sound was coming in from outside but there was just the usual dull hum of noises coming up from the yard below. As quietly as she could, so as not to rouse the sleeping Grace and Maude, she pulled one of the chairs under the open window and sat looking out as birds flew past. Still the terrible noise came at her mercilessly, it was coming from inside her head and wouldn't stop.

'Lord sev us, what's all the shoutin' an' screamin' 'bout?' Kitty muttered under her breath as she stood at the window looking down into the yard where a small group of people had gathered, forming a circle. From above they looked like the petals of a flower fanning out from a tiny pink and white shape at its centre. Then she heard the sound of Grace's door exploding open and the thud of her desperate footsteps as she ran down the stairs two at a time. Kitty stayed at the window looking out as Grace appeared in the yard below her, one by one the petals falling away, as she entered the flower's centre and dropped to her knees. The ghastly sound of the scream that left her in that moment poured along the cobbles and climbed the walls all the way to the rooftops. 'Oh Lord, tis her baby!' Poor wretch she isn't ever goin' t'get over that. Must o' fallen out o' the winda when she wurn't lookin'. She won't fergive herself fer it.' She turned and looked at Nancy who lay quietly in her cot under the table. 'Wek up girl. You wur in thar this afternoon wi' Grace Thompson, did everythin' seem alright wi' her?'

Nancy sat up and shrugged her shoulders. 'She gev me lemonade an' cookies.'

Kitty surveyed her daughter; there was something hiding in her words and a look on her face that she had seen before but couldn't name. 'Nothin' strange happened?'

Nancy shook her head.

Grace's screams went on and on like the shrill rasping of a rusty wheel as it goes round and Kitty looked out again, watching as Jacob Dyer crouched down beside Grace and laid his hand on her shoulder to comfort her as she held her child to her breast trying to shake her back into life.

'A didn't like Maude. Fat an' stupid Maude.'

With the slap of her cold words, Kitty turned to face her daughter. 'The baby's dead, don't matter you didn't like her. Havvy no feelin' fer her at all?'

Nancy didn't understand why Kitty was asking her. She didn't have any feelings herself. When her own child died she had simply gone to the stove to wet the tea and then carried on as if nothing had happened. If Nancy had no heart, it was because her mother hadn't given her one.

'Will A mek us some tay ma?'

Kitty stared at the unnatural child, even more monstrous today than she had been when she tore her way out through her body in the darkest hours of that December night. It was true she had no natural maternal feelings; but had there been anything of any merit at all to pass from mother to child, she knew it would be wasted on such a miscreation.

'Mek tay if you like.' Kitty pulled a chair up to the window and sat looking down on the tragedy, not deeply touched by it but strangely drawn in. She watched as a woman took a white pillowcase from a washing line and helped Grace to wrap the baby in it, carefully folding it around her so that only her little face, perfect and untouched, peeped out as peaceful as if she was just sleeping. Then they disappeared. 'Thems bringin' her in.' Kitty listened to the distant sound of slow, shuffling footsteps on the stairs coming up closer and closer until finally the death march reached the landing outside their door. They seemed to pause there, like they would knock and Kitty found herself holding her breath as she waited, but they moved on and she heard the sound of Grace's door shutting quietly.

Over the next two days, the police came, a sombre Reverend Wing came, an undertaker and photographer came, and women Nancy had never seen before brought containers of food that were sent away again uneaten. Then three days after the falling-day, just as Nancy had stepped out onto the landing, Grace's door opened and she stood just a few feet from her.

'Nancy.'

Nancy stared at Grace, at least she thought it was Grace, she looked a different colour and shape. More shadow than any real substance. Her hair was frizzy with strands of grey springing out, not pretty like she remembered it, her skin now a bloodless parchment laid on top of her bones.

'Nancy, will you come in?'

Nancy shook her head. 'A've chores t'do fer me ma.'

'Please, just for a moment or two, I promise not to delay you.'

She didn't want to but didn't think she could say no so said 'Okay.'

Grace stepped aside to let her into the room where, on the table, there was a small white box or a skib by another name. Nancy didn't want to go near the box so hovered near the door, but Grace trapped her as she closed it behind her and went round to the other side of the table, laying her hand gently inside the casket. 'I try to remember Nancy, try to recall what happened that day, but my mind will not release it. I remember we were having lemonade and cookies and Maude was crying but I can't remember anything else and I must!' She rubbed her forehead like she was trying to stir her memory. 'Why was the window so far open? I never open the window wide; I don't like the smells from outside.' She sat down on a chair keeping her hand inside the casket. 'Did I open the window Nancy?'

Nancy shrugged her shoulders 'A don't remember.'

'Think hard Nancy, it's important.'

'A don't remember.'

Grace looked around and began talking as if there was someone else in the room to hear her desperation. 'Maude was always trying to climb on things, I just don't understand why the chair was under the window, why would I put it there? I would never do that...' She looked confused, her words trailing off into nothing. 'We practiced your writing, Maude was crying, I was tired, so tired...'

Nancy nodded.

'Then there's nothing.' She stared down into the box. 'It's my fault, my girl deserved a better mother than me, one that could keep her safe.'

'You wur a gud mother.'

Grace looked up. 'Do you think so?' She was desperate to find some comfort and any small crumb of redemption to free her from the hell she was in.

'Aye. Better than me ma.'

The relief she craved was left wanting at

the comparison, there was no commendation of any kind in being mentioned in the same breath as Kitty Sullivan. She simply didn't care about anyone except herself and had nothing of any merit to give to anyone including her own child. With the savagery of the comparison Grace instantly fell back into the black hole of her guilt and grief.

'I don't remember you going home that day.' Grace's voice seemed far away.

Nancy hesitated before answering. 'You wur rockin' Maude, tryin' t'get her to sleep.'

'Was I? Surely I would have said goodbye to you? Why can't I remember? Was the window wide open when you left? Think Nancy, really think hard.'

'A don't know.' The hunt was really on now and Nancy began to panic. 'A have t'go.'

Grace caught the alarm in Nancy's voice.

'Let me go. You can't mek me stay here.'

Grace's face seemed to suddenly awaken with the look of someone who grasps something that has alluded them for a long time and in the searing clarity of the moment, she stood slowly, eyes fixed coldly on the child who had stolen her own. Caught! Nancy was on the pressure plate now, the rusty metal jaws would snap shut around her ankles, the hare must escape, run as fast as it could. She began to cry. 'You did open the winda. You did put the chair thar. Tisn't me fault an' you can't say tis!'

'You!' Grace rocked on her feet never taking her eyes off the murderer until her legs gave way beneath her, then, almost as the whisper of a prayer, she said. 'God forgive you for what you have done.'

Nancy turned and ran, slamming the door behind her. Back in her own room she hid in her cot under the table, making herself small, dark thoughts about Maude swirling in her head. Why did she deserve so much love and she got none? There was nothing fair in this world and everything was Maude's own stupid fault, it wasn't like she had pushed her, up to her if she wanted to climb on the chair and fall out through the open window.

She dreamt that night, a terrifying dream where the three shadows visited her again, this time Issy appearing alongside them - not as a shadow but clear and bright - all silent but loud in their accusation of her as the hideous slayer of purity and innocence.

CHAPTER 20

Losing Grace

'Who knocks at this hour on a Sunday? You'll be after stirrin' the devil wi' yer hammerin', Old South's not even rung out eight yet!' Kitty was only half awake, drugged from the sleep stolen by the rain battering heavily on the roof all night, Michael, as usual, simply not quite sober from the excesses of the evening before.

'Mr. & Mrs. Sullivan!' There was more loud knocking as Jacob Dyer's flat, depressing voice came from the other side of the door.

With the sharp jab of Kitty's bony elbow in his ribs, Michael cussed as he reluctantly tipped out of bed, staggering unsteadily towards the door. Opening it, Dyer's grey, lifeless face spun a little in front of his blurry eyes and then settled. 'What d'you want Mr. Dyer? The rent's not due; wur paid up t'date wi' you.'

'I am not here about the rent Mr. Sullivan.'

'What's the problem then t'have us tipped out o' our beds s'early?'

Dyer looked upset. 'I offer you an undeserved courtesy Mr. Sullivan if you would just give me time to speak.' Michael stepped back to let him cross the threshold and averting his eyes from Kitty, who made no effort to cover herself, Jacob Dyer continued with his mission. 'You will have new neighbours tomorrow; I have let her room.' And he glanced across the landing towards Grace's closed door.

Dropping his head Michael tried to feign some genuine measure of respect. 'God rest her soul, tis surely a terrible thing, eh Kitty, a terrible thing.' Kitty was now out of bed and standing by the stove warming herself but said nothing and joined Jacob Dyer in blankly staring out through their open door towards Grace's room.

'We haven't seen her since... well since the day o' the funeral, is she gone away then?'

Dyer nodded gravely, the shadows under his eyes melancholy crescents that sank into the crinkled skin below them.

'Must o' broke her heart poor soul. Hard fer a woman, 'specially abandoned, wi' n'man t'care fer her.'

Jacob Dyer's anger flared and Michael was sure he saw his lip trembling. 'Mrs. Thompson was not abandoned. There were those who cared for such a fine and noble woman as you would expect. Any decent man would understand that the loss of an only child in such a tragic way could cause any woman to break, lose her reason for living.'

'Oh beg yer pardon fer gettin' me facts s'wrong.' He looked over his shoulder towards Kitty and smirked, Dyer clearly had feelings for her.

'Wherever she has gone, I pray God will continue to comfort and protect her in her darkest hours.'

'Amen t'that Mr. Dyer.' Michael bowed his head; it seemed the right thing to do.

'Anyway, new tenants move in tomorrow and you're not to mention what happened in there, no need for their minds to be disturbed by such terrible events. Once imagined, the image of it might appear almost as real to them as to those of us who saw and suffered it so dreadfully.' He looked like he might cry. 'Do you understand me?' So his visit wasn't a courtesy, he was warning them off.

'No problem 'bout that, we won't say nothin', wur not ones fer gossipin' are we Kitty?'

'Thems never goin' t' hear it from us Mr. Dyer.' Then Kitty turned to Nancy who was sitting in her cot under the table listening to it all. 'An' yer not t'say nothin' 'bout it either girl, hear me?'

'No ma, A won't, A promise.' Nancy would never mention it and would try her hardest never to think of it either.

'Very well then, I will leave you.' And he went out through the open door, pausing briefly as his hand reached for the banister to brace himself, before going on down the stairs.

Shutting the door Michael stood with his back leaning against it, steadying himself, fighting the spinning room and the pounding in his head. 'A think our Mr. Dyer had teken a real fancy t'her, poor fella. He never had a chance wi' a woman like that, he needs to tek a look in the mirror! Still, life goes on eh? Let's hope wur gettin' quiet neighbours an' have heard the last o' screamin' brats through the night, not t'be disrespectful or nothin' o' course, but A don't want t'be sufferin' that n'more.'

As her father blathered on without audience, Nancy could hear Maude's crying and laughing in her head and put her hands over her ears, like she could block it out, but nothing would stop it bubbling up inside her so she dug her nails into her leg and the pain of it took away the noise in her head.

CHAPTER 21

Samuel's Secret Place

At first they just walked home together, but after a few weeks they had begun making the journey to school together too, Samuel always walking slightly apart from her and saying little when there were other people around. On days when the streets were quieter, he would help her with her spelling as they went along, short, simple words but precious to her. He would talk about the books on his father's shelf, stories of far-off lands, of legends and mysteries, of strange animals and with every step she fell further into his magical world of words and pictures until one day on their way home, he asked her if she would like to see ten thousand books.

Nancy looked down at her fingers, she knew that was ten. 'How many be ten thousand?'

'It's as many as would fill every wall of the schoolroom from floor to ceiling and then twice as much!'

Nancy was picturing it in her mind. It couldn't

be true; there couldn't be that many books in the whole of America.

'Whar be thems?'

'In a secret place but I can take you there. Would you like to see?'

She wanted to go with him more than anything, and he wasn't a stranger now, so she said *aye*. But then he started pulling back his words. 'We would have to go in the evening though, your parents would want to know where you were going, it won't work.'

'Me ma isn't home reglar an' me da comes back from his work after eight or goes drinkin'. Ma is always complainin' bout it.'

Samuel stopped and looked at her. 'I'm sorry Nancy.'

So again she knew it was true, his face told that her life should be better than this, but she shrugged it away anyway.

'Well then will you meet me on the corner of your street tonight at six o'clock?'

'What 'bout yer da? Will he let you out?'

'He has a church meeting tonight; he won't know I'm gone and we can be back home before either of our fathers walk through the door. I'll be waiting for you at six, I promise not to be late.'

She rushed through her chores and on the sixth chime of the bell at Old South she went out, careful not to look across the landing as she headed down the stairs, ran past Jacob Dyer's partly open door and stepped out onto the street where, true to his word, Samuel was waiting for her. They walked to the corner of Pine but instead of turning left to the school they turned right walking down unfamiliar streets in the falling light. The streetlights not yet lit, dusk was the cloak that hid them as they slipped silently past adults who would be interested in them for all sorts of different reasons, some good, some bad. After about ten minutes Samuel suddenly stopped next to a narrow passageway that seemed to her to lead to a dead end, although it was unlit, so it was really just that they were staring into blackness. The tall iron gate was padlocked and at the bottom a panel of wood had been wedged into its bars. Samuel looked around and then got down on his knees and started pulling at the piece of wood which looked fixed but came away easily. Behind it, two of the upright metal bars were missing, leaving a child-sized space to climb through. Leaning the piece of wood against the wall Samuel squeezed through the gap and she watched as the soles of his shoes disappeared into the darkness, she waited, then suddenly he pushed his face out between the bars making her jump. 'Come on Nancy, climb through.' She dropped down, clambered through and then sat leaning against the wall while Samuel reached back through the railings to where he had left the piece of wood and pulled it back against the gate so that it looked just as it did when they arrived.

His disembodied voice came out of the blackness. 'Hold my hand.'

She hesitated; hands clasped behind her back.

'Please Nancy, it's too dark and we'll be seen if we light a candle. I need to lead you or you might trip and hurt yourself and I can't be carrying you all the way home if you break a leg!'

Reluctantly she took hold of his hand then felt him gently pulling her into the blackness as she traced her other hand along the brick wall beside her for compass and to steady herself. Suddenly he let go of her. 'Here we are.'

She could just make out that they were standing under a large window that was high up in the wall. 'Stay there.' Straining her eyes as they began to adjust to the darkness, she watched Samuel go further down the passageway, as black disappeared into black. She was scared, what if he didn't come back for her? She didn't know where she was or how to get home. Then just as she was beginning to panic he appeared again out of the darkness carrying something. 'Got it!' And he put the large wooden box he was holding down on the ground and stepped up onto it. Taking a knife from his pocket, he flicked it open and reached up, pushing the blade in between the bottom of the window and its frame rocking it up and down until a gap opened up and he could slide his fingers underneath. Then pushing it upwards he opened it enough for them to climb through.

'You first.' And he pulled her up onto the box beside him. 'Put your hands up and hold onto the window frame then I will give you a push. There's a table on the other side, you'll be fine. Ready?' She didn't respond but he grabbed her around her legs and pushed her up anyway until she was balancing on the window frame half in and half out. Reaching down in front of her she put both hands on the table and then let her body and legs fall in behind her. Samuel looked in through the window. 'You alright?'

'A'm alright Samuel, A'm on the table.'

'Good, move over so I can climb in.' She crawled to the edge of the table and watched as he grabbed the windowsill and jumped, his top half landing on the tabletop, his long legs flailing around like he was dancing in mid-air as he wriggled in.

It seemed to her even darker inside than out. They both swung their legs down and sat side by side as Samuel reached into his pocket and took out two small candles and a box of matches. 'Hold this.' He struck the match and lit the candle she was holding lighting up his face like a beautiful glowing angel. Then he lit his own candle and slipped the matches back into his pocket. 'Hold this one too while I get down off the table.' Then he lifted her down like she was no more than a feather. 'Ready for an adventure?' She thought she was and as she lifted her candle and turned a full circle she could see they were in a large closet. A few chairs were stacked haphazardly against one wall, and on the one facing it, a broom with the widest hairy head she had ever seen was hanging from a hook. To the left of the door two mops stood in their buckets, on the shelf beside them, a feather duster and a stack of cleaning rags. She couldn't believe that all the bottles and tins of different shapes and sizes - polishing pastes for metal, waxes for floors, polishes for wood - had their own room almost as big as mamo's cottage.

Samuel walked across to the big oak door facing the window. 'This way.' He turned the shiny brass handle and opened it slowly like he wasn't sure what he would find on the other side. The unfamiliar but pleasant scent that was beeswax and books reached her before her eyes found their way, and looking up, it was like she was under the table in her cot as a low wooden ceiling hovered just above her head. In reality, they were stepping out from under an arch, one of eighteen that supported an elevated walkway and carved balustrade on three sides of the room, books below it and books above it. Was this ten thousand books? On the remaining wall three large arched windows gridded with small panes of glass - some plain, some red - loomed over them, weak moonlight casting a strange pink light through them. Six rectangular tables, perfectly straight, were placed evenly in the centre of the library, each with a glass-shade lamp at its centre and six chairs around it, also perfectly ordered. In the centre of the ceiling hung a brass and crystal chandelier, circling around it, smaller pendant lights with round glass shades that looked like huge raindrops falling from the sky.

'Well, what do you think?' Samuel spoke in a low voice hushed by his reverence for the special place.

'A've never seen a room s'big, tis like giants cud live here.'

'We'll be giants here Nancy, the words and things we learn will make us taller beings.'

'What if wur caught?'

'We won't get caught, no one ever comes until the morning, at night it's ours.'

'How d'you know?'

'Because I've been coming here for nearly two years, since I was not much older than you, no one uses libraries at night except me. It's been my secret place but I am happy to share it with you. Now, first things first, can you tell the time Nancy?'

She shook her head. 'A can count the church bells.'

'No need, I'll take care of the clock watching, we mustn't stay more than an hour.' He looked up to check the big square clock on the wall, twenty minutes past six. 'Come and look over here.' He put his hand on her shoulder and guided her along to the furthest corner of the room to the right of the big window under one of the arches, until they stood in front of a block of five shelves, their candles lighting up the rows of books in browns, greens and reds, illuminating the gold letters on the spines.

'See this shelf? I have read every book on it.'

She stared at him open mouthed.

'And half of the next shelf. That's thirty-two books so far!'

Thirty-two sounded as much as it looked on the shelf. 'Yer very clever Samuel.'

'One day I want to be a lawyer so it would be very helpful to be clever! Do you like poetry Nancy?'

'What's it 'bout?'

'Let me see; words put together in a special way, sometimes they rhyme like a song, sometimes they tell a story line by line. I think you will like it.' He ran his finger along the books on the shelf, like he was trailing a stick along railings, stopping halfway along he said, '*Aurora Leigh.*'

Nancy liked the sound of the name when he spoke it. 'Be it a girl?'

'It's this book.' And his finger tapped the spine of a brown cloth-covered book with gold writing. She made the sound of the *E* and the *B* in her head but couldn't form the words. 'It's by E. B. Browning, Elizabeth Barrett Browning, she writes magical poetry.' He pulled the book from the shelf. 'I'll read some of it to you if you like.' Then he handed her his candle to hold and pulled two more books from the shelf. 'We'll need these to wedge them.'

She kept step with him holding the candles as high as she could as he headed for the table nearest the middle-arched window. Putting down the copy of *Aurora Leigh* he placed the two other books on the table spine to spine, then taking a piece of cloth from his pocket, laid it across the books before taking the candles from her and carefully pushing their stumps down between them. 'Mustn't get wax on the covers.' He said quietly to himself.

Now he opened the book and as soft light danced on the first page, in the sacred silence of the library, he began to read to her.

"Of writing many books there is no end;
And I who have written much in prose and verse
For others' uses, will write now for mine.
Will write my story for my better self..."

She quickly fell under the spell of the word's soporific rhythm and their mesmerising sounds as her hard chair became a soft blue sofa, the candlelight like sunshine flooding the room. Eventually, eyelids dropping with the wonder of it all, she felt herself tipping forward towards the table, Samuel putting his arm out just in time to push her back before she toppled. He smiled and looked up at the clock. 'Enough for this evening, it's time we were going.'

Straightening the chairs, they carefully replaced the books and headed back into the closet closing the door behind them, leaving no trace of ever having been there, then climbed out through the window, closed it, replaced the box and checked the street before crawling out through the railings and replacing the wood panel. Back on the corner of Pine Street by just after half past seven, she was in time to put out some supper and wet the tea, before her swaying father walked through the door.

CHAPTER 22

Fallen Pilgrim

As she climbed in through the railings for the ninth time, tonight and each night visiting the library felt like entering a dream where sounds and shapes and colours formed softly, differently to the harshness of her daylight hours out in the world. The gateway to happiness was here – the wooden panel, the box, the table waiting on the other side of the window - and as their candles lit the way to the shelves and illuminated the treasures that awaited them there, they were like pilgrims to a sacred place. Over the weeks they had fallen into a pleasing, almost mechanical, rhythm. They would take their seats, prop the candles and Samuel would read to her from *Aurora Leigh* or pour out beauty from some other book he chose for her. Sometimes he would open up pages with pictures of strange animals too fantastical and curiously formed to believe true, or pictures of men and women the look of him but dressed differently or hardly dressed at all, it all bringing on wild imaginings that she couldn't get out of her head long after she left the library.

'Where were you born Nancy?'

'Kinlough.'

'In Ireland?'

'You know A wur born in Ireland.'

'Just checking, you've never mentioned Kinlough before.'

'Whar wurry born?'

'Boston.'

Nancy looked into his face searching for something that she could recognise to reconcile this piece of information.

'You're thinking I don't look like most people in Boston, my skin being so dark, well I am the same as my mother and father and was born to their colour, not the colour of this country even though I was born right here in Boston. Do you understand?'

She didn't.

'My mother and father were both born in Virginia although they moved up from the south before I was born. Life was hard there even for free people.' For a moment he seemed to slump down in his chair at the thought of it but then quickly straightened himself up, lifting his head as he continued. 'They knew there were more opportunities for work, schools for coloured children, here in Boston, somewhere my two sisters could get an education. I never knew their parents, my grandparents, but they were brought to America all the way from the Gold Coast in Africa.'

Nancy's eyes widened at the thought of a coast made of shimmering gold.

'Wait here.' He left her at the table and she watched him as he climbed the stairs up to the higher bookshelves, walked along until he stood over the third arch, and pulled a huge book from a shelf. She could see that it was heavy as he carefully made his way down the stairs again, watching his feet on the steps, with no hand free to hold the rail. Putting the book down on the table he lifted the heavy cover and then turned over page after page of pictures before reaching the middle of the book. Smoothing his hands across the paper, he flattened out the pages, opening them as wide as they would go. 'This is a map of the world Nancy.'

Nancy stared down at the flat world spread out before her as colours, lines, words and shapes arranged themselves on the pages.

'We are here.' And Samuel pointed to a tiny spot on the map.

'The library?'

Samuel laughed 'No, Massachusetts, and you travelled from here.' And he slid his finger over to the right to a tiny splodge on the page. 'That's Ireland.' It couldn't be, it was so small and she knew it to be big with no end to how far your eyes could see. 'You sailed from here to here.' He ran his finger left across the blue, but it was such a short distance on the page, and it had taken so long to travel. 'And my grandparents sailed from here to here.' He moved his finger down the page and traced a curving line up from the Gold Coast to Virginia. Sensing her confusion he said. 'It doesn't look far but it is thousands of miles Nancy. We live in a big world and I would like to travel it.'

'Leave Boston?'

'Yes, one day.'

Nancy didn't want him to go away and he could see that she was becoming upset.

'Not for a long time, don't worry, not for a very long time. I have to complete my education. My father would like me to go into the church but I want to be a lawyer.'

'Why do he want you t'go into a church?'

'Not go into a church, become a clergyman, you know, be a pastor.'

'Like Reverend Wing.'

'Who's Reverend Wing?'

'He helped me ma an' da find Pine Street. Fixed me da wi' a job.'

'He sounds like a good man. Yes, my father would like me to be a man like that, but I think I can be a man of his measure and still be a lawyer, perhaps a more useful man because of it. My father says there are too many poor souls who deserve a chance of justice in a world that is set against them, so I hope I can serve both them and God at the same time.' He looked up at the clock. 'We'd better be going. I'll put back the Atlas, you return *Aurora Leigh*. Be sure to put it back in the same place, into the gap, so that everything stays in order.'

She nodded, she understood how important it was that no one should know that they had ever been there, that they leave no trace of their visit behind them, so as Samuel went up the stairs, she slipped her book carefully back into its slot on the shelf, lining it up perfectly with the books left and right of it, like it had never been disturbed. Waiting for him to come back down, her eyes travelled the shelves and that's when she saw it, those distinctive gold letters stamped on the black band of the book's spine. She could hear the sound of her heart in her head, and in one precious moment it came back to her, just as she heard Samuel's footsteps on the stairs. 'Come on Nancy, time we were going.'

She wrapped her shawl tightly around herself and followed him out into the closet closing the door quietly behind her. Then climbing out first as usual, Samuel reached in through the window to help her down. 'Take my hand.'

'A can do it meself.'

'Okay, but be careful.'

With one hand and two flailing legs, she

scrambled down onto the box, before they made their way along the passageway and back out through the gate onto the street. On the walk home Nancy stayed quiet and kept her eyes down on her boots.

Samuel looked across at his friend. 'Are you feeling alright?'

She didn't look up, folding her arms tighter around herself.

'Have I done something to upset you?'

'No. A'm cold is all.'

But as he put his arm around her shoulders to warm her, she stopped dead in her tracks, going rigid and twisting away from him. Stricken by her reaction, Samuel immediately let go of her. 'I'm sorry Nancy, I didn't mean… I just thought I could protect you from the chill air.'

She smiled sweetly though, confusing him, and they walked on in silence until they reached the corner of Pine Street.

'Will you want to come to the library again on Wednesday?' There was hesitation in his voice. 'You don't have to; I can go alone.'

'A want t'go t'the library.'

'If you're sure.'

'A'm sure. See you the morra Samuel.' She seemed happy but in a hurry, turning from him and running towards her house, not looking back or waving goodbye like usual.

CHAPTER 23

Crime and Punishment

'Shall it be *Aurora Leigh* or *Jane Eyre* or even *Wuthering Heights*?' He held a candle up to his face casting ghostly shadows across it, twisting and contorting it to frighten her. 'Or are you too scared to hear about the wild Cathy and tormented Heathcliff alone with me here in the dark?'

'A'm not afeared but A don't want *Wutherin' Heights*.'

'Or we could look at a picture book perhaps? Your choice.'

'*Aurora Leigh*. A like how you mek it sound.'

'Again? We're nearly at the end of it and then you'll have no choice but to choose another book from the shelf unless you'll have me start all over!' He smiled at her and went to fetch the book.

As they sat close, she rested her chin in her hands as he read to her, listening to the sweet winding of the words all the way to the very last one until Samuel announced dramatically 'The

End!' but as he snapped the book closed a strange noise seemed to echo it. They looked at each other, what was it? Then in the stone silence, as they held their breath, they heard the creaking of a chair or a floorboard coming from a corner of the library near the closet door.

'Stay where you are.' A man's voice came out of the darkness as a shadow stood and stepped out from behind a large oak desk. Even in the darkness, they could see that he meant business, they were in trouble. As the man approached, Nancy caught hold of Samuel's hand under the table for reassurance.

'I am Edwin Jackson, manager of this library. You two are trespassing.'

'We're sorry sir, we know we shouldn't be here, please let us go.' The fear Samuel felt made his voice crackle and his words break like twigs.

'I do not intend to let a couple of thieves out of my sight. Your parents shall know of your crime and the law will have to take its course as it should.'

'We'd never steal from the library sir, we just like to come here to read, we meant no harm.' Samuel was as offended as he was frightened by the accusation.

'A book has gone missing and its absence cannot be accounted for in any other way except that it has been stolen. I have waited these last two nights in the library to catch the culprits and here you are.'

'It wasn't us. I swear, it wasn't us.' Samuel looked at the man and then at Nancy whose head was down.'

'You say you never took *David Copperfield* from the shelf?'

'No. We would never steal any book.' Then Samuel's confidence began to leave him, *David Copperfield*, the only book Nancy had ever owned before her mother had taken it from her. He looked at her but she didn't look back at him, instead staring up into the man's face she said. 'A didn't want t'come but Samuel said it wud be alright.'

Samuel stiffened.

'Do you say you have nothing to do with this girl?'

'It wurn't me.' Nancy began to cry.

'If it wasn't the girl then I conclude it was you boy. Did you take it? Come on now, tell the truth otherwise you're both in trouble.'

'I would never steal sir... never, but I might have borrowed it.'

'Borrowed it? If you have taken it from the library without permission any man would consider it stolen. What's your name boy, Samuel what?'

'Samuel Marshall.'

'Very well Samuel Marshall you will come with me. Child, you can get yourself out of here the way you came but know this, the gate will be sealed and the window locked from now on, so that will put an end to your visits here. Consider yourself lucky not to be taken to the police tonight. Now get yourself home. Go!'

Nancy didn't protest and getting down off her chair, pushed it back under the table to make sure it was straight and tidy like they did every night, then left Samuel to his fate without a look or a word. He was willing her to be brave, *We'll live Aurora Leigh, we'll be strong, the dogs are on us but we will not die!* but Samuel watched on sadly as she seemed so easily to abandon him. It was useless to continue to protest his innocence everyone would believe her word over his any day of the week.

'Where do you live boy?'

'Rose Street.'

'I know of it although I have never visited. Who lives there?'

'Just my father and me.'

'Your mother?'

'My mother died.'

'Then at least she will have been spared the shame of your crime. I shall speak with your father then. Put the book back on the shelf and we will go and see him now.'

'He won't be at home sir; he's out at a church meeting this evening.'

'Then we shall go and see him there.' Samuel

thought he might be sick.

The man watched while Samuel returned the book to the shelf. Then they went into the closet to lock the window before going back out through the library, down the main corridor and out the front door.

What followed was the worst of everything Samuel could have imagined. The church meeting was coming to a close, but it was well attended, so many would witness his downfall. It was the Pastor himself who greeted them at the door when Edwin Jackson knocked, opening it up to a sea of surprised faces, including his father's.

'Good evening Pastor, I am sorry to interrupt your meeting, I am Edwin Jackson.'

'How can I help you Mr. Jackson?'

'There has been some trouble at the central library, a theft, I need to speak to this boy's father.' Samuel's father was already on his feet and making his way to join the Pastor at the door, eyes fixed on his son's face, oblivious to the frenzied whispering that had begun to circulate around the room behind him.

Samuel would take a beating, he would take any fair punishment, but he could not bear the disappointment and worry in his father's eyes.

'Is it true Samuel? Does this have anything to do with you? Remember the truth will always set you free.'

'It's true that I was in the library father.'

'What were you doing there?'

'I go there sometimes in the evenings to read and learn new things.'

'At night?' Samuel's father looked at Edwin Jackson. 'The boy surely does love books sir it is true, but he has not been raised to trespass, I have raised him to respect the law.'

'Well, there is a book missing.'

'Taken by my boy?'

'On being pressed he admitted to borrowing it but he had no right to take it and I do not believe he ever intended to return it.'

'My son knows the difference between right and wrong. I do not believe he would take it without permission. Samuel?'

Samuel didn't reply. To say he took it would be a lie, if he was asked if he knew who did take it he would have to lie to protect Nancy, so he said nothing.

'Well, I think his silence speaks the truth of the matter Mr. Marshall.'

Samuel's head hung down with the weight of his father's disappointed eyes upon him.

'We'll replace the book Mr. Jackson and you have my word that my son will never be allowed to visit the library again.'

'That is not enough I'm afraid, the police will need to be notified.'

The Pastor slowly inter-laced his fingers as if he was about to pray. 'Mr. Jackson, the church will undertake to ensure the correction of Samuel's ways. Surely a criminal record is not necessary for one so young. On this occasion his passion for reading may have overtaken his good sense but he has never been in trouble before and I believe him to be a boy of good character.'

'A crime cannot go unpunished.'

'Samuel will have his punishment Mr. Jackson. He carries the stain of his actions and will have to atone for them, seek the Lord's forgiveness.'

Edwin Jackson searched the Pastor's face. 'Very well Pastor, I will leave it to you to decide how he should be punished. I suppose as he will no longer be able to visit the library, he will count that as loss, given his love of reading. I will take it no further providing the book is returned to the library tomorrow. If it is not, I shall go to the police.'

'Yes of course. Thank you, that is most charitable, God bless you.'

'I will wish you a good evening then Pastor. Mr. Marshall.'

A copy of the book, not the actual book, was taken to the library the next day. Samuel wasn't in school and wouldn't be again, punishment was to be moved away from all that he knew, leave behind his transgressions and turn a fresh page in another place with his disappointed father.

PART III: BOSTON 1862

CHAPTER 24

Book to Ashes

'Nancy please come up to the front and read for us.' It was a normal occurrence; she was the class's best reader and far and away Alice Perkins' favourite student. If she ever wanted to prove her efficacy in running the school or demonstrate her skill as a teacher to The School Committee, Nancy was the living proof of what could be hewn from even the roughest of raw materials and at presentations to visiting Aldermen of the city, she was always put forward as a shining example of what Alice Perkins could do.

For more than three years she had enthusiastically applied herself to her studies and was never happier than when she was learning something new; except perhaps for when she was being praised for it. She had the measure of how clever she was, as by unrelenting degrees, her father and occasional mother showed themselves as more stupid and ignorant to her by the day, in school too, the balance of power having completely shifted in her favour. The pretty blonde girl in the green dress, Dollie, Dumb Dollie as far as she was concerned, turned out to be officially stupid. It seemed to Nancy that the girl's tiny brain was incapable of retaining even the simplest of facts and she would cry like a baby if she was chastised for not practicing her writing or when her numbers were left wanting. It became a game in Nancy's head to count how many seconds it was before the first dumb word would come out of Dollie's mouth. What a sap!

It all came so easily to Nancy and in every subject she triumphed over her fellow students except perhaps in Geography which she just couldn't seem to navigate or retain. One by one her classmates had fallen into line and submitted to her superior intellect, she was untouchable, even the spineless Linus Mason had learnt long ago to regret sticking his tongue out or playing pranks on her. She had only had to grab that marmalade-coloured hair once and smash his freckles against a wall for him to understand that she was greater than him in every way, in that respect at least, he had proved himself a quick learner.

Now, standing confidently in front of the class Miss Perkins handed her the book, *David Copperfield* her treasure, and running her fingers across its cover the sound of Nathaniel's sweet voice came to her like it always did. Here was the only book that had ever been hers, stolen from her but then stolen back, the second crime no more or less justified than the first as they cancelled each other out. She knew every word, every phrase and drawing, every character real and known to her like she could meet them on the street any day of the week. 'Read us the first three pages please Nancy.'

Opening the book she smiled at the familiar picture of Little Em'ly looking out at the sea with her long hair blowing in the wind, then turning over the page, she began to read the treasured words. *'I AM BORN. Whether I shall turn out to be the hero of my own life, or whether that station will be held by anybody else, these pages must show...'*

But the next word was snatched from her lips by the loud bang that thundered around the walls and rattled the windows as the schoolroom door was flung open, a drunk Michael Sullivan standing in the doorway. 'Nancy Sullivan, get yerself home now or you'll be gettin' the strap!'

Miss Perkins laid her hand on Nancy's shoulder. 'Stay where you are Nancy.'

'Mr. Sullivan, how dare you burst in on my class drunk and threatening violence, please leave immediately.'

'A'll not be goin' anywhar wi'out me girl, her mother's gone an' A needs her home.' He was swaying and shuffling his feet to keep from toppling.

'You must leave now Mr. Sullivan or I shall bring the police to deal with you.'

'Me wife always said you wur high an' mighty…' He pointed a shaky, accusing finger at her and began stumbling his way up the avenue of desks, lurching from side to side, sweeping his eyes across the bewildered children, frightening them with the menacing grin on his face.

'Stay where you are. Do not come any closer Mr. Sullivan.'

He stopped, spreading his legs wide to steady himself, like he was standing on the swaying deck of a ship. 'Yer not the master o' me woman. No woman be the master o' me! A'll g'when A've the girl an' not afore.'

Alice Perkins could smell the alcohol on his breath from ten feet away and feared for both her students' safety and her own, drunk, men like him just became more of everything that was already undesirable about them when they were sober, she couldn't risk it. 'I'm sorry Nancy dear, you must go with your father, he demands it.'

'At last! She sees sense.' Michael tipped his hat mockingly giving her a deep and completely fake bow.

Nancy looked out at the sea of faces in front of her, she had fallen, in seconds all the prized elevation she had achieved, lost. Real life had collided with her dreamed for life and once again it was real life that would be the victor. Resigned to it, she put the book on the desk, then walked past her father and the rows of smug, satisfied faces, down the aisle and out of the schoolroom. Making it home before her father, she screamed at the walls, kicked at the floor and scratched her arms until they bled but nothing released her from the pain of her humiliation. By the time she heard his footsteps on the stairs, the heat of her anger had begun to turn to cold fury, she was ready for him.

'Yer mother's gone.'

'Why did you take me out of school?'

'Diddy hear what A telled you? Yer mother's left us fer gud. The bitch isn't comin' back.'

'Where's she gone?'

'Here an' thar wi' any fella not kickin' her out o' bed. Thar be plenty o' men who aren't too fussy 'bout thar skirt an' thems welcome t'her.'

'She's never been a mother to me and she's hardly ever here anyway. Good riddance to her! What does it have to do with me going to school? All the class will be laughing at me tomorrow.'

'The morra? Yer not goin' back the morra. Yer never goin' back.'

His words set off an explosion inside her and she sprang across the room, lunging at him and almost knocking him off his feet, thumping him and screaming in his face. 'You can't do it! You can't!'

He pushed her away and losing her footing she

fell down heavily hitting her head on the floor.

'Tisn't up t'you. A'm yer father an' I'll decide. Yer mother's not comin' back an' yer goin' t'have t'run the house an' do some work fer a change. Me lungs are near finished wi' the iron works an' wi' this damn war, thar's never goin' t'be a way t'keep up wi' the hunger of the furnaces, s'yer goin' t'tek care o' me from now on.'

Nancy stared up at him. Take care of him? He'd never once taken care of her or protected her from harm, never put himself aside in favour of what she needed. It was all the wrong way around. It wasn't supposed to be like this.

'I won't.'

'You will.'

'I won't.'

'Whisht girl, you'll do as A tell. Enough o' all this pointless learnin', what gud are books t'girls like you anyway? A see you hidin' away readin' when you shud be doin' chores, A knows whar you keeps yer book.'

His words flew past her like an arrow to the corner of the room where the rug covered a loose floorboard, her secret place. Crawling on her hands and knees, she scrambled for what she knew was already gone, tearing back the rug and lifting the floorboard. 'Where is it? Where have you put it?' Her voice breaking in her desperation.

'T'be sure A never thought A'd say it, but A think you can profit from a book... when yer lightin' a stove wi' it!'

If he'd had a shovel in his hands he couldn't have beaten her any harder before callously tossing her away just like Faerie, leaving nothing in her; no words, no fight. The hare had always tried to outrun him but today she gave herself up, lay down on the floor and stared up at the ceiling.

'Don't be tekin' on s'bad, twas only a stupid book. Time you wur workin' an' bringin' some money into this house instead o' lazin' 'bout. Me friend's a sweater, a man o' business, an' he knows whar thar be work fer a strong girl like you, tek the pressure off me fer once. He'll fix us up proper A'm sure, then yer poor auld da can stop workin' s'hard t'keep us out o' the workhouse.' With all the exertion of his long-winded ramblings he stumbled backwards, fell down onto the bed and with one loud snort, passed out cold as the power shifted in her favour - she was going to kill him - take the poker and bash his head in like he deserved. But then she'd be locked away and there would be no books, ever.

With the cold reality of her situation fully dawning on her, she pulled herself up from the floor, went to the stove and stared down at the ghosted words on the layers of scorched pages that were once hers. All lost to her now, except one, the illustration of Little Em'ly sitting by the sea looking out at her steadily, unblackened by the flames. She reached in and retrieved her, then picking up the poker, stoked the flames and the ashes of her book ready to boil the water for the tea.

CHAPTER 25

The inimitable Josiah Doggett

'A'm expectin' a visitor s'don't be after givin' any o' yer lip. A want yer best behaviour, mek a gud impression.'

Despite the bells of Old South ringing out their call to worship and peace to all men; she still wanted to bash his brains in for what he had done to her but said nothing and went about clearing away the remnants of their breakfast from the table. At the sound of unfamiliar footsteps on the stairs, Michael sprang from his chair, almost tripping over himself in his rush to open the door.

'Girl, this is me friend Josiah Doggett.' Michael slapped the man on the back in a friendlier way than the man seemed to like. 'Josiah, this is me daughter, Nancy.' The man stood in their doorway looking her up and down, measuring her out with his eyes, breathing heavily from the exertion of climbing the stairs. He was even shorter than her father and had a thick neck and jowly face that seemed to have no bones in it to stop his cheeks sliding into his chin. 'She's a gud girl, an' strong wi' it, didn't A tell you.'

'You did Michael, she's everything you said, pretty thing too.' He stepped inside never taking his eyes off her.

'Eh? S'pose she is, teks after her da.' Michael laughed but the man didn't join him, he just kept staring and she didn't like it.

Michael pulled out a chair for him. 'Sit me friend, sit.' Then he sat too while Nancy stood by the stove ready to reach for the poker if she needed it.

Josiah's coat gaped open as he leant back in the chair, spreading his legs wide like he was claiming the space around him, the folding of his body in the chair forcing forward his flabby paunch until it was wedged against the table. Contrary to everything that was dark about him, under the oil and grime, he was colourful - purple neckerchief, red and yellow tartan waistcoat, a once-blue shirt - a dead-man's clothes much too fine to have been his at first owning. And his voice seemed borrowed too, deep and mellow and measured with no rush in it, like it belonged to a man of more significance and breeding.

'Can we fix you some coffee?'

'No, I don't have much time, I'd rather we got down to our business.'

'O' course Josiah, yer a busy man A know.'

Nancy watched her smarmy father buttering

him up, he looked like he would happily get down and lick his boots if he asked him to, she didn't understand what this man had that her father needed so badly.

'Well now, I can set you up easy, there's plenty of work to be had if you know the right people. Mind, I could do better for you if you had more space and a place better equipped.' His eyes drifted around the cramped room. 'And it's not the kind of place for handling anything for fine folk; that's where your money is to be had. No, you would need somewhere different, I can help you out with that if you like.'

'Move?'

'Up to you.'

'But move? It suits me here an' the rent's cheap, yer auld fella Dyer downstairs don't have a brain fer business like us, cud be askin' double fer this room the auld fool.'

'I'm not pressing you, but you limit the options for the girl's work, and your profits, while you live here. Besides, word is the draft is coming and there are places in the city more friendly to avoiding conscription shall we say. There'll be officers washing through the streets of Boston soon looking for men to join the Union ranks unless you've got three hundred dollars to pay another poor beggar to go in your place. It's a poor man's fight, that's for sure.'

'A can't join the fight. Tis a young man's game

an' A'm not fit fer it, 'sides, A'm not after layin' down me life fer the Union cause, does me no fevours. Auld man Lincoln can go an' boil his head as far as A'm concerned!'

'You'd do well to keep those thoughts to yourself. I'm sure you'd do your bit if you were a well enough man Michael.' He didn't mean it and Michael didn't reply. 'Anyway, just give me the nod if you want me to put in a word for you, find you a cheap place where you can be safe from it.' He tried to sound casual but he knew he already had Michael on the hook.

'Cheap you say? Well, mebby A cud think 'bout it, cud mek sense eh girl?'

'You know, I had a feeling in my gut that you were a wise man Michael, and now you've just gone and proved it to me.' He slapped his hand on the table and smiled as he slowly nodded his head. 'I pride myself on the calibre of my business associates and it will be a pleasure to do business with you.' Nancy looked at her stupid, grinning father. He was so easily flattered, and with even the slightest of compliments, the little sense he had flew out the window. She really thought he was good at nothing except being drunk and he was a useless, ugly drunk at that.

So it was decided, they would move, somewhere near Fort Hill where Josiah's circle of associates would benefit them greatly apparently and her father could avoid the draft. Notice was given on Pine Street, Jacob Dyer seemingly completely unperturbed, perhaps even pleased, by their sudden departure. 'Plenty of folk looking for fair rent and a respectable house in this city.' And that was it, he took the money he was owed and shut the door on them.

At their new address, one room became three although she thought the sum of the space was not much more than they had at Pine Street. Three dark semi-basement rooms with no doors separating them, more accurately described as one square room and two closets, made their old room up in the roof seem bright and airy to Nancy now. Cooking, eating, gambling and drinking would all be accommodated in the square room. Their sleeping in the closet rooms. 'Well this'll do us grand eh girl?' Her father paced out the dim room, the only light given to it by a small high window in each of the doorless closet rooms. A large table and four ladder back chairs were the sum of the furniture, it was the over-sized squat-square stove, metal washtubs, mangle and the deep wooden shelves stretching from floor to ceiling that revealed the real purpose of this place, it was to be the workhouse for her not a home of any measure.

Cold, damp air clung to her skin and clothes, everything around her permeated with its musty smell and the fruity stench of the drain that ran along the street outside and leaked down the steps to their door. One of the closets had a small wooden bed in it with just space beside it to stand up if you didn't spread out too much. Michael claimed it. 'This'll do me grand.' The other, presumably used for storage, was bare with just two long wooden shelves, one at her waist height the other high up just below the ceiling. At the far end there was a tap, she'd never seen one inside a house before. 'Spece fer you under thar girl, leave it t'yer da t'fix up a bed.' So she was destined to sleep under a wooden sky again. 'Gud spece fer workin' too, Josiah's done a gud job fer us.' He didn't mean it but said it for effect. It was much worse for living than Pine Street but better equipped for Josiah's purposes for her. 'You get the stove goin' an' settle us in. A'm away t'see Josiah, fix things up wi' him.' Get drunk he meant.

Unpacking was a meagre affair quickly completed, only half a shelf taken up with their belongings, and little chance that the other half would be claimed. Lighting the stove she pulled a chair up to it as gradually the warmth began to reach her fingertips and toes. It was noisy here. Banging doors, shouting, sounds coming in from the street that you didn't have to endure when you were up on the third floor where the birds fly. She leant back in the chair and closed her eyes, fingers reaching up inside her sleeve, nails trailing the surface of her skin feeling for the roughness of scabs on her arms that needed refreshing. Then somewhere between consciousness and sleep she heard his sweet voice *Brigid, fair Brigid, always be open to happiness...*

'Hey! See what happens Josiah when A leave this house fer a moment, the girl's shirkin' at the first chance. Don't you worry, A'll be mekin' sure she's no slacker. Wek up girl!' Her father was standing behind her chair, leaning over, shaking her out of her half-sleep. Looking up at the two men from her position of disadvantage she instinctively scrambled to her feet to level the match.

'Tis all sorted eh Josiah? You start the morra wi' the laundry work. You'll tell her how it all works won't you.' Michael was swaying on his feet and fell down into the chair she had been sitting in waving his hand at Josiah as a signal to explain the arrangements to her.

'Well, it is true I have used my influence to secure regular, reliable work for you.' He paused like he was waiting for some appreciation but nothing came so he continued. 'On Mondays, Wednesdays and Fridays a hamper of linen will be delivered here for laundering, all whites. You're to have the clean laundry parcelled and ready for collection on the next delivery day. Out in the backyard there's a washing line that's only for your use, I will show you that later, and there's an awning too for when the weather's bad, rain will be no excuse for the linen not being dried and pressed ready for collection. Understand? If any other devil tries using the lines, you're to let me know, I'll deal with them.' It all tripped off his tongue so easily, and as Nancy looked around the room at all the equipment already in place, she wondered who had done the job before her and what had happened to them.

'My client is very particular, so don't let me down, my reputation is at stake and I won't have you ruining it.' Then he systematically went through the inventory of equipment; two large washtubs, a washboard, the wringer, a laundry bat and dolly, soap, bluing and starch in the drawer, three flatirons so that there would be no need to stop once she started pressing, and brown paper and string to parcel the linen which was all to be labelled according to its sets. 'That's everything for the laundry work I think.' It sounded like there was more to come. 'Now the work for Miss McCabe.' So there was more. 'You are lucky my girl to have the opportunity to work for her. She supplies hats and bonnets and the like for the fine ladies of this city and needs those embellishments…' He twirled his finger in the air. 'You know, the feathers and ribbons and things that decorate them. You will be dying them to order, in different colours, according to her list. I will take you there myself on Saturday to make the collection and delivery arrangements and so you can receive your instructions on applying the dyes. They'll write it all down, you read don't you?'

'I read very well.'

'Ah you have a clever one here Michael, spirited too, I like that.'

As promised, a basket almost as big as her arrived the next morning with a dozen sheets and two dozen pillowslips stashed inside. She decided to unload it as she went along, two sheets at a time, then last of all to tackle the pillowslips, but hardly able to get everything out on the line before it was dark, realised it would all be dampened in the morning by the dew, so brought in the first of the six sheets she had washed to finish drying them in front of the stove. She would press those first thing in the morning and then hoped the others would be dry enough by midday to bring in, press and pack up by the evening ready for collection the next morning.

By Tuesday evening it was all done and just as she placed the last parcel inside the basket and closed the lid, her blackened father came in from work. She put out bread, cheese and two thick slices of ham with a jug of beer which always successfully muted his complaining about being given a cold supper. Then thankfully he went to his bed and didn't bother her again for the evening. This was now to be the brutal, unrelenting rhythm of her days. At night exhaustion would claim her, although there was no bed for her yet, just newspapers on the floor and a blanket over her, the only small comfort, the pillow her father had given her from his bed.

By the time Saturday came, she was moving without thinking, an oiled cog in someone else's machine, forced to keep turning. With her father away to work, she washed herself quickly staying close to the stove for warmth, but just as she was wiping the wet cloth under her arms and across her shoulders, Josiah Doggett knocked, coming straight in without waiting for an answer, catching her before she could cover herself.

'Good morning Nancy.'

Jumping at his voice so close, she kept her back to him as she pulled the bodice of her dress up to cover herself, folding her arms tightly across her body.

'Don't let me interrupt you.'

'I'm finished.'

'There's no hurry if you'd like to sit and talk a while, get to know each other a little better.' He pulled out a chair and sat down, vest buttons straining, spreading himself open as usual like he was ready to receive something.

She'd sooner spit in his ugly face than talk to him. 'No, thank you.'

'Come on now, I'm just being friendly with you.' He patted his knee expectantly.

'My da says that I'm to do the work you give me but that doesn't mean I have to talk to you or even like you.' She was thinking it but didn't expect the words to come out of her mouth.

He was irritated. 'The bitch bites eh? Well hurry up then. I don't have all day.'

She grabbed her shawl from the back of the chair and went to her room, if she stood at the tap end, she would be hidden from his sight. Using her shawl like a cape to cover herself, she quickly buttoned up her bodice, listening all the time for the sound of him moving from the chair towards her, then safely dressed, she laced her boots - worn and no longer beautiful her father having cut through the stitching at the toes and heels to give her feet more space - took a deep breath and went back into the room. 'I'm ready.'

'About time, come on then.'

He sulked all the way up Milk Street, shoving his hands down into his pockets and striding out, walking so quickly that she struggled to keep up as something distantly remembered stirred an anxiety in her. At the top of Milk Street they turned left and made their way along Washington and still he didn't speak to her, not until they eventually stopped outside W. Knight's Books & Stationery.

'This is it.'

A bookshop? His words drifted past her as she stared in through the window at the books, near enough to touch, but none within reach.

'Hey, stop your daydreaming. Round here.'

Tailing Josiah as he walked around the side of the shop, she slowed down as they passed a black door with a brass plaque on it that read, *A. McCabe, Finest Fashionable Ladies' Hats, Bonnets and Caps.* To its right, the window displayed a striking blue hat on a stand with two long, shiny blue-black tail feathers that shot into the air like they belonged to a bird diving for fish, so animated in its design it looked like it might take flight at any moment. Beyond it, she could just make out the shifting shapes of the vapid women preening themselves as they tried on bonnets and fussed with their hair. 'Hey, hurry up.' Josiah was ahead of her waiting by a wooden gate, waving her over. 'Come on, you're wasting my time.' She followed him through the gate and across a small tidy yard to a green door where he neither knocked nor waited, but went straight in and up the fourteen steps to a landing that opened onto a large bright room where six women, of varying ages and sizes, sat at tables cutting, stitching and shaping hats and bonnets. The woman at the back of the workroom, who looked like she was in charge, stared at them with mild disgust, like she thought they were dirtying the clean air. 'I'm here to see Miss McCabe, she expects me.'

'You should have rung the bell downstairs. You cannot come straight in unannounced. Who calls?'

'Josiah Doggett.'

'Wait there Mr. Doggett.' She gave him a cold, warning look, then stood up and disappeared through a door behind her leaving them standing there awkwardly, locked in the disapproving gaze of the other women. Finally the door opened and the woman waved them over.

Following her into a small, poorly lit room, an old lady sat at an elaborately carved desk, her hair completely colourless in contrast to the vibrant purple bonnet she was wearing ,her face as white and wrinkled as mamo's legs. Sighing loudly at the interruption, she looked up at them through gold rimmed glasses that made her eyes look huge and her head seem too small for her body. The room was plain and painted in a sickly light brown colour, with no pictures on the walls or rugs on the floor, just the desk, a chair, and a parrot that swung its cage frantically, screeching and bobbing its head up and down excitedly at their arrival. Nancy couldn't take her eyes off it, with bright green feathers, a flash of red at its wing tips and big yellow rings around eyes that followed you, it looked like it belonged on top of a lady's hat.

'Be quiet Beauty!' The old woman raised her voice to shut the bird up.

'Mr. Doggett.'

'Miss McCabe. How nice to see you. You look very well.'

The insincere compliment bounced off her and

she just stared at him impatiently. 'Get on with it man.'

'Well, I have brought the girl as promised.'

She returned her pen to its pot and peered at Nancy. 'So this is she?'

'Yes madam, I have found you a young and fit worker, I guarantee you'll have no trouble with her at all.'

'I wonder how many would give any merit to a guarantee from you Mr. Doggett?'

Out of the corner of her eye, Nancy could see Josiah twisting his hands behind his back turning his knuckles white as they squeezed hard together, channelling the anger that was coursing through him.

'Hold out your hands child.'

Nancy stepped forward and did as she was told.

'Stubby fingers, she's not suited to anything that requires dexterity, still it's not a problem for the dying work I suppose.' She pushed back her chair and came round the desk to where Nancy was standing, the deep ruffles of her over-ornate satin dress - much more suited to a younger woman - sweeping the floor as she went. 'Do you have good eyesight girl?' It seemed an unfair question to Nancy from someone whose own eyesight was clearly so bad.

'Yes I do.'

'Yes I do, what?'

'Yes I do, thank you.'

'Not, *Thank you. Madam.*'

'Yes I do, madam.'

Nancy jumped as the parrot joined in 'I do madam, I do madam.' A bird that talked, the woman must be a witch.

'Shush Beauty I say.' She held a bony, warning finger up to the bird. 'Never seen a parrot before girl?'

'No madam, never. I didn't know they could talk neither.'

'Indeed they can, too much sometimes.' And she gave Beauty a disapproving sideways look. 'I'll give her a trial Mr. Doggett, but if her work's not up to it, or if she's any trouble, that will be the end of it.'

'She won't let you down Miss McCabe, I'll see to it.'

'Very well. Millicent! Millicent!' The woman who had shown them into the office appeared at the door. 'I will be starting this girl with dying feathers. If she does well, we will discuss her taking on the ribbon too. Give her ten gross of goose feathers to take away with her and show her how to mix the dyes and apply them. We'll start her off with just the purple, we fall behind on commissions and every fashionable lady seems to want purple these days.' She touched her own bonnet as she said it before turning to Josiah. 'Fifteen cents a gross Mr. Doggett.'

'I had expected more.'

'Take it or leave it, I am sure I can find another poor wretch to do the work.'

'Very well, I accept your terms but I would prefer payment in advance Miss McCabe, I'm sure you understand.'

'When the girl proves she can do the work and doesn't spoil ten gross of goose feathers, then you shall have your money. Now if that's everything, I have work to do.'

Josiah nodded his understanding and they both followed Millicent back out into the workroom. 'I'm sure you can find your own way home.' His business concluded, hardly bothering to feign courteousness, he tipped his hat and was gone.

Millicent showed her how to mix the dyes and dip the feathers, the way to lay them out to dry so they wouldn't stick together and the colour would be even. 'They must be fully dry before you pack them and bring them back, they'll be no use to us otherwise.' When the lesson was over, Millicent dropped ten small white bags into a sack and carefully placed the dye and the laying-out paper inside it too. 'Be off with you then and bring them back on Monday morning before ten o'clock. When you come, ring the yard-door bell and someone will come down to you. You're not to come up to the workroom from now on or go anywhere near the salon.' She nodded across the landing to a door that's top half comprised of five panes of etched glass, the centre pane with the addition of thin black strips of glass forming the letter M. 'Miss McCabe's customers would be most distressed to see a girl of your sort mingling with their finery.' It was not a new lesson for Nancy, she had already learnt that a girl like her should be invisible and say nothing, be nobody.

PART IV:
BOSTON 1864

CHAPTER 26

Death on Milk Street

She liked the walk up Milk Street. It wasn't as crowded and bustling as Washington and was home to purveyors of musical instruments, crockery and haberdashery, and the trades of plumbers, engravers and all manner of other services only afforded to the wealthy. People walked at a slower pace with no want nor need for rushing and with fewer carriages rattling by to shake your brain, there was always a pleasant percussion to the street. The gentle congeniality of the street's sounds may have made her feel comfortable but the visitors to Milk Street did not, and it was harder to lose herself than on Washington, as the *haves* completely eclipsed the *have-nots.* Here there was little on offer to those living within meagre means, the street naturally selecting only those who lived beyond the basic essentials of life, able to pay any price for their comforts.

Necessity over the years had shaped her

proficiency at wending her way up the street while keeping her eyes lowered to the sidewalk, dodging the lines, able to avoid the gaze of those with the sensibilities to be offended by the sight of a girl like her, as they considered which pieces of delicate china they would add to their collection or what fine velvets would be suitable for their drapes. Her very presence might be enough to give a lady the vapours, still today, lifting her head, she looked everyone in the eye. There was nothing to lose now.

She had kept a count of her twice-weekly visits to Miss McCabe's and each time, savouring a few stolen moments outside the bookshop, would dare to imagine herself as someone with a different life where there was time to read, before going round the side and in through the gate to ring the yard-door bell as who she really was. These precious little pockets of time went so much further than just the seconds they lasted and then, when she would stand at the green door, she would feel herself touching something gentler and finer by just being close to frivolous things that had no merit other than to make things pretty. It was always Millicent that came down to her and made the exchange, taking the dyed feathers and ribbon from her and giving her a fresh supply with instructions on the colours and quantities. From the little she was able to gather, Miss McCabe was happy with the quality of her work, so for the last eighteen months she had given her the job of dying the ribbons too. In their short, functional exchanges, Millicent didn't exactly speak kindly to her, but her voice wasn't unkind either, and she was simply the only nice woman Nancy knew.

Now, standing outside the door for the one hundred & ninety-seventh and last time, she rang the bell, took a deep breath, and waited for the familiar light tap of Millicent's footsteps coming down the stairs.

'Good morning Nancy.' Millicent had the loaded sack in her hand as usual ready to make the exchange but despite standing only inches from each other, Nancy stared out dumbly from somewhere distant, with eyes that seemed to look through her. 'Lost your tongue?'

'Good morning Millicent. I'm sorry but I won't be taking those today.'

'What do you mean?'

'I won't be coming back again, not ever.'

'Why not?'

'I'm dying.' The words came out of her mouth in a rush propelled by the relief of sharing her terrible news with another living soul.

Millicent stepped back a little. 'Lord, what is it? What does the doctor say?'

'I haven't seen a doctor, but I know I am.'

Millicent sat down on the bottom step of the stairs and stared at the pale child-woman. 'Tell me what it is that ails you.'

'These past three days I've had pains like I'm being gutted like a fish, near takes me off my feet, something is cut inside me, the blood pours out like milk from a quart jug and leaves me so weak. I am sure to have drained away completely by Friday.'

Millicent smiled cruelly at the telling of her terrible news. 'How old are you Nancy?'

'Thirteen come December I think.'

'And you say this has never happened to you before?'

'Never. That's why I know I'm dying.'

'You're not dying but you will have to learn to live with the discomfort of it all. You become a woman; it's natural and you're simply cursed with the weakness that all women must endure.'

'I'm not dying at all?'

'No, you're not but you need to prepare yourself for feeling this way every month. It will come upon you without fail and when it does you must take your rest when you can, lie down until the worst passes. You'll need rags too for the bleeding. Wait there.'

Nancy felt light-headed, not only from the shock of being about to die and then not, but because she had never thought about becoming a woman, and leaning against the doorframe to steady herself, her mind raced at the news, totally unprepared for the sudden inevitability of womanhood. A couple of minutes later Millicent returned with a small bundle of hastily folded rags and a length of blue ribbon. Looking back up the stairs over her shoulder, she lowered her voice to a hush. 'Take these. Fold the rags for thickness and secure them around your waist with the ribbon. With practice you'll get used to it.'

Nancy burst forward through the door and threw her arms around Millicent's neck, not realising just how much she wanted to keep living. 'Thank you Millicent.' She hadn't embraced anyone since mamo and felt strange and uncomfortable wanting to let go almost as soon as she felt the warmth of Millicent's body against hers but she didn't know how you were supposed to break away. Millicent took care of that as she stiffly removed the scarf of Nancy's arms from around her neck and stepped forward, gently backing her into the yard. Dropping the rags and the blue ribbon into the sack she held it out to her to take. 'See you on Monday.' And she went back inside and closed the door.

A bag full of feathers and ribbon is light, no burden at all really, but now as she made her way home she felt as if she carried a cloud in the bag that lifted her feet off the ground as she floated her way down the street. The realisation that she wanted this small life, even though it amounted to so little, took her by surprise, that she would rather feel the pain and suffering of it than feel nothing at all was a revelation to her.

What did it all add up to though? Did it mean she would become like her mother? Some days she would catch sight of the green shawl with its pink fringe, its wearer scurrying away, darting in a different direction to her for fear they might collide. That devilish woman who had carried the curse and passed it on to her, had so easily abandoned her, cut the ties that should bind a mother to her child. She had only ever loved Issy and that was only a little bit, but Nancy would have taken even that, just something to prove that she was wanted in this world by the woman who brought her into it. Kitty hadn't cried when Issy died, even in that, Nancy had failed to punish her for not loving her. If she had known that her mother would feel so little at his loss she wouldn't have squeezed the sweet banewort berries into his mouth to put him to sleep. She had only wanted to send him away so she could have some small share of the love that came to him, only the first part of the plan formed in her child's head, never considering beyond that anything that amounted to finality – she'd thought, you go, you come back. Still, the angels had taken him to heaven and she supposed he was better off out of this life that she herself clung to.

CHAPTER 27

The Quickening

The sight of her living child on the street this morning made her stomach flip over as the not-yet child inside her made its first move to be felt. In a moment of sudden realisation, it was all she could do not to speckle the sidewalk as everything that had been tasteless going down, rose up as sour, burning bile in her throat.

Over the last few weeks she had completely disregarded the occasional feelings of sickness, and as she'd continued her bleeds, had totally missed this new child's silent approach. Now the slap of her shocking fate hit her with its full force as she fell backwards into the shadows of an alleyway, leaning her traumatised bones against a wall to keep herself upright. Clamping her mouth shut against vomiting she looked down at her body. She was thinner than ever, but then that had been so when she carried her other babies as they drained her of everything, her condition not showing until the last month of her term. There was no denying it, the quickening was here and as she laid her hand on her belly she knew she would have to take care of it, even though it was more difficult to arrange these days as the laws of men were changing and it was women who were paying the price for their interfering, their bodies not their own to command as men laid claim to them, deciding what could and could not be allowed in the name of propriety and decency.

Her mind raced at the thought of it. She would have to be discreet in finding someone who could be trusted to make sure it slipped away quietly, not some gossiping hag who blabbed on every street corner to anyone with ears to listen. She could take the pennyroyal but it was probably too late for that now. No, Polly at The White Horse would know someone, she'd already let four slip away herself and seemed untouched by it, she would help her to take care of things.

Her own mother had told her how it could be done with plants that wash out your insides and set everything straight again, she had made it sound as mundane and necessary as washing laundry but as her plans to banish the child rushed through her head, Kitty realised that this was different; she wanted this child and the sudden, unwelcome longing for it made her panic. For all its impossibilities and impracticalities, something in her unthought but known yearned for this man's child, to reproduce something of him. She was a fool! He would abandon her at the first mention of a child and probably see his wife and his loveless marriage as a much less complicated prospect in his life, no she must get rid of it, but then the child inside her, his child, seemed to jump violently in protest as if it were connected to her thoughts and she quietened her thinking to try and settle it.

For years starvation had stalked her and so she had always thought it the lack of food that left her feeling dull and empty, that the pains inside her could be satisfied if only there were food rather than the constant gnawing and fear of the days when it wouldn't come, but plentiful food had found its place in her life since they'd arrived in Boston, with it the realisation that she wasn't sated by it and the hunger in her didn't disappear. She felt hollow all the time, withered by the paltry scraps of emotional sustenance that came to her from her family, any meagre morsels of anything not completely selfish or contemptable making her feel worse, feeding and growing a poison inside her that would spill out and destroy everything around her. She had wanted to stop it but just couldn't help herself, so she had got out, removed herself from Michael and the child.

Leaving Michael had cost her nothing as she had never cared for him, in fact her loathing towards him had been the only constant in their marriage, it was true that she didn't care for

Nancy either but knew she owed her something more than she was able to give her, the girl would stand a better chance without her. For the first time in years Grace Thompson came to her mind and recalling the look on her face as she gazed down on her poor dead child, Kitty knew that even though death had separated them, a grave would never separate Grace from her daughter. Even as she had looked on at the terrible tragedy, she had been intrigued by the unbreakable bond between mother and child, felt a strange longing for such an enduring, unshakable connection to any living thing in her own life and then on one ordinary day it had come, her closed and disregarded heart prised open by a man who was right for her.

He looked beyond her hard shell and saw something in her that she didn't know herself was there, and as the words exchanged between them met kindly without combat and with no need for victory or spite, both happily surrendered to the fullness they brought to each other. For the first time in her life she had felt safe, not from the harshness of the world, but from herself, as a different order to things was defined with everything she had learnt to depend on taking a lower place in things - her looks, the shape of her body. Estranged from love her whole life she still recognised it when it came.

She played the conversation of telling him

about her news in her head, perhaps there was a chance and he would choose her and this child, but then one of the reasons she wanted him was because he was decent and loyal, so would she ruin the very thing she prized? Then as she swung over to the other side of the argument, she considered that something so fine deserved a chance and couldn't be wrong, surely all can be justified in the name of love. The listening child fluttered contentedly inside her, yes, she would take a chance, risk everything and place it all before him to do with as he would, even accept it if he turned her away.

Pulling her shawl tighter around her she stepped out onto the street where all seemed unchanged by her news, she would do it tonight, pray that his reply would mean there was no need for the pennyroyal.

PART V: BOSTON
1869

CHAPTER 28

Reunion

Not one of them would be able to land a punch on target but they crowed and boasted about how they could have laid either one of them out flat in half the time. Jimmy Riley and John Baxter had gone thirty-seven rounds neither one able to keep the other down on the ground for long. Her father had done well though, backing the dog that just wouldn't lie down, able to stagger to his feet one extra time. 'A've never seen such a poor fight wi' neither o' them hardly able t'come up t'the mark after the first couple o' rounds. How thems kept goin' s'long A'm hanged if A know, spent more o' their time on the ropes than fightin', twas a poor show fer sure.' Michael critiqued the fight like some kind of expert rather than the paunchy, ignorant spectator he was.

'Poor show for John Baxter, his head looked like an exploded melon by the end, only a mother could love him looking like that!' Josiah pulled a contorted face. 'Anyway, you won didn't you, what are you complaining about?'

'Well s'pose A did alright but A'm after a bit more entertainment fer me money, cud've done better meself.' Jumping out of his chair he lifted his fists up in front of his face and began jabbing at thin air, ducking the invisible blows that were coming in his direction, too stiff and weighed down with alcohol to lift his feet, only able to shuffle on the spot. Then losing his balance, he fell back down into his chair, a loud, unedifying, belch erupting from his gaping mouth with the force of his hard landing.

'You're blind as a bat, they'd be on you before you saw them coming! No my friend, you're too heavy and slow to dodge a fist heading in your direction, besides one knuckle in your face and you'd be out cold Michael Sullivan boxer extraordinaire!' Josiah laughed and slapped Michael's back.

'Yer too matey yerself t'get out o' anyone's way. You'd be more dangerous if you fell on them!' Jack and Thad joined in with the laughter, Josiah did indeed seem to get fatter by the day.

'Ah, shut up! I'll take you on any time, just try me.'

'Don't be tekin' on so. Have a drink an' settle yerself down.'

Nancy turned her back on the four useless drunks round their table, and raising the jug to her face, spat quietly and generously into it.

‘Bring the beer girl, me friends have a thirst on them.’

Placing the jug on the table she looked with hidden delight at her spittle floating on the top as it mixed with the froth, but then as she leant over, Josiah reached round behind her and pulled her down onto his knee, his greasy hands pinning her arms to her sides. ‘Get off me! You better let me go or you’ll regret it.’ She twisted and strained to get free, her flailing legs too short to reach the floor and find the footing she needed to get herself upright again. Despite the curtain of hair that fell over her face blurring her vision, looking out from behind its cover, she couldn’t escape that up close he was even more disgusting. His tongue was too big for his mouth pushing out his pink fat lips like they were two greasy sausages and hairs poked out of his nostrils and ears like the dirty bristles of a yard brush. He was losing his hair and pink patches of his scalp shone through the remaining wiry tufts while a snowdrift of small white flakes of skin sprinkled his eyebrows and moustache. She closed her eyes to try and shut the look of him out but nothing could block the rancid smell of his breath as he pulled her in even closer.

‘Your daughter’s not very sociable again this evening Michael, you need to have a word with her about that sharp tongue of hers, teach her some manners.’

Jack and Thad quietened down as the mood began to turn while Michael's glassy eyes gradually focussed on Nancy. 'Like her mother, don't know when she's well off, that's her problem. All A've sacrificed fer her over the years, not a bit o' gratitude fer it.'

'Are you like your mother Nancy? I've heard so much about her, I hear she is very friendly, very popular by all accounts if you know what I mean!'

Michael slammed his hand on the table. 'If anyone is goin' t'insult Kitty, tis goin' t'be me, d'you hear?'

'Now who's taking on? I'm just jesting; no need for you to be getting worked up about it. No man could hold on to a woman like that, no man would want to!'

'She didn't leave me, A threw her out.'

'Oh I see. You threw her out. Yes, I'm sure you did.' The inebriated Jack and Thad found Josiah stupidly entertaining as he gave them a comical smile at Michael's expense, then as he was basking in their admiration, Nancy bent down and bit his arm. 'Ah! Bitch!'

As he let go of her, she sprang to her feet and grabbed for the nearest weapon; the laundry bat that was resting against the wall next to the stove. Grasping it with both hands she raised it up ready to bring it down on him. 'Touch me again and I swear I'll kill you.'

Josiah got to his feet as she held the bat

suspended in mid-air. 'You hit me with that and it will be jail for you girl, mark my words.'

'I don't care. It can't be any worse than this.'

'I think you might care missy. There will be dozens more men not as kindly as me ready to take their pleasure and you'll have no laundry bat or any other thing to fend them off. Locked in a cell, it won't be friends who hold the key to it, you'll be as helpless as a rat in a trap for sure.'

She stood her ground holding his gaze.

'Leave the girl alone Josiah, if you keep eggravatin' her, you can't be complainin' if she hits back at you. C'mon yer holdin' the game up!'

'Ah you're not worth it.' Josiah dropped down onto the chair and picked up his beer. 'There are plenty of young ladies in this city who are most partial to the charms of Josiah Doggett. A few pretty words, a trinket or two, they're easily had. You would do well to learn how things work my girl. You're only heading in one direction in this life so you might as well get used to it. Deal the cards Michael.'

As they started up their game again, Nancy put down the bat and surveyed the four brainless men, she'd like to kill them all, the world would be no worse off for the loss of them, but instead she headed towards the door.

'Whar you goin' girl?'

'None of your business.'

'Get back here.' Michael vainly tried to exercise

some authority over her.

Ignoring him, she went out, slamming the door behind her as loudly as she could to make her point. Up on the street she punched the wall as her anger burst out and her skin split open, the sight of her bloodied knuckles shocking her into a cold calmness, although still ready to go thirty-seven rounds with any one of them who pushed her any further.

'Been in a fight miss?' An old man who had been standing looking down on a pigeon that was hobbling around in circles on the sidewalk, its wing limp and drooping, called over to her. Then picking up the injured bird, shuffled over, all the time staring down at her bloodied hand.

'Leave me alone.'

'As long as you're not being bothered by no one. My bones are old but I'm still up for the fight if someone's knockin' you about, just say the word.'

'What's it to you?'

'Well nothin' I suppose as long as the other beggar came off worse! Can't abide men who beat their women.'

'Don't worry, I'll take care of him, both of them.'

The shabbily dressed man smiled at her. If he hadn't been upright and moving, he would have just looked like a pile of discarded rags. The pigeon squirmed in his hands 'Good. Well then, I'll wish you a good evenin' miss.'

As he tipped his hat unsteadily she stared at the crescent of congealed blood above his left ear. 'Ah, been in a bit of bother myself this evenin'. My old legs can't carry me as fast as they used to and I find there's always someone doin' the chasin'!'

She stared down at the fidgeting pigeon. 'Are you going to eat it?'

'Eat it!' He raised the broken bird up close to his face smiling at it, nose to beak. 'No, I'm goin' to fix it. With a bit of help she'll fly again.'

'It's just a pigeon.'

'One of God's creatures and born to fly, that's all I know.'

He must be crazy and backing away from him she headed off up Pearl Street looking back over her shoulder to see the stupid old fool opening his coat and tenderly placing the pigeon inside, before gently wrapping its protection back over the startled bird and shuffling away with his precious cargo on board. 'Mad!'

Eventually she found herself on Washington Street and looking up at the clear night sky, tried to shut out the soulless buildings towering over her, imagining instead the majestic mountains of home. A hundred lights shone out through the shop and restaurant windows softly pooling on the sidewalk lighting her way, but still, tonight like every night, she felt outside of it all, moving like a ghost among people who lived and breathed and had a place in the world. A little way ahead of her, a carriage pulled up and a well-dressed man of about her father's age stepped down, followed by a young woman who he handed down onto the sidewalk. Small and attractive, even from a distance her wide smile and open face showed she had never known hardship and Nancy hated her for it. Mostly though she was struck by the dress she was wearing, emerald green, the colour of her jealousy, with black trim and a beaded bodice that brought frame to her pale skin perfectly. As the two stood on the sidewalk another man, familiar to her, stepped out of the carriage to join them. Raven black hair curled down onto his collar, eyes almost as dark, lit this evening by a streetlamp rather than by the light of a candle.

If she didn't move any closer perhaps he wouldn't see her but some long forgotten invisible thread connecting them pulled his head around until he was looking directly at her. Silently he mouthed her name before sending the man and the young woman on into the restaurant ahead of him. She stayed rooted to the spot as he began to walk towards her, the hare ready to run but unable to move.

As he approached her he was slowly shaking his head. 'Nancy, is it really you?'

'Yes, Samuel, it's me.' She hid her bloodied hand behind her back.

He looked like he would cry. 'You look as lovely as ever.'

'That's not true. Don't tease me Samuel.'

'I mean it Nancy.'

She believed him but couldn't look into his face. 'I'm sorry.' Her words drifted out of her as a whisper.

'Sorry about what?'

'Sorry about what happened in the library that night of course.'

He hesitated before answering. 'You mustn't blame yourself; it was my fault. You were frightened and you panicked. I should never have taken you there in the first place but I wanted to share it with you.'

'I'm glad you did. Those times in the library, well, I felt like I belonged to something. I'd never felt that before, like I had a place in things.' With the sudden aching memory of it, her words came out in a rush and she was embarrassed that she had given her enduring feelings away so easily.

'Well then, we shall both look back on it fondly and forget the unfortunate events that followed, all a long time ago.'

She nodded. 'How is your father?'

'He is in very good health and age doesn't seem to slow him down one bit! He still enthusiastically gives every free moment to the church and I hope I shall be half the man he is one day. How are your parents?' Do you all still fly with the birds at Pine Street?'

She stared down at the ground. 'I haven't seen

my mother these nearly seven years, well not close up, she keeps company round and about the city and I catch sight of her sometimes...' Her voice trailed off. 'My father, well he can be found the same, still a useless drunk.'

'You deserved better Nancy.'

She shrugged her shoulders. 'We live near Fort Hill now. My father was keen to dodge conscription so he moved us there.'

'Were you able to finish school?'

She shook her head. 'My father took me out of school when I was ten.'

'Why?'

'So he could have me working all the hours to fund his drinking while he gambled with his so-called friends. Anyway, what use is an education to a girl like me, it only teaches you about everything you'll never have.'

'I am so sorry Nancy; I had dared over the years to hope better for you.' His words hung in the air between them. So he had thought about her too.

'It's okay, I'm used to it.' Now she looked up into his lovely face. 'You look very well Samuel.'

'I am, thank you. I find myself most fortunate to be apprenticed to a highly respected attorney here in Boston. He has been very good to me and thinks I have great promise. If all goes according to plan I hope to be practicing law within two years.'

'It was always your dream. Will you stay in

Boston?'

'To begin with, yes, the restlessness I once felt seems to have left me and the city offers me great opportunities.'

'I am sure you will be a fine attorney.'

'Well, I will surely be most unusual amongst my peers.' There was so much loaded into those few simple words but he smiled at her without any trace of bitterness. 'What of your future Nancy?'

She shrugged her shoulders.

'I hope that, well… you might find a way out of your situation.'

'I was told only but an hour ago that my life heads in one direction and I should accept it. No, there is nothing better for me Samuel.'

'But Nancy, you're clever and bright, please don't waste it.'

'It's easy for you, you're a man.'

'A coloured man. I know what it is to overcome prejudice every day; prove to people that I am more than the colour of my skin.'

'It still puts you above me.' There was dull resignation in her voice as their conversation seemed to reach a dead-end. 'You'd better be getting back to your friends, you don't want them to come looking for you and to find you talking with me. Who was that woman anyway?'

Samuel hesitated. 'Nancy, I am engaged to be married. Her name is Clara and she is as good as she is pretty, I am sure you would like her.'

With those words she felt the blow of an invisible door slamming shut in her face. 'She looks rich, I can see that any man looking for advantage in life would be attracted to that.'

Samuel physically shook with the slap of her words. 'Nancy, why are you being so unkind, so bitter?'

'You can afford not to be bitter, I cannot. Goodbye Samuel, I hope you'll be happy.' She didn't mean it and left him standing in the street, the boy that could have been hers, now someone else's love. She didn't care, everything always ended up being spoilt or taken away from her anyway, fulfilling Josiah's prophesy about her life would be easy.

By the time she got home the card game had broken up and her father was alone, lying on his bed, snoring loudly. She stood looking down at him, mouth open, stinking breath putrefying the air around him. Even the flies weren't attracted to his stench and hummed at a distance in the main room avoiding his closet, except one that had ventured in and lay dead on the small table beside his bed. She picked it up, examined its fat blue-black body and folded hairy legs, then dropped it into his gaping mouth.

CHAPTER 29

M is for McCabe

Everything looked just the same as it did the first time she stood in front of Miss McCabe's desk nearly six years ago, like the old woman had never moved from her chair, the only sign that she had, her bonnet, which was a different colour, bright red and even more gawdy. She wore the same heavy satin dress although it was faded and she no longer filled it, so shrunken that Nancy thought if it weren't for its heavy ruffles as an anchor, the merest gust of wind could blow her away like a feather. The parrot was quiet but watchful.

'Millicent puts in a good word for you and tells me that you would like to be considered for a place in the workroom?' As she spoke she didn't look up from the papers she was studying on her desk.

'Yes madam.'

'And what makes you think you are suitable to work in such a respectable establishment as this in close proximity to fine things?'

'I'm a hard worker madam and I would like the chance to better myself.'

'Better yourself at my expense?' She looked up now and stared at her over the top of her glasses.

Despite the anger that flushed Nancy's cheeks, she spoke steadily and calmly. 'I have been dying feathers and ribbons for you these past nearly six years, I have never missed a delivery and I had hoped you would be satisfied that I am a reliable worker madam?'

'You've been paid for it haven't you? You do me no favours.'

'Yes madam, you have been very good to me, I am grateful for the work.' She hoped flattery would take the sharp edge off their exchange.

'Hmm, I would think so. Well, I am satisfied I suppose but then the dying work does not call for much skill.' She drummed her fingers on the desk like it was helping her to think. 'Does Mr. Doggett know you are here?'

'No madam.'

'As the agent for your work, so to speak, I think he would be disappointed to lose the income from the existing arrangement, you would be working for me directly if you were to take up a permanent position in the workroom and Mr. Doggett would receive no benefit from it.'

Nancy said nothing.

'Still, I am sure I can take care of our Mr.

Doggett.'

'Mr. Doggett, Mr. Doggett.'

'Be quiet Beauty, don't interrupt me.'

The bird strutted up and down its perch, head bobbing as it flapped its wings furiously either with indignation at the reprimand or simply because it didn't like Josiah Doggett either.

'I have an opening for a cutter, one of my girls... what's her name Millicent?' She wafted her hand in the air like she could command the answer to come to her.'

'Rachel, madam.'

'Yes, Rachel leaves to marry a grocer. Pah! Her life will be potatoes and turnips and a man who will have her minding shop from dawn to dusk, his prospects are poor and she will be joining him in them. Love seems to have driven the girl to madness; she has lost all sense and perspective it would seem.'

It didn't sound so terrible to Nancy but Miss McCabe was clearly irritated that the girl had chosen marriage over working at the milliners.

'You will need an accurate eye and a steady hand for what is required. Do you have these things?'

'I think so madam.'

'Well do you or don't you?'

'I do madam.'

'Very well then, I shall take you at your word and trial you for a week. Millicent will train you in what is required and then I will decide if you are up to it. If you are not, you will return to dying the feathers and ribbons, although fashions are changing and flowers and lace, pretty rosettes and the like, are more the thing elegant ladies are wearing these days. Isn't that correct Millicent?'

'Yes, madam, you are right of course as always.'

'I expect all my girls in the workroom to be clean and tidy so be sure your cap is always laundered and you must scrub your hands and fingernails every day. Clean boots too or you will be sent home. Millicent will arrange a work overall for you. You can start on Monday.'

'Thank you madam. You won't regret taking me on.'

'It will be up to you whether I regret it or not. I will speak with Mr. Doggett and let him know about your trial. No doubt he will want to try and benefit from your situation so be prepared, I find he is at his most diligent when profiting from the labours of other's hands.'

'Yes madam.'

'Very well, away with you then.'

Miss McCabe was right, Josiah took the news very badly and headed to Pearl Street as soon as she informed him of Nancy's change of circumstances and the possibility of her coming into *McCabe's* direct employ, he wasn't going to let her slip out of his grasp. Alone when he burst through the door, he grabbed her by the wrists, swinging her round to face him, his anger frothing the spittle at the corners of his mouth. 'Going behind my back eh? Ungrateful bitch! After all I've done for you and your father, this is how you repay me. Getting above yourself I think. You would be wise to stay on the right side of me missy.'

'Get off me!' She twisted and pulled to get free but he was too strong and held her clamped up close to his stinking body.

'You owe me so if you get your job in the workroom, I'll want my share, we wouldn't want any unfortunate accidents to come upon you, I'm sure you understand me?'

'Let me go.'

'Tell me you understand!' He gripped her wrists tighter to push his point more effectively.

'Yes.'

Letting go he pushed her away. 'Good, best to be a clever girl if you know what's good for you. You'll still have to do the laundry mind; I'm not for letting my other customers down.'

'There won't be time for the laundry too.'

'You have evenings and nights don't you? You'll have to work them that's all.'

She wouldn't fight him for now; she would save that for later when her job in the workroom was fixed and advantage had shifted in her favour. Once she was safely in Miss McCabe's direct employ she would flick him off like the blood sucking flea he was. With a regular wage put into her own hands, perhaps she could move out and find a room somewhere, get away from him and her useless father, put an end to this dead-end life they had consigned her to.

She put Josiah's threats out of her mind and when Monday came, she walked up Milk Street with a new feeling, hope. Could people see that she was on her way to do a respectable job among respectable people, did she look as different as she felt this morning? Arriving at the yard door she rang the bell as usual, then checked herself, smoothing her dress and making sure no dust had dulled the shine on her boots. Last night she had scrubbed her hands raw and soaked her nails in soapy boiling water to remove any traces of the dye that stained her nails, now, eyes set straight ahead, she was ready. As she heard the familiar sound of Millicent's footsteps coming down the stairs she felt open to the happiness that was flowing in her direction, then there she was, going up the stairs to her new life.

Millicent walked Nancy around the workshop introducing her to the other women and explaining what they all did. Some worked at wooden hat blocks shaping and embellishing colourful bonnets, others worked with magnifying glasses stitching tiny beads and ornate rosettes in intricate patterns, while two of the women spent their days braiding straw making the stiff unyielding golden stems seem as soft and pliant as silken hair. Each in turn stared at her without speaking or smiling before returning to their work. Introductions over, Nancy was given a stool in the corner next to Millicent at the end of a long bench table and as she looked down at the novelty of her clean hands and shiny boots, she felt like someone else.

Millicent passed her a starched white overall and as she put it on she realised she had never worn anything as impractical, life had always been too dirty to consider it. 'We'll start with cutting felt, it's the most forgiving of materials and won't give you too much trouble. Once you've mastered cutting it to a pattern, Rachel will show you how to manage the difficulties of velvet and silk, these take more skill and are too expensive to waste so there is no room for error.' As Millicent began to unroll the black felt, Nancy watched as one of the women attached colourful goose feathers she herself had dyed in her squalid room in Pearl Street to a green bonnet, each would be individually stitched and placed at just the right angle to show them off to their best effect and the wearer would never know that a poor, dirty girl's hands had played a part in its creation.

As the week progressed, Millicent seemed pleased with her work; she was dexterous and accurate and quickly learnt the tricky ways of the expensive fabrics. Not one piece she cut had been wasted, much to Rachel's frustration, it had taken her weeks to tame the slippery, fraying materials that Nancy seemed to master so easily. She would catch the-bride-to-be staring at her, willing her to make a mistake, but she didn't. The work was enjoyable; she liked the quiet industry of the workroom and relished the feel of the scissors as she directed perfect cuts into fabric that gave no resistance to their sharp blades. As the end of the week approached, she knew the job was hers. 'Miss McCabe asks to see you tomorrow afternoon and I'll be happy to commend you to her Nancy. You have a natural aptitude for the work and I think you'll do very well here at *McCabe's*.' As Millicent spoke she was at the same time checking the finish on a straw bonnet with a pink sash, running her fingers around the edges to check their smoothness. Then placing it on a block, Nancy watched as she tied the sash and stood back to check the balance of its structure.

'Thank you Millicent, I enjoy it very much.'

Millicent smiled at her. 'Well I think this bonnet will do very well, what do you say?'

'Yes, it's perfect.'

'Well then, can you take it through into the salon for me please, put it on the empty stand nearest the door.'

'Me?'

'Yes you. There's no one in there.'

'But will it be alright?'

'What do you mean?'

'Well I've never been on the other side of the door.'

'And neither will you if we have customers in there, but it's empty, so off you go and be sure to tie the bow neatly to its best effect.'

Nancy smoothed her already perfectly clean hands on her overall, carefully untied the bonnet's satin bow and took it from its block, holding it aloft like it was a crown of jewels. Over the last week she had observed through the door she would now enter - and from the respectable distance of the workroom - the silhouettes of twittering women as the blues and pinks of their dresses danced and flickered across the glass. Listened to the sounds of their excitement as hats were tried on and expensive ones, or twos, or threes were chosen to go with this dress or that, but now as she approached it, the black M loomed larger like it was warning her off, this fragile glass door as solid a separation of different lives as anyone could imagine. This side of it you wanted for it all, on the other, its excesses were almost too much to bear.

Bridging the line of separation from the hard wooden floor of the landing to the soft, thick carpet on the other side, the muffled sound of the salon made her feel like she had something stuffed in her ears as the carpet soaked up the hard surface sounds of the glass and the wood and the plaster. Sun poured in through three big windows, its light bouncing back around the room from two large mirrors that stood against the facing wall. Painted pink and blue flowers wound their way on their stems around the room imitating the fresh posies that were placed precisely on small round tables, and a dozen or more wooden hat stands, with sturdy barley-twist stems, were positioned in a curved shape, heads without bodies, standing as tall as her. The stand nearest the door was empty as Millicent had said it would be so she carefully lifted the bonnet and placed it on top, tied the sash - pulling out the loops so that they were as fulsome and generous as possible - then stood back and checked her work. Even though it was only her hands that placed it, the bonnet looked as fine as all the others, and she was happy she had shown it off to its best effect.

Glancing back towards the closed door, she approached one of the full-length mirrors, then took off her white overall, staring with revulsion at her reflection as she took in the flat brown of her dress which seemed to suck all the colour out of the room and make her look dirty in contrast to the whites and pastels around her. It wasn't what she was wearing that shocked her, it was the woman staring back at her. Despite everything she would have wanted to do to avoid it, when had she become her mother? Shouldn't she have felt herself taking her shape, the look of her? Quickly putting her overall back on in the hope she could cover up the horror of the woman underneath, she turned to face her mute crescent audience – *what are you staring at?* - and as her eye curved along the line of bonnets, she imagined the hatstands transformed into the silly women who would giggle and fuss over which one to choose. Walking to the end of the line, she looked up at an elaborate blue bonnet with a purple velvet sash and a halo of frothing white flowers around the crown, picturing the plain and pointless woman desperate to be noticed who would wear it, then without taking her eyes from it, her fingers felt for one of the pins threaded through the collar of her overall and reaching up, she pushed its sharp point through the top of the bonnet. Rachel had worked on it, delivered this blue and purple creation to the salon, she was sure to be blamed for the injury the pin would inflict. Alas, the departed cannot defend themselves and all would say that it was better she had left *McCabe's*, too careless. Small victories. Smiling to herself, she checked she had left no dirty marks on the carpet, then went back out into the workroom.

The next day as planned Nancy stood straight and tall in front of Miss McCabe's desk with Millicent beside her ready to share in her triumph.

'Millicent gives a very favourable report of your trial this week.'

Nancy turned and smiled at Millicent.

'It would seem you have a natural ability for the work.'

'Thank you madam.'

'However, as I have always believed, work you can depend on but romantic love you cannot. It never runs smooth for those foolish enough to enter into it and so I am afraid I will not be offering you the position of a cutter in the workroom.' She put down her pen and smiled up at Nancy. 'The silly girl will not be marrying her grocer; he has taken up with another young woman who brings money to his business. Such is love, when affection is measured in dollars, it's for fools!'

She had been sure the job would be hers. Stupid! Stupid! Stupid! 'But Miss McCabe, I have done a good job.' She looked over at Millicent to back her up.

'There's nothing to be done. There simply isn't the work. I'm sorry, but there it is.'

The ground was shifting under her feet again and as she stumbled a little, Millicent put out her hand to steady her. 'But you promised me the job would be mine if I proved myself.'

'Rachel is no longer leaving us so there is no job to offer you.'

The parrot was strangely quiet like it knew

an injustice had been served and she imagined opening the cage door and Beauty flying out straight into Miss McCabe's bonnet, tangling its body in its beads and ribbons, getting caught up in her wiry hair, pecking at the dried-up witch until her face and hat were the same colour.

'Well? Lost your tongue girl?'

'No madam, but it seems that whatever I get is taken away from me, I'm disappointed that's all.'

'Life is full of disappointments I find but a girl like you will always get by.'

'Yes madam.' A girl like her had to learn to reconcile with defeat.

'You can return to dying the feathers and ribbons then for as long as we need them. If anything else becomes available, we will let you know.'

'Yes madam.'

'Very well, hand back your overall before you leave.' And she picked up her pen and began scratching away as if Nancy had already left the room.

Back out in the workroom, Nancy surveyed the snivelling Rachel - the spurned bride-to-be who had cost her the job - and thought of the pin. Keeping her voice low Millicent laid her hand gently on Nancy's arm. 'I'm so sorry, Rachel must have gone to Miss McCabe direct, I didn't know she was staying.'

Nancy shrugged off the sympathy. 'It's Miss

McCabe's loss.' Her words were defiant but belied her disappointment, she felt beaten.

'Perhaps something else will come up.'

'Nothing will and better I don't wish for it.' And the hare was stripped again as she unbuttoned her overall and handed it to Millicent.

'Don't lose heart.'

'Good things don't happen to girls like me. I'm used to it.'

Millicent hesitated. 'Shall you take the feathers and ribbons with you today then; it will save you a trip tomorrow?'

With those words the door shut firmly on Nancy's dream of making something of herself as her claustrophobic room at Pearl Street reclaimed her. 'If you like.'

Millicent bagged the ribbons and feathers while Nancy stood waiting awkwardly all the lowered eyes in the room intently watching her ruination. When she was finally back out in the yard she screamed out her disappointment and anger at the top of her voice then made her way home.

To her surprise and dismay, her father and Josiah were waiting for her.

'See what the cat dragged in!'

She ignored them and took the bag of feathers and ribbons to her closet. She didn't have the stomach for them this evening and they'd better not push her. Anyway, what was her father doing in the house at this time, it wasn't even seven o'clock? Delaying as long as she could, she went back into the main room averting her eyes from the two idiots who had clearly been drinking for a while, then went to the stove to make a pot of coffee.

'Why not join us in something a little stronger?'

She looked over at Josiah but didn't respond.

'Haven't I always said your daughter has no fun in her Michael, she needs to learn how to enjoy herself a little.'

'She'll have n'time fer fun now me job's gone, time she wur lookin' after me properly.'

Nancy almost dropped the coffee pot. 'You've lost your job?

'Gev it up. Thems been tekin' advantage o' me gud nature fer years. A'm sick o' it so A've told them what t'do wi' thar stinkin' job. A'm never goin' back thar, me an' Iron Street are finished fer gud. 'Sides, A've been doin' well wi' a few wagers recently, A seem t'have the knack fer pickin' a winner these days, reckon A'll tek the easy money thanks.'

'That won't last and we can't manage without your wages. You'll have to get another job.'

'What 'bout yer fancy new job? We'll be fine if you pull yer weight thar, 'sides, Josiah says Miss McCabe is a very rich woman, keeps a lob o' cash on the premises by all accounts, A reckon she wudn't miss a bit o' it if yer smart enough t'lay yer hands on it.'

'Steal you mean.'

'Well A wudn't put it s'crude, more a few little bonuses fer being a hard worker eh?'

'You can forget that, I didn't get the job and won't be working there, so you'll have to find your beer money somewhere else.'

'What? A thought the job wur certain, how'd you mess it up?'

Nancy ignored her father.

'A'm talkin' t'you, answer me!'

'Michael, Michael, give the girl a chance... Nancy dear, have you vexed Miss McCabe in some way? I would be most disappointed to learn that you have let her down?'

'It was her that let me down! The job was promised to me but turns out her word isn't to be trusted any more than yours!'

'Harsh words, be careful little vixen. Still, all is not lost, I have been thinking there are other more lucrative ways for an attractive young woman to make a living... and I am always happy to make the introductions.'

Michael gave Josiah a sideways look but said nothing.

Nancy fully understood his foul proposition. 'I already break my back to line your pockets; I'll never lie on it to make you or any other man a profit! Find another sap!'

'Well it's true, you have so many other options you could consider. You'd be wise to think about it.' He laughed and went back to his beer. 'Women eh Michael? Strange creatures. Can't live with them, can't live without.'

Michael looked up at Nancy blankly and said nothing.

She felt trapped. 'I'm going out!'

'Hey whar you goin'? What 'bout me supper?'

'Get it yourself and I hope you choke!' She slammed the door behind her, went up the steps and ran up Pearl Street jumping the lines between the flaggs, hoping the rush of the wind would help her cast off the stifling inevitability of her bleak future, her mind racing with dead-end ideas, until finally she slowed her pace and began to breathe more steadily. Winding her way through the streets she tried to clear her head, she mustn't overthink it or she would never leave so when Old South rang out ten, she made her way home; going back for now would give her the chance to plan her escape on her own terms. When she got back she was relieved to find Josiah gone and her father already snoring in his bed. Sure he wouldn't wake again for the evening, she went to her closet and getting down on her knees pulled back her bedding, tugging at a piece of loose skirting in the corner that damp had long since separated from the wall. Reaching down behind it into a small hole, careful not to let the coins jangle, she pulled out the heavy black pouch that had travelled with them from Ireland and emptied the contents out onto her blanket.

All the household payments had been hers to manage and swindling her innumerate father out of a nickel most weeks since moving to Pearl Street, here they were, stacked in twenty-two piles of ten with another five loose coins, eleven dollars and twenty-five cents, enough to buy a small freedom.

CHAPTER 30

The White Horse

'Josiah Doggett! Good to see you my old friend. It's been a long time.' The landlord slapped him so hard on the back it rattled the teeth in Josiah's head. Not a friend but a sap who would spend good money this evening and was sure to lose handsomely at poker to the landlord's great profit. 'You look weary, let me bring you a drink to revive you. If you're feeling lucky, there's a game tonight and an opportunity to fill your pockets with gold, will you join us?'

'I prefer to play with men known to me.' More easily cheat he meant.

'Well think about it, you don't have to decide now, the night is still young. Perhaps you'd like some company for the evening though, help pass the time more pleasantly?' He gave Josiah a slow wink.

'Just get me a beer, I've no need of the flea-ridden strumpets that hang around these parts and no need of the pox!'

'Well I think I am offended my friend.' Raising his eyebrows he gave Josiah a faint smile of indignation. 'Only the most delightful of young ladies frequent The White Horse, but yes a drink first, it will oil the way to a most enjoyable evening I'm sure.'

As the landlord went off to fetch his drink Josiah Doggett looked down at his trembling hands and knew he was losing his grip in more ways than one. His hair was all but gone now and his leather belt strained on its final notch as his waist continued to expand with life's excesses. His eyesight was beginning to fail him too, especially in the evenings when the light faded, and he found himself squinting to try and sharpen his focus. Never having given any mind to getting old, he cursed the march of time as his bones ached and his tongue found yet another tooth that wobbled in his mouth, still, the beer would dull the pain of it and take away the rotten taste. Tonight, through narrowed blurry eyes, he looked around the tavern at the happy intoxicated crowd but the change of scenery did nothing to lift his spirits and he felt no part of it.

'One beer for the gentleman.' The landlord slapped the liquid gold down on the table with a flourish. 'Now are you sure I can't get you anything else my friend?'

'Nothing. Leave me be.' And he shoved a coin across the table at him.

'Yes of course, I will leave you to enjoy it, just shout when you're ready for another.'

The taste of the beer did make him feel better and he called for another and another although the third time it wasn't brought by the landlord but by a woman who seemed quiet and polite, pretty too. Looking up into dark eyes that smiled back at him she put the beer down on the table. 'Can A get you anythin' else? Wud you like a little company this evenin'?'

Now he took in the sum of her, not young but not faded either, tall and shapely he thought. Yes, altogether quite pleasing to the eye.

He nodded. 'Yes, sit.'

She pulled a stool round and sat close to him. 'A'm Catherine.'

'Josiah.'

'Pleased t'meet you Josiah. A've not seen you in here afore.'

'It's been a long time since I was in this part of the city. Just fancied a change and a Saturday night seemed as good a time as any. Fort Hill is more my regular patch.'

She nodded. 'An' what d'you do Josiah?'

'I'm a successful man of business.'

'G'wan, tell me more.'

'Well, I have many wealthy and influential customers in the city who rely on my good services, more than one man's share but there it is. Industrious men like me with a sound head for business can sniff out opportunities others miss and still prosper in this city.' He smiled and tapped his nose.

'That be very impressive Josiah. A'm sure yer family are proud o' you.'

'I've no family.'

'A'm the sem. Tis a lonely life t'be sure...' She smiled at him and laid her hand on top of his for the briefest moment before taking it away again.

'I've got friends though, oh, lots of friends.'

'A'm sure you do, thems bound t'be drawn t'such a successful man.'

'Yes, yes, there's many who do well to count Josiah Doggett as a friend and well, I like to help an unfortunate soul in this life in any way I can; I think it's my Christian duty to share my good fortune with others.'

'That's very generous, thar not be many who wud be s'kind hearted.'

Josiah was performing well and he could see her growing appreciation for all his fine qualities. 'My friend Michael only said to me the other day *I don't know what would have become of me and Nancy if you hadn't helped us out so generous.* Fair swelled my heart.'

'Did he? Michael an' Nancy you say?'

'Yes, Michael Sullivan. Helped him and is daughter out when his wife left him a few years back. Abandoned them both she did, bad business, but there you are.' The woman looked on silently as he drained his glass and slapped it back down onto the table, grinning at her, pleased with himself as his story got into its stride. 'Now the girl, she's turned into a beauty, that's for sure, I've been biding my time there but soon she'll be for breaking a few hearts if I have anything to do with it.' For the first time he noticed how pale her skin was, it seemed almost colourless to him now.

'How auld is the girl?'

'Oh I don't know, sixteen, seventeen, thereabouts. Ripe for the picking though.'

'And you'll arrange the pickin'?'

'Yes, I know men who will be respectful and considerate, nothing rough if you know what I mean.'

'A know exactly what you mean.' She pulled her green shawl with its faded pink fringe tighter around her shoulders as if a cold draught had suddenly cut across her.

'I'll take care of her like she was my own daughter, don't worry about that.'

'Like yer own child?...'

Josiah smiled and shrugged his shoulders 'She won't want for anything if she's a good girl that's for sure. Pretty dresses and bonnets, if she's after having them, bring a better class of customer with deeper pockets so we'll both benefit.' He winked at her but the woman didn't blink and just stared back at him. She seemed twitchy for some reason, kicking her foot against the leg of the table, rattling his empty glass.

'I think you're getting impatient for a drink Catherine; will you join me?'

'A have t'go, you can drink alone.' She spat the words out.

'Eh? What's this about? I thought we were getting on fine.'

'Think again.' She put her hands flat on the table to push herself up, like her legs wouldn't hold her, then got up and left him.

'Stupid bitch!' He shouted after her but she didn't turn around, then waving his hand in the air, he called out to the landlord. 'Bring me another drink and be quick about it.'

Five beers later, all watered-down and overcharged, Josiah Doggett staggered out of The White Horse and pulled his collar up against the chill evening air. He would finish the night at Michael's; he was surely the nearest thing he had to a friend and he needed to be with friends tonight. Walking slowly he concentrated on not tripping on the uneven cobbles as his feet disobeyed him, his body almost bent double, as the uneasy feeling that had taken root in his gut churned his insides, tying them in knots. Turning the corner onto Pearl Street, running his hand along the back of his neck, he tried to rub away the invisible, hostile presence that had held on to him since leaving The White Horse, if he didn't know better he might even imagine someone was following him. He shrugged it off, knowing well the phantom of intoxication, at one moment a benevolent friend in all your merriment, the next, a dark revenant force that stole your equanimity.

When he arrived at the Sullivans' he found the usual crowd, with Jack and Thad already settled into the game of poker and Michael appearing to be doing very well out of it. He eyed the already half emptied whiskey bottle. 'Friends! I come to join you! Aren't you going to offer me a glass?' The men looked up at Josiah swaying in the doorway but Nancy didn't even glance in his direction as she set out their supper of bread and ham.

'Looks like you've already had a few.' Michael was irritated, he always did better at cards when Josiah wasn't there holding court, putting him off his game.

'Ah the night is young, time for plenty more my friend.' He lurched across the room and pulled out a chair, falling down into it. As he eyed Nancy moving silently around the table, the bitterness of the night's events rose up in his throat enough to make him choke. 'These women need to be taught a lesson, what are they without men to give them a life, nothing.'

'Whar you talkin' 'bout? Some wench got the better o' you this evenin'?' The men laughed at Josiah's expense but he was not going to be the object of their derision and with a need to reinstate his power, he caught hold of Nancy's wrist as she leant across the table, swinging his other arm around her waist. 'What is it you women want eh?'

'Not a man like you that's for sure.' And she pulled her arm away, twisting her body out of his grasp.

The men laughed again and Michael punched his friend's arm playfully. 'That told you Josiah! You'll never learn!'

Josiah sat back in his chair spreading himself out; he would have to play this a different way. 'I've been thinking, time I took a wife, have myself a few home comforts. How'd you fancy me as a son-in-law Michael?'

Beer exploded out of Michael's mouth spraying the table and everyone around it. 'Yer drunk! Marry Nancy? She's just told you, she wudn't havvy.'

'Marry you? I'll throw myself in the river first!' She meant it.

'No need to be so ungrateful. There would be plenty of advantages to being Mrs. Josiah Doggett, you'd be wise to consider it.'

Nancy realised that even in his drunkenness he was serious and slowly backed away from the table to where the laundry bat leant against the wall, it would come to her rescue again if she had to fight her way out of there.

'Think about it Michael, I can give her a good

life, bring you some grandchildren to bounce on your knee.'

Nancy watched her father with horror as she saw Josiah's ugly proposition slowly working its way through his tiny brain.

Michael laughed. 'Yer never goin' t'capture this one, she's too wild fer you Josiah. She'd be the death o' you.'

'I think with time you might come to see my point of view and how it might be, well, advantageous to you shall we say, unless you prefer the girl to be the head of you of course.'

'Eh?'

'I thought you were the master of this house Michael, but seems your daughter makes the decisions, my mistake.' He knew exactly how to play Michael and bring him round to his way of thinking.

'She knows who's in charge eh girl?'

Nancy stood in stunned silence with her back against the wall and Josiah saw her hand close around the handle of the bat.

'Don't you be raising that thing against me again.'

She grabbed it anyway and held it up ready. 'Don't any one of you touch me, I mean it!'

'Put it down girl, that's no way to respond to a proposal of marriage, calm yourself.' Josiah laughed at her. 'You just need to get used to the idea that's all. Deal me in Michael.'

That was it; tomorrow she would leave.

When midnight came and Josiah left Pearl Street, he had both won the night at cards and in convincing Michael of the merits of his marital plans although he'd probably have to work on him again once he'd sobered up. Yes, he was back on top, but as it began to rain, the uneasy feeling he'd had earlier dropped down on him again and he quickened his step to try and dodge it.

CHAPTER 31

Run Dry

'Poor fella, they must have come at him from behind.' Two policemen stood over the body sprawled out on the cobbles and then one crouched down to get a better look. 'He'd had a few drinks for sure, stinks like he spent the night at the Burkhardt Brewery.' Reaching under the body and pulling back the man's coat, he felt inside one of his trouser pockets and finding a wallet, flipped open the clasp. 'He's still got money on him, plenty of it, so it wasn't a mugging, some other motive for his murder.' Now as he patted the vest pocket nearest him he felt the bulge of something hard and pushing his fingers down inside pulled out a silver penknife with a carved wooden handle, as he did, tangling his hand in a silver chain that disappeared into the pocket on the other side. Closing his hand around the watch at the chain's end, he yanked at it, but the clip held fast to the vest cloth and the man's body twitched as if it was coming back to life, so he pulled harder until the cloth tore and gave way and the body stayed still. 'Gotcha! No point holding on to it old fella; no use to you now your time's run out.' That was it, nothing else on him 'Not carrying any papers, unfortunate, but there it is.'

It was a lifeless Josiah Doggett that lay face down in the street, a glistening crown of red around his head and run completely dry, unable to ever tell anyone what had happened to him. His attacker had been proficient and one fatal blow across the back of his head had afforded him the undeserved mercy of dying instantly as his skull cracked open and all his lights went out. It was the unexpected rising up of a powerful primal instinct that did for Josiah Doggett, not the bluntness of mere physical strength, but a blind unstoppable fury that nature dictated must be satisfied.

The other bluecoat slowly circled the corpse taking a cursory look around its margins for a weapon or any other visible evidence of what or who killed him but there was nothing. Lazily sweeping his eyes wider around the street, pools of gaslight shimmered on the wet cobbles but no human life was illuminated by it, just the vermin and strays that sought the shadows away from its light. They had the convenience tonight of no witnesses and so everything could be taken care of quickly.

'It was a woman's scream that brought us to him so we know somebody saw something.' The policeman who was crouching down took one more look at the sticky, red gash on the back of Josiah's head and then stood up, knees cracking in protest. 'We know there are always eyes on the street but they don't always choose to tell, no, they don't want to be accused of having anything to do with it.'

Slowly turning Josiah's possessions over in his hands, he gave the other policeman a familiar nod, then slipped them all into his coat pocket. 'I'll file the report as a mugging with nothing of any value left on him. I don't expect an investigation unless someone comes forward and demands it, although I suspect this man doesn't have a wife, no evidence that any woman's hand has helped him with his turn out.' He looked down dispassionately at the shabby-looking man whose pockets he had emptied. 'Even the newspapers won't be interested in this one so he won't be getting his moment of fame.' He straightened up and stretched his back for the final summing up. 'There's nothing for us to go on and if no one claims him, well, he'll have the ending of all the other lost souls in this city, terrible pity, but there it is.'

CHAPTER 32

Between the Lines

Gut burning from too much cheap whiskey and feeling sore that fortune had turned against him in the evening's game of poker, tossing and turning in his bed, Michael cursed Josiah Doggett's luck, although he had a growing suspicion that he had been cheating so luck probably had little to do with it. Then before he could even settle his circling irritance with Josiah, Kitty invaded his thoughts as he tried to remember a time when they didn't despise each other, when they were content to be in the same room, but he couldn't reach it. He'd deserved better from a wife that was for sure, a little tenderness, some respect. He'd never have married her if she hadn't trapped him by getting herself pregnant, even in that, she'd poisoned the girl against him and made him look small and inadequate at every opportunity. She'd even lost him his son, starved him of her milk, dried Issy out until there was nothing left of life flowing through his body, the memory of it after so many years still able to ice the blood coursing through his veins. Grandchildren though, a grandson, now that would bring him some cheer. He could convince Josiah to name him Michael, carry on the name his own father had passed to him, secure himself a sliver of immortality. The boy would look up to him, give him some respect and he'd be good to him, buy him toys and candy, teach him to box. Eventually, the pleasant ramblings of his mind eased his agitation and steadied his breathing until, in the early hours of the morning, he finally drifted into sleep content that this, as yet unmade boy, would right all the wrongs levelled against him over the years by the women in his life.

On the other side of the wall Nancy lay awake listening to the sounds of the night - banging, scuttling, dripping, shouting - waiting for the rasp of her father snoring in his bed, then at six o'clock just as it was getting light its rhythmic sound finally came, so quietly gathering her belongings together, and tearing away the poems she had written on paper scraps from the shelf so there would be nothing left of her, she retrieved the bag of coins forcing its bulk down into her bodice for safe keeping. She gave her room a final look. Like a prisoner on their liberation day nothing here had ever brought her any comfort, it had amounted to containment in a doorless box with inescapable and unrelenting misery as her jailor, still she was nervous to leave it and everything she knew. Stopping on her way past her father's room to take one final look at him, Nancy realised she felt nothing at their parting except relief that the giant presence of this small man in her life was finally over. Whispering, 'I wish I'd never known you as my father, I might have imagined you as something better,' she turned her face away from him for the last time and left. She was going to get far away from Fort Hill, somewhere her father and Josiah wouldn't find her, somewhere they would be considered unwelcome visitors and recognised for being the low-living vermin they were. Closing the door quietly behind her she went up the steps and onto the street standing still for a moment to wear her freedom for the first time, it didn't matter that she was homeless, Pearl Street had been a poor excuse for anything that felt like a refuge anyway, just a squalid square of stale air and despondency.

As she walked through the awakening city she entertained herself by imagining Josiah's fury when he found she was gone. He would rail and cuss, consider himself unjustly wronged, unable to do anything about it, hah! she had finally emptied out any power he had over her. As she delighted in the fall of Josiah Doggett she didn't know that someone had already drained him out, left him dead on the street, and that she herself had often felt the blunt edge of the cruel hand that did it, a hand that had never once offered her any protection until last night. As for her father, in his state of unjustified abandonment, she knew he would turn to drink as he always did, enlist the friend that never solved a single problem but dulled the pain of his reality. He would be as helpless as a baby, unable to look after himself, the world set against him now there was no one to do everything for him.

As familiar streets ran out, eventually a repeating line of shop windows lit by the sun guided her along Tremont Street for the first time, and as she became aware of the heavy pouch in her bodice weighing her down, knew she could buy something, she wouldn't do it of course but played with the idea in her head just for the feel of it. Approaching the end of the block a flash of blue in one of the windows caught her eye. As she got closer, she could see it was a glorious gown, the manikin wearing it so life-like that it seemed as if it had just that moment turned away from the window to show off the bustle and sweep of shining fabric that fell from the bodice and its tiny waist like a silk waterfall, splashing and pooling on the ground, inky blue like an ocean you could drown in. Drawn in nearer, she touched the glass and traced a finger along the line of its silhouette, feeling the smoothness of the glass under her finger and imagining it was the silk. Beyond the gown's loveliness, inside the shop, she could see that on one side high wooden shelves were stacked with bolts of material in every colour graduating from white to black and on the other, a long, low wood and glass cabinet showed off reels of ribbons and cards of beads and buttons enough for a thousand dresses. A young woman in a neat, crimson-coloured dress was standing behind the counter serving a customer and another, dressed as if her twin, was holding up a piece of purple velvet as a woman ran her fingers lightly across its surface checking its quality. Nose pressed up against the glass now, she was falling into the beauty of it all and as her gaze came back to the dress, her eyes gliding along its generous folds, she knew she would do just about anything to have it, spend every nickel.

'It's very elegant isn't it?' A woman was standing beside her, joining her in looking in through the window, taking in the spectacle of the dress.

'I've never seen anything so perfect in my whole life.'

'Yes, I am very partial to it myself. Blue is my favourite colour.'

Neither of them took their eyes off it.

'Are you going to buy it?' Nancy blurted out the question before she could stop it.

The woman laughed 'Well, I suppose in a way, I already have. This is my shop you see.'

‘Yours?’ Nancy turned to face the woman. She was well-dressed, not loudly so but with all the elegance of her clothes in the arrangement and stitching of them rather than the easy effect of showy embellishments. Somewhere in her middle years, with hazel eyes and pale skin, she had a kind face and a genuine smile. It was Grace. As panic struck her, she didn’t dare blink or move a muscle in her face for fear of giving herself away, but as she looked into Grace’s face, the steady gaze she returned reassured Nancy that she hadn’t been recognised.

‘Yes, I’ve been here five years now and the business does well, it keeps me busy and my mind occupied which is a very good thing. The good Lord has been merciful to me poor wretch that I am.’ She glanced towards the shop window like it would reassure her that it really had been her salvation and smiled sadly to herself at something lost but still vivid to her mind. Then with a complete change of tempo, as if she was suddenly in a hurry, she said, ‘Well I had better be going, I have a very particular customer who doesn’t like to be kept waiting for a moment!’ and she winked at Nancy before pushing open the door to go into the shop, but as the bell above the door rang out her entrance she suddenly stopped, like she stood at the open window in the moment before the fall. Staying perfectly still, balancing there as lifeless as the wax manikin, her knuckles turning white as she squeezed the doorknob, she didn't turn around and spoke in little more than a sigh. 'Perhaps you will have a blue dress of your own one day.' Then she went inside and shut the door on her.

Nancy stared after her as something long held in cracked wide open. *It wasn't my fault. Maude shouldn't have done it. You could have loved me instead…* The shock of seeing Grace and the feelings it gave life to began colliding as dark mis-shapen fragments of thought that her brain couldn't assemble, threaded through them, the stinging injustice of it all, no room for remorse about poor dead Maude. Thrown off balance, she leant against the shop window, her mind tumbling over and over, the voice in her head telling her that wherever there had been fault it hadn't been hers, it had been the making of others, life always asking too much of her, expecting her to be the one to bend to their shaping of things; dance to their tune. Now as always, she stood outside her own life surveying the failing players in it, watching them mould it to their own ends, finding herself shut out. She put her fingers in her ears to try and block out their noise, 'shut up, shut up, shut up!' people staring at her; the hare standing on the plate screaming before the jaws snap shut. Run, run, run!

Unknown to her or any other living being,

something had been stolen from her when she entered the world as those first breaths spurned her lungs, the loss of them vital in moulding and shaping her life; crystallising the living of it. And that wasn't all that had been taken from her before she had even got started, hadn't she been born an orphan? With no parent to consider her a precious child under their protection, instead like Aurora Leigh, she had poured herself along the veins of others and made the living answer for the dead, her starved blood giving daily life to her enduring sense of separation and otherness. With no power born to her to affect the direction of her life, she had been the victim, as crime after crime came against her.

Her child's share of love had been plundered too, her brother taking it when he went away, his leaving making no difference to her lot, with all the love that had found a home in him never coming back to find her. Issy had fallen asleep forever but wasn't he still better off, better the memory of love in death than never having it at all, you were someone and really here if you were loved. Maude had known it even if she hadn't deserved it, in life and in death the riches of a mother's love had been hers, Grace's broken heart an enduring testament to that love, not blunted by loss but sharpened by it. So what was wrong with her? Why had no one ever loved her, not even mamo? Her grandmother -

doomfully bound to the consequences of the ill-matched union between her parents - had been trapped into caring for her and hadn't come to it freely, escaping from the burden of it at the first opportunity. Treachery. There should be no absolution for a betrayal, no reward of a kiss for those who claim to love you but cast you adrift, even if they are your mamo.

Held hostage by the constant noise in her head she made her way blindly along more unfamiliar streets until she found herself outside the gates of the common, undecided about whether to go in, the railings and sweet swirling air stirring her memory of the garden at Cole Hall and marmalade with Nathaniel in the room of sunshine. Her thoughts tripped away from her again to a time when he had spread his wings over her and she had found light in the shadow of them, thought she was seen and special, but she was just someone, nobody really, because hadn't he sent her away and so easily moved on and spread them over another wretched child who had sat on the ground crying as she watched on, already forgotten. Crime after crime... She pulled herself back from the memories that tried to suck her in. Yesterday she would have walked past, today she must do things differently, so she went in.

Making herself small so she wouldn't be noticed, she wove in and out between the Elm trees, the heady spectrum of greens and blues and browns enveloping her as she trailed her fingers along the gnarled trunks of trees and looked up at the birds chattering above her, all the while resisting the overwhelming urge to take off her boots and walk barefoot on the grass as she was carried back to something long behind her. Water, flecked silver, flickered in the distance and drew her on but standing now at its edge she saw that none flowed at Frog Pond, it was only the towering fountain at the centre of the lake spouting high into the air above the treetops that moved the water before it showered down peppering the surface of the lake with stars as the sun set the droplets alight. She put down her bag, closed her eyes and listened, light-headedly swaying with the intoxicating memory of the stream in Kinlough, the sound of the ocean at Donegal Bay.

'Are you alright miss?' A man's voice came from behind her. 'Are you unwell?'

She opened her eyes and steadied herself, turning to see a tall, too-colourfully dressed man with eyes bluer than the lake approaching her and as there was no one else near them, she realised he must be talking to her.

'I don't need your help thank you, I just took a faint, I'm quite well.'

The man – as handsome as Steerforth – smiled at her. 'Perhaps you should sit a while until the feeling passes. I would certainly suggest you step back from the edge of the lake.'

'What business is it of yours?'

'Not my business at all but I find I cannot help myself if I see someone about to fall into a lake and meet a watery end. I am sorry to have bothered you if you would prefer to drown, that is your prerogative of course!'

She didn't understand why he was smiling at her. 'I can take care of myself.' No one ever really helps you for nothing, there's always a price to be paid and she would be in debt to no man now, although her cold resolve faltered a little at the thought of the guileless old man with the pigeon.

'I am sure you can. Well then, I will wish you good day miss and hope that you stay out of the lake!' He laughed, tipped his hat and left her to her fate. She watched him as he slowly circumvented the pond before going out through the Beacon Street gate and disappearing beyond the trees. It was a sign, peculiar folk like him with probably more money than sense would be in abundance here, there would be employment opportunities for her and plenty of people who felt compelled to do a good deed to make themselves feel better. So, tracing his steps, she went out through the same gate, her nerves suddenly getting the better of her as the grand houses of wealthy merchants and professional gentlemen coldly loomed over her offering no welcome to a stranger of her sort.

Taking advantage of the cover the trees offered, she hid in their shadows to steel herself until she felt ready to be exposed by the light, then uninvited but determined, she knocked on the first of the doors of the fine houses on Spruce Street, followed by Chestnut and Walnut, but all were shut in her face or not opened at all to a raggedy looking girl. Even Joy Street brought none. Finally, late in the afternoon, midway down Pinckney Street, a door opened to her and stayed open, the lady of the house in desperate need of a maid to help her run her boarding house, Nancy playing on her predicament perfectly. The woman, Mrs. Dean, would take her without references but she would be out on the street again if she proved anything less than hard-working and trustworthy, so in her hour of need, Nancy had easily convinced her that she was those things and more.

Her new home was an attic room, just a box room really, but what it lacked in comforts it made up for in the privacy it afforded her and for the first time in her life she had her own door. She made little mark on it but one day she would have pretty things to fill the drawers and a dress fine enough for hanging. She found the work easy compared to her labours at Pearl Street and ate as well as the boarders, after a few weeks, even noticing a pinch of fat around her waist as she began to gain weight. Mrs. Dean was a widow - although she so often mentioned her Mr. Dean it was as if he still lived in the house moving invisibly from room to room - and even if she was finickity and tedious, she was by equal measure fair and deliciously easy for Nancy to take advantage of. Best of all were the evenings at Pinckney Street. After the boarders had been served their meals and all the dishes had been cleaned and put away, time was her own and *hallelujah,* Mrs. Dean had a shelf full of books! Nancy's ambition was to read them all and whenever she lit the lamp in her room in readiness to enter into a book's pages, she would dip her finger into the pot of marmalade she kept by her bed and Nathaniel would come to her from somewhere lost to her now, then careful not to get any of its sticky sweetness on the cover, she would catch the distant echo of Samuel's voice in her head saying *Aurora Leigh have you completed your task of reading your book today?* Yes, she would complete the task over and over again, never tiring of it and the way the words gave to you so freely.

Silhouetted against the light of the lamp she looked around her room as it illuminated the darkness bringing shape and form to everything ordinary it touched and knew that whenever light had fallen on her, she had taken no shape or colour in it, that she had remained unseen. So if she had reshaped the light that had entered and passed through her, twisted and inverted its purity and poured all the goodness out of it, then she couldn't be blamed for the dark image she projected. Like a meddling phantom, David Copperfield had tried its hardest to write the pages of her life – and although it was true that once a girl had sat by a stream and longed to be the hero of her own - a real life isn't to be lived vicariously and you must live it as just yourself, try to make your own way in the world without anyone's help, depend on no one. And yet, somewhere between the lines written of sadness and disappointment, her pages told of being touched by angels, held by grace, lifted up on the wings of kindness. So had she written a false account of her life so far, not been truthful when she blamed others for her lot?

Tonight, with the protection of her own door, she would leave the past behind, try to write a different future for herself, so reaching under her pillow she pulled out a small, precious scrap of folded paper, yellowed and scorched at its edges. Unfolding it she carefully flattened it out on the bed's blue counterpane – Little Em'ly looking back at her as she always did with her steady, unchanging gaze - then taking a pencil from her pocket, pulled down her sleeves to cover old scars, and with no need of Grace's hand wrapped around hers to guide it, began to write. *If I open myself to happiness, will it come?* As she stared down at what she had written the pencil twitched in her hand, then scoring through the words *will it* - almost tearing the paper as she hurriedly deleted them - she corrected their order and wrote *IT WILL...*

Printed in Dunstable, United Kingdom

76674771R00204